I'M A FOOL TO KILL YOU

I'M A FOOL TO KILL YOU

A 'Rat Pack' Mystery

Robert J. Randisi

severn House

This first world edition published 2010
in Great Britain and in the USA by
SEVERN HOUSE PUBLISHERS LTD of
9–15 High Street, Sutton, Surrey, England, SM1 1DF.
Trade paperback edition first published
in Great Britain and the USA 2011 by
SEVERN HOUSE PUBLISHERS LTD.

British Library Cataloguing in Publication Data

Randisi, Robert J.
  I'm a fool to kill you.
  1. Gardner, Ava, 1922–1990 – Fiction. 2. Rat Pack
  (Entertainers) – Fiction. 3. Private investigators – United
  States – Fiction. 4. Las Vegas (Nev.) – Fiction.
  5. Detective and mystery stories.
  I. Title
  813.5'4-dc22

ISBN-13: 978-0-7278-6940-1   (cased)
ISBN-13: 978-1-84751-287-1   (trade paper)

All Severn House titles are printed on acid-free paper.

Severn House Publishers support The Forest Stewardship Council [FSC],
the leading international forest certification organisation. All our titles that
are printed on Greenpeace-approved FSC-certified paper carry the FSC logo.

Mixed Sources
Product group from well-managed
forests and other controlled sources
www.fsc.org Cert no. SA-COC-1565
© 1996 Forest Stewardship Council

Typeset by Palimpsest Book Production Ltd.,
Falkirk, Stirlingshire, Scotland.
Printed and bound in Great Britain by the
MPG Books Group, Bodmin, Cornwall.

To Marthayn, I'd be a
fool to want anyone else.

'I'm A Fool To Want You'
Words & Music by Jack Wolf, Joel Herron,
Frank Sinatra, 1957.

PROLOGUE

I

Las Vegas, Fall, 2003

Jenny Phillips was a looker.

She had the prettiest blue eyes, the kind of nose you'd see on statues of a Roman princess, and a helluva rack on her. Maybe I should have felt like a dirty old man, looking her up and down as she stood in the doorway of her apartment, but she was only eighteen years younger than I was.

She was sixty-five.

'Wow,' I said. 'You look great.'

'For an old lady?' she asked, smiling.

'Look who you're talkin' to,' I said. 'People are gonna think you're my daughter.'

She reached out and straightened my tie.

'You're a handsome old gent, Eddie G.' she said. 'Don't look a day over seventy-five.'

'Why are people always telling an octogenarian he looks young?'

'I didn't say young,' she said. 'I gave you about eight years, but you still look like an old geezer.'

'Thanks very much,' I said. 'The car's downstairs. Are you ready?'

'Do I need a shawl, or a jacket?' she asked.

'Jacket,' I said. 'It's getting cool.'

'I'll be right back.'

I watched her ass as she walked away from me. Still firm and sassy. Sorry, but I'm an old-fashioned guy. I still think the way I did back in the 60s, when I was eyeing every waitress and showgirl's ass that went by at the Sands.

She came back, stepped into the hall and closed the door

behind her, made sure it was locked. Then she turned and kissed me on the cheek.

'What was that for?' I asked.

She smiled fondly, wiped off the lipstick with her thumb and said, 'That was for looking at my ass as I walked away.'

'I don't have much of a choice, Jen,' I said. 'It's a great ass.'

'I love Ava Gardner,' Jenny said in the limo.

I didn't comment.

'I mean, in *Mogambo*? Why does anyone even look at Grace Kelly?'

'I agree.'

'So you like her movies?'

'Why else would I invite you to an Ava Gardner retrospective?' I asked.

'Well, you know how much I like her.'

'Yes, I do.'

The limo stopped and Jenny looked out the window.

'Where are we going?'

'Dinner first,' I said. 'We have plenty of time.'

This was my sixth date with Jenny. I kept count because ever since I was a young man I'd never been able to get past the sixth date, except for my wives, and you can guess where those relationships went.

So I took Jenny to my favorite Italian restaurant, my usual table. Which was always for two. I ordered for both of us. She liked that. I liked the way she was staring across the table at me. I was amazed at how smooth the skin of her face was, wondered if she'd had some work. I didn't think so, though, because there were some lines in her neck and at the corners of her mouth and eyes. She would have had those smoothed out as well. I decided she just had extraordinary skin. And her hair was still mostly black, with some grey streaks, worn long. On her, sixty-five was the new fifty.

'Do you know why I like you, Eddie?'

'I could guess,' I said, 'and I might get lucky, but I'd rather hear it from you.'

'You have manners,' she said. 'Old world manners.'

'Me?' I said. 'I'm still a kid from Brooklyn; inside, I mean.'

'Well, the man on the outside has a lot of polish.'

'And that's why you like me.'

'That's one of the reasons.'

The waiter came with wine, bread and olive oil. He poured; I tasted and nodded like I knew what I was doing. I would have preferred beer, but over the years I had learned a little about wine. For instance, I learned that after you taste it you're supposed to nod.

'Should you be drinking that?' Jenny asked. 'Eating bread and pasta?'

'Why not?'

'Your diabetes?'

'Look,' I said, 'my toes are numb, and my fingertips are getting there. I'm out with a beautiful woman, and I probably won't be able to feel the softness of your skin, but at least I can taste the wine, and the bread and the pasta.'

'You can't feel my skin?' she asked, looking sad.

I reached over and touched her wrist with the fingertips of my right hand.

'Hardly,' I said.

She reached across the table and touched my mouth.

'Your lips aren't numb, are they?'

I took hold of her, ran my lips over the back of her hand.

'Smooth and soft,' I said, kissing it.

'If you're good tonight,' she said, 'maybe I'll let you feel more than my hand.'

I frowned, then sighed and pushed away the wine and the bread.

'Tell you what, Jen,' I said, 'I'll just eat the pasta.'

She blew a kiss across the table. I may have been eighty-three years old but, on occasion, I was still pretty virile.

This was one such occasion . . .

A fter her veal and my pasta I ordered her a tiramisu for dessert.

'Nothing for you, Eddie?' the waiter asked.

'Just coffee, Luigi.'

He nodded.

'You are being good,' she said.

'I'm keeping my eyes on the carrot at the end of the stick.'

She laughed.

'That's the first time I've ever been called a carrot.'

'I'm a romantic devil.'

'Romantic,' she said, looking at her watch. 'Do we have time—'

'Don't worry,' I said. 'I've got it all timed out. We'll be there for the opening credits of *The Barefoot Contessa*.'

'The *Barefoot Contessa* and *Mogambo*,' she said, shaking her head. 'Two of my favorite movies with my favorite actress and my favorite man.'

'Bogie or Gable?' I asked.

'Who's talking about them?'

The dessert came and I watched her eat.

'You remind me of her, you know,' I said.

'I do? Of who?'

'Ava Gardner.'

'Yeah, right . . . Eddie, don't worry, you're going to get lucky tonight.'

'I'm serious.'

'OK,' she said, 'in which movie?'

'Not in any movie,' I said, 'I mean in person. In real life.'

She stopped with her fork halfway to her mouth, then put it down and leaned forward.

'Eddie . . . you knew her? You knew Ava Gardner?'

'Would that surprise you?'

'Well . . . no, I guess not. After all, you are Eddie G., a Vegas legend, friends with all the Rat Pack.'

'Well, I was kind of an acquaintance of Peter's. We never really got along. And I'm no legend. I just had some special friends.'

'Like Marilyn Monroe?' she asked. 'And Ava Gardner?'

'Among others.'

There had been a magazine article out a few months ago about the Rat Pack women. Alongside ran a sidebar about me and Marilyn. There had been enough material for more than a sidebar, but I'd made sure that most of the research disappeared. So when I met Jenny at a party at a friend's house and we were introduced, she knew who I was. I like to think we would have connected anyway, but what are you gonna do?

'Eddie,' she said, 'you have to tell me about her.'

'What do you want to know?'

'What was she like?'

'She was a great broad,' I said.

'That's all?'

I took a deep breath, sorry that I'd even mentioned it. I'd gotten carried away with the moment.

'Eddie,' she asked, 'did you sleep with Ava Gardner?'

'Are you kidding?' I asked. 'Frank would have killed me.'

I turned around, waved at Luigi to bring me the check.

'That's not a denial,' she said.

'Jenny, we have to leave now if we're gonna make the movie.'

'Damn you, Eddie,' she said, as I pulled her chair out, 'maybe you won't get lucky tonight.'

'That's not fair.'

She crossed her arms beneath her breasts and stared at me.

'I tell you what,' I said. 'We'll talk about it after the movies.'

'You promise?'

'I promise.'

* * *

I had gotten us perfect seats for the movies. Not too close, not too far away. Either way, I had to put on my glasses.

'You better come through, Eddie,' Jenny whispered in my ear.

I passed her the popcorn as the lights went down and the credits began to roll.

My big crush in the 60s had been Angie Dickinson, who I had finally met thanks to my association with Frank and Dean. Ava Gardner, however, had always been unattainable to me. She was a goddess on the screen – had actually played Venus, the Goddess of Love in the movie, *One Touch of Venus* – but her unattainable status stemmed from the fact that she was Frank's ex-wife when I met her. Ex-wife but still the love of his life.

I had to figure out just how much I wanted to tell Jenny about me and Ava Gardner. So while her eyes were riveted to the screen, I let my mind drift back . . .

ONE

Las Vegas, Sept., 1962

The dealer's name was Rachel. She was young, pretty, stacked.

The only thing that kept her from being showgirl material was that she was too short. So we lucked into getting her as a blackjack dealer—and I lucked into getting her at one of the tables in my pit.

I hadn't had anything to do with hiring her, and I didn't much mind having her at one of my tables, but even from where I was standing I could see that she was – at best – inept. Not only was she clumsy with the cards, but she wasn't standing when she was supposed to stand, or hitting when she was supposed to hit. In short, she was a looker, but she was costing us money.

I waved over Zack, one of our regular dealers, and told him, 'Relieve Rachel.'

'I'd love to relieve her of—' he started, wiggling his eyebrows.

'Just do it, Zack.'

'But . . . it ain't time.'

'Yes,' I said, 'it is. And then send her right over to me.'

'Uh, sure, boss,' he said, once he realized I was serious.

He went over and tapped her on the shoulder. She frowned at him, listened to what he had to say, then looked over at me. I nodded. She put her cards down, clapped her hands together once, then left the table.

'Mr G., I—'

'Take the rest of the day, Rachel.'

'But . . . why?'

'We'll have a talk tomorrow morning.'

She stared at me and asked, 'Like . . . over breakfast?'

'What?' Then I realized what she meant, and felt stupid.

'No, no, it's nothing like that, kid. Geez, I'm not hittin' on you!'

'Oh. Well then, wha—'

'I'm the boss, right?'

'Right.'

'So I'm tellin' you to take the rest of the day off, with pay, come to work tomorrow, and then we'll talk. OK?'

She stared at me like she still didn't think I was on the up-and-up, then said, 'OK, Mr G.'

'Good. Now get outta here.'

She shrugged, turned and walked away. Every male head within sight of her shapely butt watched it leave, including me. Then I turned and saw the dealers all looking at me, wondering if I was fucking her.

'Deal!' I growled at them. Now all I had to do was figure out what to do with her, because she was never going to make a good blackjack dealer.

Later in the day Dean Martin showed up at the blackjack tables. He, Frank and Sammy were all in town to play the Sands. It wasn't the entire Summit – not without Joey and Peter – but it would do. The Copa Room would be filled the next three nights.

'Hey Dino,' I said.

'Eddie G.,' he said, shaking my hand warmly. 'Good to see you, Pally.'

He looked sharp in an expensive suit, his only jewelry a watch and a pinky ring on his left hand.

'You wanna play a little? Or deal?' Dino was known to deal a little blackjack and pay the pretty ladies off on 22.

'No, not today,' he begged off. 'I'm just here checking on a friend. Well, the friend of a friend . . . of a friend.'

'You're making me dizzy.'

'You know how it works. Friend of a friend of a friend?' He had a cigarette in his right hand, held it between his forefinger and middle finger and used his thumb to bend his nose.

'Oh, a friend of Momo's?' Momo was Sam Giancana, number one man in the mob in those days. And a good friend of Frank's. He would like to have been friends with Dean, but the wise guys didn't fascinate Dean the way they did Frank. If Dean was doing a favor for Momo, his favor really was for the Leader.

'Now you got the picture, Pally. So where is she?' He looked around. 'I'm supposed to check on her.'

'On who? Where's who?'

'Rachel.'

I swallowed and asked, 'Rachel?'

'Yeah, she's supposed to be the new dealer. Didn't Jack tell you?'

'He told me he hired her,' I said. 'He didn't tell me why, or who she was. Who is she?'

'Just somebody's . . . niece.'

Right, I thought, somebody's *Goumada* was more like it.

'So where is she?'

'I gave her the rest of the day off.'

'Isn't this her first day?' Dean asked.

'Well, yeah . . .'

'Oh boy,' Dean said, 'was she that bad?'

'No, I just – we need to find somethin' – I have to talk to Jack in the morning about her.'

'Look, Eddie,' Dino said, 'you don't have to hide anything from me. I'm just doin' somebody a favor by asking.'

'The truth is,' I said, still being careful, 'she needs more training.'

'More training?'

'Some training,' I said. 'She needs training . . . in something.'

'She as good looking as I heard?'

'Oh yeah . . .'

'Well, OK,' he said, spreading his hands. 'Listen, you wanna get some dinner later?'

'Sure.' When would I ever turn down Dean Martin's invite to dinner?

'Good,' he said. 'There'll be a car out front after the show.'

'What about Frank?'

'He's got Nancy and the kids in town, gonna be spending time with them.'

'And Sammy?'

'Yeah, May's with him, so it'll just be you and me. That OK?'

'Fine with me, Dean.'

'Good, see you then.'

Dean waved, turned and walked back across the casino floor.

I was going to have to approach this very carefully with Jack. Although I wished he had told me we were dealing with some mob boss's 'niece.' But the bottom line for Jack should also be that she was costing the casino money. All I was going to do was suggest that we get her some training as . . . something.

I got called back to the pit to OK a limit increase, and then got busy the rest of my shift. Afterward, I went to the locker room where I kept some extra clothes and changed into something appropriate for having dinner with Dean Martin.

TWO

Dinner with Dean after a show was usually a raucous affair. Frank, Sammy, Joey, Peter, sometimes other friends like Buddy Hackett and Buddy Lester (a comic actor and friend who had appeared in *Ocean's 11*), or Tony Curtis and Janet Leigh might show up. But on this particular night it was just Dino and me, and I gotta tell you, it was a thrill. I'd known Dean personally for a couple of years then, ever since the filming of *Ocean's 11*. I was a huge fan long before that, but although I now considered us to be friends, it was still a kick having dinner with him and getting all his attention.

We were at the Bootlegger Bistro on the South Strip, a traditional Italian restaurant that both Dean and Frank often patronized. The owner and the waitresses all made a fuss over Dean until he asked them to go away so he and I could talk.

See? That's what I mean. What a kick!

We talked about families – his, not mine – films he was going to make, and attempts to lure him to weekly television.

At one point he said, 'We've talked about me enough, Eddie. What's goin' on with you?'

I told him I was still happy in the pit at the Sands, still had my little house away from the strip, and was still single with nobody regular in my life.

That was a mistake. He then went on about how important it was for me to find a woman, settle down and have a family. I told him none of that was really in my plans.

'What happened to that pretty waitress you were seein'?' he asked. 'What was her name?'

'That didn't last, Dean, and she moved on. She doesn't live in Vegas anymore.' I was hoping he'd let it drop.

He did. Instead, we talked a bit about Marilyn Monroe, and how her recent death had affected us both. He said the movie he was supposed to be doing with her got scrubbed. He wouldn't hear of them replacing her.

I had met Marilyn through Dean, helped her survive a crisis, and was one of the last people she called before her death, a supposed – and apparent – accidental overdose just the previous month.

Dean told me he was looking at some scripts, wanted to do another western, but was also looking at a series of spy novels written by someone named Donald Hamilton. The character's name was Matt Helm, and he was some kind of super spy. Or, at least, that was the way Dean was thinking of playing him.

We finished dinner and had some coffee and cannoli for dessert.

'Have you seen Frank yet?' he asked me.

'No, not yet. Why, is there something wrong? Does he have a problem?'

'No, no, nothing like that,' Dean said. 'At least not that I know of. It's just . . .'

'Just what?'

'He's kind of different when he's around Nancy and his kids.'

'Different how?'

'Oh, sort of on his best behavior, you know? He doesn't want to give Nancy any reason to not let him see the kids.'

'Are they all here with him?'

'Yep, Nancy, Frank Jr. and Tina.'

'Aren't they over eighteen?' I asked.

'Not Tina,' Dean said. 'She's fourteen. Frank Jr. is eighteen, Nancy's twenty-two and a beauty. Their mother could still keep him from seeing Tina if she wanted to.'

'So Frank's gonna behave, huh?' I said, smiling. 'I don't think I've ever seen that side of him.'

'Well, he'll be the same on stage and in the steam room,' Dean pointed out. 'It's just when he's around his family, you know?'

We went back to talking about Dean's kids after that, which was OK with me. He was proud of them. He was thinking that Dino Jr. was going to follow in his footsteps, but he was equally talented as a musician and a tennis player. He thought the kid would probably make a good pro tennis player.

Deanna, his daughter, was also talented, had a fine singing voice.

'Well,' I said, 'if you end up going on television with a weekly show, you could always have them on.'

'You know, you're right,' he said. 'I could do that. I could also have Nancy and Frank Jr. on. They both sing very well.'

'Not Tina?'

'Tina's the brainy one,' he said. 'I bet if the other two have a career in show business it'll be with her behind the scenes. In fact, I'll bet she'd be a great producer.'

It was nice to hear how proud Dean was not only of his own kids, but of Frank's as well. To my way of thinking, this was the sign of a real friend.

THREE

As we continued our dinner we talked about other members of the extended family. Sammy was doing well and was happy with May. Peter was still on the outs with Frank over the JFK thing. I asked Dean if he had tried to intercede on his behalf but he said he stayed out of other people's politics, and that's what 'this' was all about.

'Is Frank still mad at Bing Crosby because JFK stayed there instead?'

'That's the odd part,' Dean said. 'No, he isn't. In fact, we're gonna do another film, this one called *Robin and The Seven Hoods*, and Frank wants to give Bing the part that was originally gonna be played by Peter.'

'That is odd,' I said. 'Why not be mad at Bing?'

'I don't know,' Dean said. 'He's not mad at him, or JFK. Only Peter.'

'That doesn't sound right.'

'Well, maybe you can talk to Frank about it. He values your opinions.'

'Oh, no,' I said, 'I'm with you when it comes to people's politics. Besides, I've never been that crazy about Peter.'

'Why is that?'

'I don't know,' I said. 'Maybe it's that snooty British attitude of his.'

Before we left the restaurant we managed to somehow get on the subject of Dean's old partner, Jerry Lewis.

'Seems Frank thinks I should appear on Jerry's Labor Day telethon.'

'I guess Frank doesn't feel the same way about stayin' out of other people's business.'

'Well, it's not a political thing, between Jerry and me, and Frank likes to see himself as a Mr Fix-It.'

'With other people's relationships?'

Dean nodded.

'Are you gonna do it?' I asked.

'Nah,' he said. 'Maybe some day, but not this year.'

I had met Jerry only once, when he played the Sands, but had not spent any time talking to him. I knew Jack Entratter considered him a friend, but Jack had lots of friends I didn't talk to.

Dean paid the bill and we got back in the limo and returned to the Sands.

'Nightcap?' I asked him, in the lobby.

'No, I don't think so.' People were pointing at him and staring. Any minute one of them was going to come over and ask for an autograph.

'I'm gonna go upstairs and call Jeannie and the kids. I miss 'em when I'm away.' He slapped me on the back and said, 'Give the family thing some thought, Eddie. I'm tellin' ya, it's great.'

'See you tomorrow, Dean,' I said. 'Maybe I'll come and see the show.'

'You do that. I think we're gonna drag Buddy Lester up there since Joey's not in town.'

'I'd like to see that.'

'OK, see ya then, Pally.'

'Say hello to Jeannie for me. She was a real help when I was in L.A. a few months back.'

'I'll tell her.'

He headed for the elevator and I headed for the casino floor. Technically, I wasn't on the clock, but I usually liked to walk through if I was around, see how things were going.

As I walked past my pit one of the dealer's called out, 'Mr Entratter was lookin' for you, Eddie.'

'He say what he wanted?'

'Not to me,' the dealer said.

'How long ago?'

''Bout an hour.'

'OK, thanks.'

'What do I tell him if he comes back?'

'Tell him you heard I went out to dinner with Dean Martin.'

FOUR

The next morning I drove up to the Sands, stopped to take in the marquee. The day before it had said FRANK SINATRA, DEAN MARTIN, SAMMY DAVIS JR. On this morning it said NAT KING COLE, and below that TONY LABELLA in the lounge. Later that morning I watched from my pit as Jack Entratter walked across the casino floor towards me. He had a determined look on his face, one that said he either had indigestion, or a problem. Or maybe one was causing the other. As usual, his shoulders were straining the seams of an expensive suit.

I stepped out to meet him, and to keep our conversation away from the tables.

'What's up, Boss?' I asked.

'Have you seen Ava Gardner?'

'In which movie?'

'Don't be a wise guy, Eddie,' he said. 'Have you seen her in the casino?'

'Ava Gardner? Here?' My heart started beating faster just at the thought. 'If she was here I missed her, Jack. What the hell—'

'Somebody said they saw her in the lobby of the hotel – twice,' he said. 'Once coming in, and then going out. Very upset, apparently.'

'When?'

'This morning. Seems she came in and left within half-an-hour – if it was her.'

'Who saw her?'

'I don't know,' he said. 'Word's gettin' around. You know how that works. Nobody ever remembers where something like that got started. That don't stop them from spreadin' it around, though.'

'How are you gonna find out if she was actually here, Jack?'

He smiled at me and poked me in the chest with a thick forefinger. 'I'm not, Eddie. You are. I'll be in my office. Let me know what you find out.' He started away, then stopped and turned. 'Oh, and stop the word from going around. I don't want to hear it again.'

'Why me?' I asked.

'Because you're the guy, Eddie,' he said. Only he said, 'The Guy,' with capital letters. 'You're my go-to-guy, right?'

'But why, Jack.'

'Why what?'

'Why do you want to know if it was Ava?' I asked. 'I mean, we get lots of celebrities here. It's Vegas.'

'Because I'm the boss,' he said, 'and I'm tellin' you to find out for me. Do you need more than that, Eddie?'

'Ya know what, Jack?' I said. 'I kinda do. I mean, after all this time workin' for you, doin' what you say without question—'

'Ha!'

'—I need an explanation for this one.'

He hesitated, then said, 'OK, Eddie. This is not just a celebrity, this is Ava. Frank's Ava. If she came here it was to see him, but then she ran out. I wanna know why before it gets back to Frank. That enough?'

He was looking out for Frank, like always.

'Yeah, OK,' I said. 'That's enough.'

'Thank you,' he said, and started to walk away.

'Wait, Jack!'

He'd taken two steps, stopped and turned, frowning.

'What about Frank?' I asked.

'What about him?'

'Well . . . can I just ask him if he's seen her?'

Entratter rubbed his jaw thoughtfully.

'I don't see why not, but he's got his ex-wife here, and his kids,' he said. 'Tread lightly.'

'I always do, Jack,' I said, 'when it comes to the guys.'

'Check with Dean first,' he suggested. 'Maybe you won't have to bother Frank. Those guys usually know everything about each other.'

'I'll do that,' I said. 'I had dinner with him last night, but do you know where he is now?'

'I can't do your job for you, Eddie,' he said. 'You know Dino. Check the golf course. I heard Jack Benny's in town. They're probably playing.'

Entratter started to walk away, then stopped and turned, raising his arm like he forgot something.

'What's with Rachel?' he asked. 'She's in my office, sayin' you sent her home yesterday.'

'She's got two left hands, Jack,' I said, scowling at him. 'And she doesn't have the head for a dealer. And why the hell didn't you tell me she was some mob guy's *goumada*?'

'You didn't ask,' he said. 'Besides, I'm the boss. That means I don't have to explain everything to you. Right?'

'But Jack . . . does she have to be a dealer?'

'No, she don't,' Jack said. 'Why don't you just find something else for her to do?'

'Why do I have to—' I started to ask, again.

'Because I foisted her off on you,' he answered, cutting me off. 'You don't want her? Foist her off on someone else. But don't let it interfere with finding out about Ava.'

'You got it, Boss.'

Since I was going to have to leave the casino floor – and probably the building – I needed somebody to cover my pit for me. One of my floormen was just weeks away from becoming a pit boss himself, so I asked him to take my place for the day.

'Just today, Eddie?' he asked.

I grinned and said, 'I'm hoping it won't be much longer than that, Phil, but if it is you'll be the first to know.'

'Anythin' you wanna tell me before you leave?' he asked.

'Yeah,' I told him, 'just don't piss off any of my regulars.'

Then I went in search of Ava Gardner.

FIVE

The last film I'd seen Ava in was *On The Beach*, with Gregory Peck. That had been in fifty-nine, three years ago. She'd done an Italian film with Dirk Bogarde in sixty, *The Angel Wore Red*, but I hadn't seen it yet. Since then she'd been off the screen, living in Madrid and supposedly trotting around the globe. Only a few months back I'd heard that she'd started production on a new film called *Fifty-Five Days at Peking*, with Charlton Heston and David Niven. I didn't know if that movie had wrapped or not, but if not what would she be doing in Las Vegas?

The answer was obvious. She would have been looking for Frank. They had been divorced since fifty-seven, but being friends with Frank I knew that he stilled loved her, and she still loved him. They tried to stay friends, but they mixed like dynamite and fire. Frank had once said to me, very sadly, 'I love her, and God damn me for it.'

I went to the hotel lobby to talk to the staff, hoping to find out who had actually seen Ava in the building. But there had been a shift change. If a bellman or desk clerk had seen her, they had gone home. I decided to go outside and talk to the valets. That's where I lucked out.

'Yeah, I saw 'er,' a valet named Kenny said. He had enough acne to make him look like Howdy Doody. 'Got out of a cab, went inside, came running out again a little while later.'

'Where'd she go?'

'Got into another cab.'

'Did you hear where she told the cabbie to take her?' I asked.

'I didn't hear, but I figured it must be the airport,' Kenny said.

'Which cab was it?'

'It was an Ace cab.'

'You know which one?'

'I don't know the number,' he said, 'but the cabbie's name is Leo.'

'Is he in line now?' I asked.

Kenny looked over at the line of cabs waiting for fares and said, 'No, he's not back yet.'

I thought about going to the airport to find him, but he might have been on his way back.

'Kenny, if he comes back in the next ten or fifteen minutes I'll be in the lobby,' I told the valet. 'Tell him there's a ten in it for him if he comes in and talks to me.'

'What's it about, Eddie?' he asked.

'Just do it, Kenny. OK? As a favor?'

'Sure thing, Eddie.' I gave him a five spot and went back into the hotel.

SIX

I used one of the phones behind the front desk to call Ted Silver, who worked in Security at McCarran Airport. I had to wait a while for him to come on the line. In those days the airport – named for Senator Pat McCarran – was pretty small, so he came on the line quick.

'Eddie G., my man,' Ted said. 'What can I do for you, brother?'

'Ava Gardner.'

'Sign me up.'

'I need to know if she flew in or out of Vegas in the past couple of hours.'

'You're kiddin', right?'

'Not kidding, Ted,' I said. 'In fact, she may be in the airport right now. Or stepping out of a cab.'

'Jesus,' he said, 'what the hell am I doin' on the phone with you?'

'Find out for me, Ted.'

'And whataya want me to do with her if she's here?' he

asked. 'You want me to hold 'er here? She run out on a marker?'

Good question. What did I want? Entratter didn't say anything about bringing her back to the Sands.

'No, no,' I said, 'don't detain her. I just need to know if she was here. And where she goes.'

'That's it?'

'That's it.'

'What's it about, Eddie?' he asked. 'Did she run out on a debt?'

'Just do it for me, Ted. OK?'

'OK, Eddie,' Ted said. 'I'll give ya a call back at the Sands, right?'

'Right. Thanks, Ted.'

'Tickets to a show, right?'

'Whenever you want.'

'I'll be talkin' to ya.'

I hung up, nodded my thanks to the people behind the desk and got out of their way.

I decided not to bother Dean Martin with this. Frank had told me on more than one occasion that we were friends, and that I could talk to him anytime. On the other side of the desk I found a house phone and asked for Frank Sinatra's suite, made arrangements to see him.

But in the end I decided to go ahead and check with Dean before seeing Frank. I knew how volatile Frank's relationship with Ava had always been. Maybe I could avoid throwing wood on that fire.

I found out Dean had arranged for a tee time at the Desert Inn Golf Course. The last time I bothered him there he'd been playing a round with Bob Hope. This time – according to Jack Entratter – I might've been interrupting a round with Jack Benny.

I found Mack Gray, Dean's Man Friday, in the clubhouse bar. After we shook hands he confirmed that Dean was on the course with Jack Benny.

'You want I could drive ya out there?' he asked.

'You know what hole they'll be on?'

'We could probably figure it out,' he said. 'Come on.'

We got a golf cart and after Mack wedged his bulk behind the wheel, we took off. Several times as he executed a bend I thought Mack's weight was going to overturn us. But somehow he managed to keep the cart upright.

As we drove I asked Mack if he knew anything about Ava Gardner, any recent news.

'I know what I hear the boss talk about,' he said. 'She took some time off from movies, but just made one recently. I think she finished last month.'

'Where did they shoot?'

'Spain. I think that was the only reason she did it. She ain't made a Hollywood movie since nineteen sixty.'

Some of that I already knew.

'There they are,' he said.

They were on the tee for the eighth hole. As we drove toward them Dean noticed us, must have recognized Mack behind the wheel. He said something to the other men – presumably Jack Benny – and walked towards us.

'What's goin' on, Eddie?' he asked, as I got out of the cart. With my weight gone the thing almost tipped over on Mack, but he quickly got out before that happened.

'I just wanted to ask you a couple of quick questions before I bother Frank with them,' I said.

Jack Benny looked over at us, and then checked his watch.

'I won't keep you long, Dean,' I said. 'I don't want to get Mr Benny mad.'

'Don't worry,' Dean said, 'He'll sulk a bit, but when I beat him he's going to blame you.' He put his right hand in the pocket of his white pants, leaned on the golf club with his left. 'What's this about Eddie?'

'Word's goin' around the hotel that Ava was there this morning.'

'Ava? I thought she was in Spain.'

'That's what I thought. So you didn't see her? Or hear anything?'

'No.'

'Nothin' from Frank?'

'Nope,' he said, shaking his head. 'If he saw her he hasn't told me.'

'Would Frank bring Ava to Vegas while his kids were here?' I asked.

'Maybe,' he said. 'After all, she was their step-mother for a while.'

'But would he bring her while their real mom was here?'

'No,' Dean said, shaking his head, 'that'd be looking for trouble.'

'Well,' I said, 'I guess I'm gonna have to ask him if he's seen her. Entratter wants me to find out if she was really here.'

'Well, ask him, then,' Dean said. 'Maybe he did see her, but he sure wouldn't mix her with Nancy.'

I nodded.

'Thanks Dean.'

'Anything else?' he asked 'Or can I get back to my game?'

'How's it goin', Boss?' Mack asked.

'You and me are gonna eat in style tonight, Big Guy,' Dean said, 'on Mr Benny's dime.'

'That'll make 'im cry,' Mack said.

'Let me know what happens, Eddie,' Dean said, and returned to his game.

As we drove back to the clubhouse I said to Mack, 'It should be interesting to have dinner with Jack Benny, huh?'

'Oh, Mr Benny won't be there.'

'But Dean said you'd be having dinner with him.'

'We're gonna have dinner *on* him,' Mack said. 'If he loses and has to buy two dinners, he sure ain't gonna wanna buy a third!'

SEVEN

When I knocked on the door I was surprised when it was answered by a beautiful young girl of twenty-two. She was blonde, slender, wearing a mini-skirt and white boots.

'Well, hello,' she said.

'Hello,' I said. 'I was looking for Frank—'

He came up behind her, cutting me off with his appearance.

'Eddie!' he said. 'I want you to meet my daughter, Nancy.'

'The famous Eddie G.,' she said, with a smile. 'This is a pleasure.'

'I can see why your dad is so proud of you,' I said. 'You're beautiful.'

'And talented,' Frank said. 'She sings like an angel.'

'Daddy, I'm more interested in the fact that Eddie thinks I'm beautiful,' she said, boldly looking me in the eyes. I had the feeling this young lady was going to be a force to be reckoned with as she got older.

'Maybe we could have a drink some time—' she started, but her father cut her off.

'Oh, no,' he said, pushing her out the door. I had to step aside to let her go. She smelled wonderful. 'Eddie's too old for you, little girl. You just run along. We have business.'

'Oh, Daddy . . .'

'Go!' he said.

She took a few steps down the hall and when she was out of his sight held her hand to her ear and mouthed, 'Call me.'

Frank was casually dressed and waved me in, a big welcoming smile on his face. I stepped into the suite, where it was safe.

'Hey, my man Eddie,' he said, closing the door behind me. He pumped my hand. He was dressed casually, open collar shirt, grey slacks, and a pair of slippers. 'Great to see you, Clyde. What brings you here?'

'Where's George?' I asked, looking around.

George Jacobs was to Frank what Mack Gray was to Dean.

'Down the hall,' Frank said. 'I got a separate suite for Nancy and the kids. I'm having George look after them. You wanna drink?'

'No, thanks,' I said. 'I'm not gonna take up too much of your time, Frank. I just have a question.'

'OK.' He folded his arms and shrugged. 'Shoot.'

'Did you see Ava today?'

'Ava?' He dropped his arms. 'Why? Is she here?' His blues eyes lit up as they always did when he spoke of her, or heard her name.

'I guess that means you didn't see her, then.'

'No, no, I haven't seen her' He frowned. '*Was* she here?'

'I don't know,' I said. 'That's what I'm trying to find out. One of our valets said he saw her, but he could've been mistaken. I'm checking with the airport now.'

Frank walked to the bar, hesitated, then changed his mind about a drink. Instead, he just leaned on the bar with both hands.

'Maybe,' he said, 'she was here, and somehow . . .'

'Somehow what?'

'Found out that my family was here.' He turned to face me. 'She wouldn't have wanted Nancy to see her.' I knew he was talking about his ex-wife, not his daughter.

'Would she just run out?' I asked. 'Without even leavin' you a message?'

'Run?'

'The valet said she came out in a hurry, got into a cab,' I explained. 'I'm waiting to talk to the cab driver who might've picked her up.'

'When was this supposed to have happened?' Frank asked.

'Jack came to me a little while ago.'

'So this morning?'

'Yes.'

'I was in the lobby this morning,' he said, 'briefly, but with my family, my ex. She could've seen me.' He scratched his head. 'Damn it. You gotta find her for me, Eddie.'

'I'm lookin', Frank.'

'No,' he said, 'I know Entratter wants you to find her so that I won't worry. He's trying to protect me. But I mean you've got to find her *for me*, talk to her. Find out what's wrong. If she came here without calling first, then something's wrong. She wanted to see me for some reason.'

'So maybe she saw you with Nancy, got jealous and ran out.'

'No, Ava wouldn't get jealous of Nancy,' Frank said.

'Come on, Eddie. I know you. If she's in town you can find her. Then bring her to me so I can find out what she needs.'

'And then what?'

'Then I'll give it to her,' he said, with a helpless shrug. 'Whatever it is.'

EIGHT

I left Frank's suite and went back downstairs. I'd left word at the desk to hold the cab driver if he came in while I was with Frank. He hadn't. But as I was standing there a driver came in and I recognized him immediately, though not by name. I knew him the way I knew a hundred cab drivers in town: by face. This one was particularly memorable, because it looked like a map, with peaks and crevices earned over years of hard working and living.

'Mr Gianelli?' he said. 'Kenny said you wanted to see me?' I was groping for his name when he saved me. 'I'm Leo Rossi.'

'Of course, Leo,' I said. 'Thanks for coming in. Leo, did you have Ava Gardner in your cab today?'

'You know,' he said, 'I thought that was her, but I wasn't sure. I mean . . . this broad gets in my cab and she's a looker, ya know? But they look different when they're not up on the screen, ya know? And she had dark glasses, and . . . I think she mighta been cryin'. What reason would a big movie star have to cry? They got it all.'

'Yeah, I know,' I said. 'Where'd you take her, Leo?'

'The airport.'

'Did she say what flight she would be on? Or where she was going?'

'Geez, Mr G., I didn't . . . I mean, we didn't talk, other then her tellin' me where ta take her, ya know? I mean . . . geez, Ava Gardner. Wait till I tell the wife. I mean, I get stars in my cab all the time, ya know, but . . . geez . . .'

'OK, Leo, OK,' I said. 'I've got eyes at the airport. Maybe I'll get something from them. Thanks. Wait, I owe you ten—'

'That's OK, Mr G.,' Leo said. 'Ya don't got to pay me. I'm glad ta help.'

'Leo, would you and your wife like to see a show? Frank, Dean and Sammy?'

'Geez, Mr G., my wife'd love it,' Leo said, eyes wide. 'That'd be great.'

'I'll leave tickets for you,' I said. 'Just mention my name.'

'Thanks, Mr G.'

He hurried back to work.

'Eddie?'

I turned. One of the desk clerks was holding his phone out.

'Call for you.'

'Thanks, Sean.' I accepted the phone. It smelled like the clerk's Hai Karate. 'Hello?'

'Eddie? Ted Silver.'

'Whataya got for me, Ted?'

'Ava Gardner came in on a Hughes Air Line shuttle from L.A. this mornin',' Ted said.

'And?'

'And it looks like she just went back the same way.'

'And then what?'

'I don't have any way of knowing that,' Ted said. 'You'd have to check with the airport in L.A.'

'Yeah, you're right,' I said. 'You got a name for me there?'

'Hang on.' He came back on and gave me the name of somebody at LAX who could help me.

'OK, Ted. Thanks. I'll leave tickets for you, as usual.'

'Sure thing, Eddie. Thanks.'

I hung up, then dialed the number he'd given me and asked for Ben Hoff.

'This is Hoff,' a gruff man's voice came on the phone.

I told him who I was, who'd given me his name, and what I needed.

'You're the guy who gets Teddy tickets to shows, right?' Hoff asked.

'That's right.'

'Will I get tickets for this?'

'Any time, Ben,' I said. 'You just tell me when you're in town.'

'OK,' he said. 'Ava Gardner. Well, that shouldn't be too hard. Where do I call you back?'

I gave him the number of the hotel.

'OK, Mr Gianelli,' Hoff said. 'I'll get back to you as quick as I can.'

'I appreciate it, Ben,' I said. 'And just call me Eddie.'

I hung up, glad I was going to be able to figure this out without having to actually go to L.A.

I had to go to L.A.

Ben called me back and said, 'Miss Gardner came in on a flight from Vegas, didn't go out on any other flights.'

'Are you sure?' I asked. 'Did you check international flights? She lives in Spain.'

'I checked all flights, local and domestic,' he said. 'I promise you, Eddie, she's still someplace in L.A.'

I thought fast. I could have asked my P.I. friend, Danny Bardini, to go to L.A. and check on her, but the last time I did that – earlier in the year with Marilyn – Danny had a rough time of it and almost got killed. I also could have called Fred Otash, the Hollywood P.I. who had helped me find Danny, but that didn't mean I trusted him. Not completely, anyway. After all, he did work in Hollywood.

'OK, look, Ben, find out for me if she took a cab. I'm flying in as soon as I can get a flight.'

'Need help with that?'

'I can get help on this end, but thanks.'

'No problem. Call me any time, Eddie.'

'You let me know when you're in Vegas, Ben,' I said, and hung up.

I had options: take a flight, get Jack to set it up for me, pay for the ticket; get Frank to do it; call Ted Silver at the airport, have him do it; use the Sands helicopter.

I decided to let Jack do it. I didn't want to bother Frank

anymore while he had his kids with him, while Ted Silver probably could have gotten me on a flight, I'd still have to pay for it and then get the money back from Jack. So, cut out the middle man, let Jack get me the ticket.

I waved thanks to the desk clerk for the phone again and headed for Jack's office.

NINE

I had to see Jack and Frank before I left. Jack's girl gave me a disapproving look as I breezed past her into his office. I had come to terms with the fact that she didn't like me and never would, so I just stopped trying.

'You got somethin' for me already?' Jack asked as I sat across from him.

'I need you to get me on a flight to L.A.,' I said.

'Why are you goin' to L.A.?' he asked. 'Last time you went there you almost got killed.'

'According to both airports, Ava Gardner flew to Vegas and back, but didn't fly out of L.A. So she's still there.'

'Where?'

'That I don't know,' I said. 'I've got to go and find out.'

'Wait, wait,' he said. 'Hold your horses. So Ava was here this mornin'?'

'Yes.'

'And did she see Frank?' 'No.'

'Well, then . . .' Jack said, sitting back and spreading his hands.

'Well then . . . what?'

'Why are you going to L.A.?' he asked. 'You did what I asked you to do. You found out if it was her, and it was. And she's gone. Go back to work.'

'I can't do that, Jack.'

'Why not?'

'Frank wants me to find her, and see what she was doing here.'

'So you had to talk to Frank?' he asked.

'Yes,' I said, 'don't worry, I trod lightly, as you suggested.'

'I'm sure you did.'

'I'll go talk to Frank now,' I said. 'Would you call him and see if he's in his suite?'

'And if he isn't I'll locate him for you,' he said. 'And I'll get you your flight.'

'Which the Sands will pay for?'

'Of course,' he said, with the phone in his hand. I heard a buzz from the outer office and then he said, 'See if you can locate Frank Sinatra for me. Thanks.' He hung up without saying his girl's name. I wondered if I'd ever heard it, then decided I didn't care enough to ask.

'I'll get packed,' I said, rising from my chair. 'I'll check in with you to see where Frank is.'

By the time I packed an overnight bag, using just what I had in my locker, Jack had found Frank and arranged for me to meet him for a drink in the Silver Queen Lounge. Frank was sitting at the bar, having just signed autographs for a couple of middle-aged broads. There was a drink on the bar in front of him.

'Glad to see you, Clyde,' he said. 'Do you know that most of the time, if I'm sitting with somebody, folks don't bother me for autographs? It's when I'm sittin' alone they think they can come over.'

'Guess they figure they're not interruptin' anything, Frank,' I said.

'You wanna drink?'

'Just a beer,' I said. 'I'm headin' for the airport.'

'This about Ava?' he asked, after waving at the bartender to bring me a beer.

'Yeah,' I said, 'I'm goin' to L.A. Apparently she stopped there and didn't catch another flight to, well . . . anywhere.'

'Not to Spain?'

'No.'

'So where is she now?'

'I don't know,' I said. 'That's what I'm goin' there to find out.'

'Eddie, I didn't mean for you to miss work—'

'Don't worry, the Sands will pay me, and take care of my expenses.'

'You sure Jack will do that?' Frank asked. 'I mean, if you need money—'

'No, I'm fine, Frank,' I said. 'Just a quick flight to L.A. and a little talk with Ava, once I find her.'

'Try the Beverly Hills Hotel,' Frank said. 'You might find her there in a bungalow.'

'Maybe I could call—'

'She wouldn't use her real name,' he said. 'And the staff would cover for her. No, you're right, you'll have to go and see if she's there.'

'OK.'

'I wonder why she flew under her real name?' Frank asked.

'That's somethin' else I'll ask her,' I said.

'Call me as soon as you see her,' Frank said. 'In fact, you can put her on the phone with me. Maybe then we'll get some answers.'

'OK, Frank.'

I got off the bar stool without having touched my beer. He grabbed my arm.

'Sit down a minute,' he said. 'There are things you should know about Ava.'

I sat, sipped my beer.

'Like what?'

'She's at an age where she's feeling vulnerable. You've got to be careful with her.'

Vulnerable was not a word I had heard used to describe Ava Gardner. Fiery, maybe, even wild. Not vulnerable.

'What do you mean?'

'She's not happy,' Frank said. 'She thinks she's gettin older.'

'We're all gettin' older, Frank.'

'Ava doesn't like what she sees when she looks in the mirror,' Frank said. 'And she's become hard to get along with. She gave them a helluva time on her last film, *Fifty-Five Days at Peking*.'

'How do you know that?'

'I got it from Chuck Heston and Bernie Gordon, the screenwriter. Gordon says she was drinkin' a lot. Heston says her behavior was the worst he's ever seen from a colleague.' Frank shrugged. 'He's a bit of a stiff, but she still musta been pretty bad.'

'So she's a drunk?'

'Maybe,' he said, 'but I think her problems go further than just drying out.'

'You try to talk to her about it?'

'I called her a couple of times, but we got into fights,' he said. 'But if I could see her face to face . . . maybe I could get her to open up.' He looked at me. 'Or maybe you can.'

'Me? She doesn't even know me.'

'I think I mentioned you to her once or twice,' he said. 'And you're good with people, Eddie. You're real good. Look what you did for Marilyn.'

'I got there too late,' I said. In answer to her call I'd driven the night she died from Vegas to L.A. to see Marilyn but there were cops all over there when I arrived.

'We were all too late for Marilyn, Eddie,' Frank said. 'Too little, or too late. But I don't want that to be the case with Ava.'

'I understand, Frank,' I said. 'I'll do what I can. I promise.'

'Thanks, Eddie,' he said. 'Thanks a lot.'

TEN

When I got to the airport in L.A. I met with security man Ben Hoff, he of the gruff voice, a big, beefy guy in his thirties who pumped my hand enthusiastically. He had black hair that was soaked with Brylcreem.

'Glad to meet ya, Eddie,' he said. 'Real glad.'

'Did you find me a cab driver, Ben?' I asked.

'Yeah, I found the guy who picked her up,' he said. 'Come on. When you called me from McCarran I got ahold of him and made him wait in the security office. He's a little pissed off, but I told him it would be worth his while.'

'How worth his while?'

'Fifty should do it.'

'OK,' I said. 'Let's go.'

Maybe I should have taken some expense money from Frank, after all.

Hoff walked me to the security office where a small, middle-aged man was sitting on a stool, his knees bouncing up and down with anxiety.

'Hey, Ben,' he said, popping to his feet when he saw Hoff, 'come on, I gotta make a livin'.'

'Take it easy, Larry,' Hoff said, 'this is the fella I was tellin' you about. Wants ta talk to you.'

'My name's Eddie Gianelli, Larry,' I said. 'I'm trying to find Ava Gardner. Ben tells me she was in your cab this morning.'

Larry's eyes narrowed and took on a crafty glint in his eyes.

'She mighta been,' he said. 'I get lots of broads in my cab.'

'Yeah, well this one you'd remember, wouldn't you?' I asked.

I looked at Ben Hoff, who nodded at me.

I took a fifty from my wallet and held it out to Larry.

'That's all I get?' the cab driver asked.

'Take it, Larry,' Hoff snapped.

'Yeah, yeah,' Larry said, snatching the bill from my hand, 'so she was in my cab.'

'Where did you take her?'

He hesitated.

'Larry!' Hoff said.

'I drove her to the Beverly Hills Hotel.'

'OK,' I said, 'take me there.'

'For how much?'

'The going rate,' I said, 'plus twenty bucks.'

'I'm your man,' Larry said. He grabbed my suitcase from my hand. 'Let's go.'

'Thanks, Ben,' I said, shaking the security man's hand.

'Anytime, Eddie.'

'See you in Vegas,' I said, and followed the cabbie.

Larry stopped his cab in front of the hotel and hesitated before getting out.

'Did you wait to see her walk in?' I asked.

'Well . . . I watched her walk, if that's what ya mean,' Larry said. 'Come on, it's Ava Gardner, right? So yeah, I saw her go in.'

'OK.' I grabbed my suitcase and started to get out.

'You want me to wait?' he asked. 'You're gonna need wheels, right?'

'Yeah, I might,' I said. I paid the fare, gave him the extra twenty, and then another ten. 'OK, wait. And keep the meter running.'

'Sure thing!'

I got out of the cab, hesitated, then decided to leave my overnight bag. Even if Larry took off on me, there wasn't anything of value in there anyway.

I walked up to the front door and entered, crossed the lobby to the front desk.

'Can I help you, sir?' a polite, impeccably dressed desk clerk asked.

'Yes, could you tell me what room or bungalow Miss Ava Gardner is in?'

'Sir?'

'Ava Gardner.'

'I don't believe Miss Gardner is in the hotel, sir,' the man said.

'I think she is,' I said. 'I just spoke to a cab driver who brought her here from the airport.'

'Sir,' the clerk said, 'even if she was here it's against hotel policy—'

I was tempted to invoke Frank's name, but five minutes after I spoke it, it probably would have made it into the newspaper.

If Ava was registered under an assumed name, and I knew that name, maybe that would have gotten me further.

'OK,' I said, 'thanks.'

I searched the lobby and found the public phones. I called Jack Entratter in Vegas.

'You in trouble already?' he asked.

'No,' I said. 'I just need you to ask Frank something for me.'

'What's that?'

'If Ava used an assumed name to register at a hotel, what does he think it would be?'

'That's what you want to know?'

'That's it.'

'Where are you?'

'Beverly Hills Hotel, but I'm on a pay phone. Here's the number.'

'I'll call you back the minute I find out somethin',' he said.

'OK. I'm gonna check the bungalows, but I should be in the lobby or the bar when the phone rings.'

'Frank's in the building,' he said. 'It shouldn't be long.'

'Thanks Jack.'

ELEVEN

My plan had been to go out to the bungalows and look around, but that could have gotten me arrested as a peeping tom.

Instead, I decided to go into the bar, have a drink, and wait. But first I went back out to the cab.

'I'm gonna be longer than I thought,' I told Larry. 'You want to come in and have a drink in the bar?'

'In there?' he asked. 'Where the movie stars drink? Sure thing!'

'OK,' I said, as he got out of his cab, 'but turn off the meter.'

'Aw, Mr Gianelli,' he said, 'you didn't think I'd leave it runnin', didja?'

'No, of course not,' I said, 'and my name's Eddie G., Larry.'

'OK, Mr G.,' he said. 'Let's go.'

We went into the building, entered the Polo Lounge and sat at the bar. Right off the bat I spotted Debbie Reynolds having lunch with somebody. Howard Duff and Ida Lupino were at a corner table, Steve Lawrence and Eydie Gorme in a booth. I had to keep Larry rooted to his stool so he didn't charge anybody.

'You're a cab driver in Hollywood,' I said. 'I would think this was old hat to you.'

'You kiddin'?' he asked. 'A star's a star, man.'

'Eddie?'

I turned and saw Joey Bishop walking toward me. There was a woman behind him, but all I could see was blonde hair and a shapely figure.

'Hey, Eddie G.,' he said. 'What're you doin' out of Vegas?'

I got off my stool and shook hands with him.

'They let me out once in a while, Joe.'

'What are ya doin' here?' he asked.

'I'm here on some Sands business, Joe,' I said.

'Trackin' down some bad debts?'

'You got it. Oh, this is my friend, Larry.'

'Hey, Larry,' Joey said, shaking hands. He stepped aside so we could see the woman behind him. I found myself looking at the second most beautiful overbite I'd ever seen this side of Gene Tierney.

'This is my TV wife, Abby Dalton. We were just gonna have lunch. Honey, this is Eddie Gianelli, and his friend, Larry.'

'Geez,' Larry said, staring at Abby.

'The famous Eddie G.,' Abby said, with a dazzling smile. 'I've heard so much about you. It's a pleasure to meet you.'

'Miss Dalton—'

'Oh, no,' she said, 'any friend of my TV husband's is a

friend of mine. You call me Abby. In fact, you can call me any time you want.'

'Hey, hey,' Joey said, 'no fair flirtin' right in front of your husband.'

Joey pulled Abby away from me.

'Can you have a bite with us?' she asked.

'I'm sorry, no,' I said. 'I'm, uh, waiting for somebody.'

'It was good to see you, Eddie.'

'You too, Joey,' I said. 'Hey, Abby, if you ever get to Vegas—'

'I was born in Vegas, Eddie,' she said. 'Next time I come to see my folks I'll look you up.'

'You do that.'

As they walked away to a table Larry said, 'Damn, that babe was comin' on to ya. That happen a lot?'

'Once in a while,' I said.

'Maybe,' he said, when we had our drinks – a couple of beers – 'we should go look by the pool? Maybe Miss Gardner's there? Or some other movie stars?'

'Relax, Larry,' I said. 'It's lunch time. They'll be flocking in here pretty soon.'

'I could just go up to Debbie Reynolds and ask—'

'No,' I said, 'leave her alone. She's doin' business. Like most of these people.'

'Hey, Eddie!'

I turned and got a quick kiss on the cheek from Eydie Gorme.

'We've got to run, Eddie,' Steve Lawrence said, 'but we wanted to say hi.'

'Hey, Steve,' I said, 'I love *Go Away Little Girl*.' He had a number one hit that year with that song.

'Thanks a lot, Eddie.'

I gave Eydie a squeeze and shook Steve's hand and they went on their way.

'Geez, everybody know you?' Larry asked.

'No,' I said, 'just some.'

I was starting to feel dumb about using the pay phone. There was no guarantee I'd hear it, or that anyone would pick it up when it rang. And if someone did answer it, would they come looking for me? I should have had Jack call me at the front desk. Then they could have paged me, which might have given me some credence with the desk clerk.

'If a movie star walks in,' Larry said, 'maybe they can help ya find her?'

'You think all movie stars know each other, Larry?' I asked.

'Hell, Mr G.,' he said, 'Hollywood's a small town. Yeah, everybody knows everybody. Look how many know you? And you ain't from here.'

'Wait here,' I told Larry. 'Have another beer. I'm gonna make a phone call.'

'Sure.'

I put money on the bar to cover the drinks, then went back out into the lobby.

I was walking towards the pay phone to call Jack again when it rang. I stepped in, closed the door and answered.

'Eddie?'

'Hey, Jack.'

'Frank says when Ava was first put under contract the studio wanted to call her Lucy Johnson, but she wouldn't go for it. She insisted on using her real name. But she uses Johnson sometimes as an alias.'

'OK,' I said. 'I'll try that. Listen, if you don't hear from me in twenty minutes call me at the hotel and have the desk page me.'

'What for?'

'I'm just trying to raise my profile here, Jack,' I said. 'Being paged in the Polo Lounge will do that.'

'I didn't know you went in for that sort of thing, Eddie.'

'Just call me.'

'I'll have my girl do it.'

'She won't,' I said. 'She hates me.'

'We'll take care of it,' Jack said, and hung up.

TWELVE

'Who?' the clerk asked.

'Lucy Johnson,' I repeated. 'Do you have a Lucy Johnson registered?'

The man looked confused.

'Come on,' I said. 'It's not that hard a question to answer.'

'Um, I'll check, sir.'

'You do that.'

He checked his registration records, even though I knew he didn't have to.

'Look,' I said, as he started to sweat, 'call your manager. I'll talk to him.'

Relieved, he said, 'Yes, sir.'

He picked up his phone, dialed three numbers and said, 'Mr Gentry, I need you out here. Yes, sir, it's very important.'

He hung up and looked at me.

'He's comin' right out.'

'That wasn't so hard, was it?' I asked.

'No, sir,' he said, 'but I'm just tryin' to do my job, sir.'

'Ain't we all?' I asked.

I saw three more celebrities walk through the lobby while we waited for the manager. I knew them by sight, they didn't know me, at all. One of them was that guy who played in the T.V. western *Sugarfoot*. Will Hutchins, that was it. Another one was the guy with the mustache from *Hawaiian Eye*. Used to be all you saw in the Beverly Hills Hotel lobby was movie stars. At least, that's what I heard.

When the Manager appeared he was older and, if possible, more dapper than the desk clerk. It was easy to see this was in the desk clerk's future.

'What is it, Leon?' he asked the clerk.

'Um, this gent wants to know what room Lucy Johnson is in.'

'Lucy Johnson?' The Manager looked at me.

'That's right,' I said.

'Do you have business with Miss Johnson?' the Manager asked. 'You see, we guarantee our guests' privacy—'

'I understand that,' I said, 'but it's important I speak with Miss Gardner – I mean, Miss Johnson.'

It wasn't a slip of the tongue. I just wanted to make sure we all knew who we were really talking about.

'Are you, uh, from the studio?' he asked.

'No,' I said, 'my business is much more personal than that, if you know what I mean.'

Suddenly, as if a light had been turned on in his head, the Manager smiled.

'Oh, I understand,' he said. I could tell by the look on his face that he thought he understood, but I knew he really didn't. Now I had to decide if I wanted him to keep thinking what I thought he was thinking.

'Please,' he said, 'come with me. I will escort you to her bungalow.'

OK, well, this was what I'd wanted, and it looked like I'd succeeded, so why try to talk him out of it now?

'Lead on.'

I followed him out to the bungalows, and down a path toward one of them.

'I was a little confused,' he said, as we walked, 'because Miss Johnson usually prefers the company of much younger, um . . .'

'Men?' I asked.

'Well, yes,' he said. 'I mean, uh, no offense.'

'None taken,' I said. 'I guess everyone needs a little more seasoning once in a while, huh?'

'Yes,' he said, 'yes, indeed.'

We approached one of the bungalows and he turned to give me a smile that was meant to convey some sort of bond we were sharing.

'Will you knock,' he said, 'or shall I?'

I stepped forward and knocked on the door. We waited, and I realized I was holding my breath. I had never seen Ava Gardner in person.

When the door opened she squinted her eyes against the
light, held her hand up for shade. Ava Gardner was sex in
a bottle – a wine bottle, still corked. Sexy and beautiful on
the outside, but once the cork was popped . . .

Frank said she didn't like what she saw when she looked
in a mirror these days, but when I looked at her it was like
a punch in the stomach. She was Venus, Maria Vargas from
The Barefoot Contessa, but to me she'd always be Honey
Bear Kelly from *Mogambo*. Her black hair was cut Honey
Bear short, her skin pale and smooth. And the green eyes,
oh the green eyes, even squinted and shaded they were
amazing . . .

'Mr Gentry,' she said, 'I thought I made it clear I did not
want to be disturbed.'

'Uh, this gentleman asked for you by name, Madam,' he
stammered. 'I mean, uh, he asked for Lucy Johnson.'

She looked at me for the first time, and I saw Ava, the
sexual predator. She looked me up and down and asked,
'Who the hell are you?'

'I've come on behalf of Frank'

She stared at me for a few minutes, then looked at the
Manager and said, 'It's all right, Mr Gentry.'

'Yes, Ma'am.'

She showed him her index finger and added, 'But no one
else, understand?'

'I understand.' He actually bowed to her, and backed
away.

As he scurried back down the path she looked at me and
said, 'Come on in, you must be Eddie G.'

THIRTEEN

I stepped into the bungalow and closed the door.

Ava Gardner was wearing jeans with the cuffs rolled
up and a man's shirt with the sleeves rolled up. Her feet
were bare. Just my luck she'd have to be wearing the

"Mogambo" look. My chest felt tight. She looked and smelled like sex. Somehow, the cigarette she was holding just added to the look.

I was as nervous as a school boy on prom night.

'Drink?' she asked.

'Yes, thanks,' I said.

She went to a sidebar and poured out two glasses of something. She walked across the room and handed me a highball glass. It smelled like bourbon. Good bourbon.

'You know who I am?' I asked.

'Eddie G.?' she said. 'Yes, I've heard Frank talk about you. He likes you.'

'I'm here because of Frank, Miss Gardner.'

'Oh, no,' she said, with a lazy smile, 'just call me Ava, Eddie.'

I realized then that this wasn't the first glass of bourbon she'd had that day. Though I couldn't figure how she'd had time to have too many drinks. She'd flown into Vegas, stopped at the Sands, then flown out of Vegas to L.A., and taken a cab here to the hotel. She'd probably beaten me by a couple of hours. OK, yeah, that was time enough to down quite a few drinks.

'Frank sent you?' she asked. 'How did he know I was here?'

'He didn't,' I said. 'Word got around that you were at the Sands this morning, and left just as abruptly as you arrived.'

She drank some bourbon, swirled the rest in her glass, watching as it went round and round.

'Oh, yes,' she said. 'I saw Frank with Nancy and Tina in the lobby, and . . . I ran.' She shrugged and looked at me. 'I panicked and ran. All the way back here.'

'Ava, Frank figures it must've been somethin' very impor tant to bring you there without calling him first.'

'Important?' she asked. 'I guess that depends on which side you're on, Eddie.'

'Frank's on your side, Ava,' I said. 'So am I.'

She ran one hand through her short black hair, pulling at it, then shook her head.

'I don't know, Eddie,' she said. 'I don't know. Things have been . . . happening.'

'What things?'

'My life, it's unraveling,' she said. She looked down at her drink again, then drained it and walked back to the sidebar. She poured herself another glass, spilling a little bit from the decanter, then missing when she went to put the top back in.

'Ava,' I said, 'maybe we should have some coffee—'

'I don't want any coffee, Eddie,' she said, turning to face me. 'Coffee doesn't help. This is the only thing that helps.' She drank from her glass.

'Well then, maybe we can sit and talk about it.'

'I know who you are, Eddie,' she said, walking around the room slowly. 'But that doesn't mean we're friends. Why would I talk to you?'

'I told you,' I said. 'Frank sent me.'

'Because he couldn't come himself, right?'

'He doesn't know where you are, Ava,' I said. 'Maybe if we call him-'

'No!' she said, abruptly. 'No, we can't call Frank, not now. He's with his family.'

'I'm sure he can take some time to talk to you on the phone.'

She dropped herself down on the sofa, letting her hands and head hang. I watched the glass she held, waiting for it to fall to the ground.

I put my glass down and moved closer to her. There were armchairs on either side of the sofa, so I sat down in one.

'Eddie, Eddie,' she said, shaking her head, 'it'll take more than a phone call.'

'Ava—'

'Papa's dead,' she said. 'He did it to himself. Maybe he had the right idea.'

'Papa?'

'I've ruined my career, my life . . .' She lifted her head and looked at me. Her eyes were wet with tears. 'Look at me, Eddie. Look at me. I'm hideous.'

Good God, woman, I thought to myself, you're a fucking Goddess! Even looking tired, worn out, with tears in her eyes, she was a Goddess.

'Eddie—' she said, and then the glass dropped.

As it hit the floor and shattered she keeled over. I might have caught the glass, but instead I caught her. Suddenly, I had my arms full of Ava Gardner, but not the way I might have dreamed it.

FOURTEEN

I lifted her in my arms and carried her to the bedroom. The bed was made, so I laid her right on top of the spread. I lifted her head, pulled a pillow out from beneath the covers, then lowered her head gently on to it. I stood up and looked down at her.

Ava Gardner, every man's dark Goddess, as opposed to Marilyn, who had been every man's blonde Goddess. But Marilyn was gone. Ava was still here. I'd failed Marilyn, hadn't been able to help her. Maybe I'd be able to help Ava. When she woke up.

I left the bedroom and pulled the door closed behind me. That was when I remembered I'd left Larry the cab driver in the Polo Lounge. I went out the front door, also closing it gently behind me. Right now what Ava needed was sleep. I decided when I came back I'd bring her some food and coffee. But at the moment I had to settle with Larry.

I followed the path back to the hotel and found that business in the Polo Lounge had picked up considerably. Larry must have been happily ogling movie stars. I wondered how a cab driver in Hollywood had avoided becoming jaded.

I peered into the lounge and didn't see Larry at the bar. A man walking out stopped short when he saw me, then smiled and stuck out his hand.

'Eddie,' Johnny Carson said. 'What a surprise seein' you here.'

'Hey, Johnny' I said, 'how's the *Tonight Show* goin''?'

He had recently taken over the show from Jack Paar, which were some big shoes to fill.

'They haven't fired me yet. Saddled me with this big jamoke named Ed McMohan. I think they're going to have to dump him, or I'll only be doin' this for a couple of years. Good to see you, Ed.'

'You, too, John.'

As I reached the front desk I noticed there was some commotion in the lobby. A crowd was gathered, excited about something. I heard the word 'ambulance' and went to the desk.

'What's going on?' I asked the clerk.

'Fella left the Polo Lounge and when he got outside somebody attacked him.'

'What fella?' I asked.

'I don't know,' the clerk said. 'I think he was a cab driver.'

'Cab driver? What happened, exactly?'

'Like I said. Somebody attacked him, beat him up. They took him away in an ambulance.'

'Jesus,' I said. 'What the hell . . .'

The clerk shrugged.

'He got a call, and when he went outside—'

'A call? When?'

'A little while ago,' he said. 'One of our bell hops went through the lobby, and into the Polo Lounge, paging . . . somebody.'

'And?'

'And . . . he took the call.'

'Where is he?' I asked. 'The boy?'

The clerk rang the bell on his desk and an old guy appeared. He looked to be about sixty.

'This is Randy,' the clerk said.

'Randy, my name is Eddie Gianelli.'

'You're Mr Gianelli?'

'That's right. The man you paged with a call earlier . . .'

'The call was for an Eddie Gianelli,' Randy said, 'but the cab driver, he took it.'

'That's because he was waiting for me,' I said.

'The guy who got beat up?' Randy asked, looking surprised. 'He was with you?'

'Yeah,' I said, 'the guy who got beat up.' I looked at the clerk. 'Can you find out what hospital he was taken to?'

'Sure, Mr Gianelli.'

'And his condition,' I said. 'Whether or not they kept him there.'

'Sure, I'll find out everything,' the clerk said.

'Thanks. Oh, and I need some food to take to Miss Gardner – I mean, to Miss Johnson's bungalow.'

'Just tell me what you want,' Randy said, 'and I'll bring it over personally as soon as it's ready.'

'No, no,' I said, changing my mind. 'She's asleep now. I'll call when I want the food.'

'What would you like?' the clerk asked.

'I don't know,' I said. 'A hamburger platter . . . maybe a steak dinner? And a large pot of coffee, with two cups.'

'Anything else?'

'Iced water,' I said.

When I got back to Ava's bungalow I looked in on her. She was still asleep. I picked up my glass and freshened it with some bourbon. I'm sure a cab driver got into a lot of arguments during the course of a day, but had Larry gotten somebody mad enough at him to wait outside the hotel and beat him up?

Or had he been beaten up because he took a call in my name?

Was that supposed to be me in the ambulance, and if so, why?

FIFTEEN

I called Jack, filled him in, told him where I was. He said he'd pass the information on to Frank.

It was late in the afternoon when the phone rang. By then I had talked to the hospital and found out Larry's last name, and his condition. I snatched it up on the first ring, so it wouldn't wake Ava.

'Eddie? How is she?'

'She's asleep now, Frank, has been for a couple of hours. I have the feeling it's the first sleep she's gotten for a while.'

'But did you get a chance to talk to her?'

'Briefly, but she didn't tell me much. Just that her life was unraveling.'

'She's told me that on the phone, too,' he said, 'but not why.'

'She's not very forthcoming about that, Frank,' I said. 'And if she won't tell you, she certainly won't tell me.'

'Maybe she will,' Frank said. 'Keep asking, Eddie. I can't come there right now, but maybe in a few days . . .'

'She knows you're with your family. She understands.'

'Eddie . . . is she drinkin'?'

'Yes.'

'A lot?'

'Who can tell what a lot is, Frank?' I said. 'She's sleeping because she passed out. Maybe from exhaustion, maybe from drinkin', maybe a combination of both.'

'OK,' Frank said. 'OK, Eddie. You need anything?'

'Some answers.'

'For what?'

I told him about the cabbie picking up a call for me, and then being hauled off to the hospital.

'How bad was he hurt?'

'I talked to some sawbones a little while ago. He was hurt badly enough to be admitted, but he's not in danger of dying. Some broken bones and a lot of bruises,' I said. 'I'm gonna go and see him when I get a chance, and I want to take care of his medical bills.'

'I'll do that,' Frank said. 'You can count on me.'

I had planned on the Sands footing the bill, but I said, 'Thanks, Frank.'

'Why do you think he was jumped?'

'I'll know more when I've spoken to him. Maybe whoever beat him up said something. I still don't know if he was jumped because he's him, or they thought he was me.'

'Why would somebody wanna jump you?' he asked. 'You're only there because of Ava.'

'I know,' I said. 'I need answers, from the cabbie and from Ava.'

'Maybe she's in trouble, Eddie,' he said.

'Yeah,' I said, 'and maybe I am too.'

SIXTEEN

The phone call had caused Ava to stir. I figured she was close to waking up, so I called the desk and asked for the food to be delivered to the room. The knock at the door when Randy arrived did what the phone couldn't do. As I was setting the food on the table, Ava came out of the bedroom, rubbing her face.

'Eddie?'

'That's me,' I said.

'I–I thought it was a fucking dream.'

'Nope,' I said. 'I'm here. You hungry?'

'No,' she said, as if the thought of food made her sick, 'I have a fucking headache and I need a shower.'

'OK,' I said, 'have a shower, and then you can at least have some coffee.'

'Coffee,' she said. 'OK, that doesn't sound too bad. I'll be right out.'

I nodded, and she went back into the bedroom, leaving the door open. Next I heard the shower turn on and – despite my best efforts – I couldn't help imagining Ava under the spray, soaping herself.

I set the food out on the table, a burger-and-fries platter and a full steak dinner, as I had ordered. I didn't know which one I would eat. I figured once Ava came out of the shower she'd be hungry, and I planned to let her have her choice.

I had a cup of coffee while I waited, trying to drown out the sound of the water. Even if Ava was in trouble, why would somebody have wanted to jump me? I'd only just come on the scene. I didn't even know anything yet.

I carried my coffee cup to the front window and looked out. Was there somebody still lurking out there? It was getting dark. What would they do when they had the cover of darkness to help them?

I heard the water go off, so I walked to the coffee pot and poured out a cup. Ava came out of the bedroom wearing a silk robe tightly belted at her waist. Her hair was wet, skin still damp, which made the silk do interesting things to her body. I could easily tell that her nipples were not only large, but dark.

I was in better shape when she was in the shower. At least I could try to block the images from my mind. There was no blocking out the way she looked in that robe.

I handed her the coffee.

'Thank you.' She sipped it. 'Suddenly I'm a bit hungry.'

I lifted the covers from both trays.

'Burger or steak?' I asked.

'Believe it or not, I'm a burger-and-fries girl,' she said. 'My rural upbringing.'

'Burger it is, then,' I said, moving the plate over in front of her as she sat down. I sat and pulled the steak plate in front of me. I didn't care for brussels sprouts, but the baked potato looked good.

I poured two glasses of cold water.

'I suppose you called Frank?' she asked.

'I spoke to him.'

'Is he coming?'

'Uh, no,' I said. When I saw her face fall I added, 'I told him not to.'

'Why the hell not?'

'Because something's going on,' I said, 'and I want to find out what it is before I give Frank the all clear.'

'You're protecting him?'

'I hope I'm protecting us all,' I said.

'From what?' she asked.

'That's what I'm hoping you'll tell me.'

She lifted the burger and bit into it – a real bite, not a dainty lady bite. Even without make-up she was easily the most beautiful woman I had ever seen eat a hamburger.

I picked up my knife and fork and cut a hunk of steak. It was a bit chewy. I'd had much better at the Sands.

'Ava?'

'Why do you want to get yourself involved in my problems, Eddie?' she asked, wearily.

'Because I want to help you.'

'Because Frank asked you?'

'That's part of it.'

'What's the other part?'

'Maybe it's because I fell in love with you when I saw *One Touch of Venus*,' I said, 'or it could be the shower scene in *Mogambo*.'

She finished chewing, swallowed and smiled.

'Is any of that fucking true?'

'Well,' I said, 'maybe the *Mogambo* part.'

'Everybody fell in love with Grace Kelly in that movie,' she said.

'Oh, not everybody,' I said. 'Definitely not me.'

She popped a French fry in her mouth and said, 'You're sweet.'

'And you're being evasive.'

'I'm not,' she said. 'I'm trying to eat.' She took one more bite of the hamburger and then put it down with an air of finality.

'Jesus, I must look a fucking sight,' she said, suddenly.

'Ava—'

She stood up.

'I have to get dressed and put my face on,' she said. She headed for the bedroom.

'What about your burger?'

'You finish it.'

The steak wasn't getting any better so I grabbed her burger and took a bite. Well done. I put it down. I had a couple of fries, wondering if she had any reason to go out a window. Or maybe there were French doors from the bedroom.

Why would Ava run from me?

SEVENTEEN

I went out the front door and around to the side. It was almost dark, and the light was on in the bedroom. I peered in her window, saw her seated in front of a vanity applying her make-up, wearing only a pair of panties. I stared at her beautiful back for a few moments too long and started to feel like a peeping ton, so I quickly backed away. It seemed to suddenly get dark and I became nervous about getting jumped, like Larry, so I hurried back to the front door and went inside.

I was sitting at the table, nibbling on fries, when she came back out wearing a pair of tight blue capris and a white blouse with cropped sleeves. Her hair was still damp, but it looked like she meant it to be that way. She had done her eyes up with lashes and eye shadow, and her lips were red. She looked great.

'Did you enjoy the view?' she asked.

'The view?'

'From outside my window.'

'I, uh, was just making sure you didn't, uh . . .' I stammered.

'You thought I was going to go out the fucking window?' she asked, laughing. 'Why the hell would I do that?'

'I don't know, Ava,' I said. 'I don't know what you're runnin' from.'

'What makes you think I'm running from anything?' she demanded.

'Because you've either been runnin' or hidin' since this morning,' I said.

'Jesus,' she said, 'has it only been one day?'

She sat down in an armchair.

'I need a cigarette.'

I looked around. There was a box on a nearby table, and a lighter. I handed her one and lit it for her.

'Thanks,' she said, as she let out a plume of smoke.

'How long has it been, Ava?' I asked. 'How long have you been running?'

She put one hand to her head.

'Eddie, that's just it,' she said. 'I really don't know.'

'When were you last at home? In Spain?'

'Days ago, I guess,' she said. 'There's been a lot of drinking, a lot of . . . men, since I finished the shoot on *Fifty-Five Days* with Chuck Heston. That . . . didn't go that well. The rushes . . . my skin looks like . . . parchment in that movie.'

'I doubt your skin could ever look like that, Ava,' I said.

She glanced up at me and I wanted to fall into her eyes – as much of a cliché as that sounds. She grabbed my hand, held the back of it to her cheek.

'You don't think so, Eddie?' she asked. 'You don't think it feels . . . rough?'

I rubbed my hand along her face and said, 'I don't think I've ever felt anything smoother, or softer.'

Then I got self-conscious and pulled my hand away. She was, after all, Frank's ex, and I was there representing him.

She drew on the cigarette again and said, 'I decided to leave Spain for a while, travel . . . Actually, that's not true. I was approached to be in a film that Blake Edwards is shooting in Rome called *The Pink Panther*. The Producer, Martin Jurow, came to see me. He found me in Madrid and practically begged me to be in it. It should have been flattering, but instead it went to my head. I was . . . horrible to them, demanded that they move the shoot from Rome to Madrid to accommodate me. Finally, Jurow slipped a note underneath my door.'

'Uninviting you?' I asked.

She nodded.

'I can't blame them, really,' she said. 'Since then I have

been all over Europe, to New York, here in L.A. and then
. . . nothing.'

'What do you mean, nothing?'

'I mean, I can't remember. I . . . blacked out. And I woke
up in a hotel room in Chicago.'

'What hotel?'

'The Drake, I think.'

'And what else?'

'I had . . . blood on my hands.'

'Blood? Are you sure?'

'Yes,' she said.

'What did you do?'

'I washed it off. I checked my clothes. There was blood
there, too.'

'Where are those clothes?'

'I . . . packed them for some reason, but when I got
here I threw them in the back of the closet in the
bedroom.'

'Wait here.'

I went into the bedroom to the closet. In the back, on
the floor, in a crumpled mess I found a blouse and a bra,
both stained with what looked like blood. But there was
also a silk nightie with blood on it, as well. And the towel
she must have used to dry her hands was stained red. I
wrapped the blouse, bra and nightie in the towel and left
them there, then went back to her.

'Was I dreaming that too?' she asked.

'No,' I said. 'There's blood on them all right.'

'Oh God . . .'

I crouched down in front of her and took her by the
shoulders, forcing her to look me in the eyes.

'Come on, Ava. Think. What happened?'

'I . . . don't know. I have been thinking for the past three
days. I can't recall.'

'All right,' I said, 'tell me this. How much time did you
lose in this blackout?'

'I . . . I figured it was about forty hours.'

Eight hours shy of two days. A lot of damage could be
done in that much time.

I was about to ask another question when there was a knock at the door.

'Eddie!' She became very frightened.

'Go into the bedroom,' I told her. 'Stay there. It might just be a bell boy coming for the dishes, but don't come out. You'll be able to hear what's being said.'

'All right.'

She hurried into the bedroom, leaving the door ajar.

EIGHTEEN

I opened the door, half expecting and fully hoping it would be Randy, the bell boy. It wasn't. It was two guys in suits with 'cop' written across their foreheads.

'Are you Eddie Gianelli?' one of them asked.

'Who's askin'?'

They both showed me their nice shiny detective badges.

'L.A.P.D.,' one of them said. 'Detectives Reasoner and Crider.'

'Which is which?' I asked.

'I'm Reasoner,' the spokesman said. He was a little shorter and broader than his partner, but they were both about the same age, mid-forties. My guess was they had been partners for a long time. 'Would you mind coming with us?'

'What's this about?' I asked.

'A cab driver named Larry Carver,' Crider said. 'Although, it seems somebody might have thought he was you.'

'I see. Couldn't I come down to headquarters in the morning and make a statement?'

'I'm afraid we're on the job now, Mr Gianelli,' Crider said. 'We need you to come now. I'm sure your friend, Miss Johnson, won't mind.'

It seemed they didn't know that Lucy Johnson was Ava Gardner. That was good.

'Would you mind if I tell her where I'm going?' I asked. 'She's in the, uh, bedroom.'

The two men exchanged a glance that wasn't hard to read.

'Sure,' Reasoner said, 'go ahead.'

'Can I tell her when I'll be back?'

'Before morning,' Crider said, then added, 'probably.'

'Probably,' I said, nodding. 'Thanks. I'll be right back.'

'Wouldn't be another way out in that bedroom, would there, Mr Gianelli?'

'Actually, there isn't,' I said, 'but why would that thought occur to you, Detective? I haven't done anything I should be running away from.'

'That's good to hear,' Reasoner said. 'We'll just wait here, sir.'

Those detectives were being a little too nice, for my taste. Not what I was used to from the Vegas cops.

I backed away into the bungalow, but left the front door wide open. I walked into the bedroom, kept that door closed. Ava rushed up to me.

'Who is it, Eddie?'

'It's the police,' I said, 'they want to talk to me about what happened outside earlier tonight.'

'That man who was beat up?'

'I think so,' I said, 'but I'll have to go with them to find out for sure. I'll be back in a little while.'

'Are you sure?' she asked. 'I mean, are you sure you should go with them?'

'I don't think they're asking, Ava,' I said.

'Do they know about me?'

'No,' I said, 'they referred to you as Lucy Johnson. They don't know who you really are, and I think we should keep it that way.'

'I think so too, Eddie.'

'Unless you want the police to help you find out what happened, Ava.'

'No!' she said, eyes wide. 'No, Eddie. For all I know . . . I hurt somebody. Or . . . or killed somebody. I can't go to the police. There'd be publicity!'

'OK, Ava, OK,' I said. 'I've got to get goin' before they come lookin' for me.'

'Eddie—' she said, and abruptly gave me a big hug. I held her tight and breathed in her scent. I found out later that she wore Acqua di Parma.

'I'll be back as soon as I can.'

I left her standing in the middle of the bedroom.

NINETEEN

They didn't take me to their headquarters, as I'd thought they would. They took me to the Cedars-Sinai Medical Center.

'This is where the cab driver, Larry Carver, was taken after somebody worked him over,' Reasoner said, as we got out of their car. 'We understand he was waiting for you in the lounge?'

'That's right.'

'Why?' Crider asked.

'He drove me there from the airport,' I said. 'I thought I'd need him, so I asked him to wait.'

'Cabbies usually wait in the cab,' Reasoner said, 'with the meter running.'

'I made a deal with him to come inside and wait,' I said. 'I was gonna use him for the rest of my errands.'

'Your errands,' Crider said, 'we'll get to those later, Mr Gianelli.'

'Let's go inside,' Reasoner said.

We entered the hospital through the front door, not the emergency entrance. Just inside we stopped.

'This is as good a place as any,' Reasoner said. 'You took the cab from the airport?'

'That's right.'

'You mind tellin' us where you came in from, Mr Gianelli?'

'Las Vegas.'

'Now we can get to your errands,' Crider said. 'What brought you to L.A.?'

I'd had time in the car to think about what my answer would be if they asked this question.

'There are several high rollers living here who owe the Sands quite a bit of money,' I said. 'I came to collect.'

'Does the Sands usually send pit bosses to collect their debts?' Crider asked. Of course, they had checked me out already and knew half the answers I was giving them – the true half.

'They do when the players are whales,' I said, 'my whales. See, I brought these guys into the casino, I OK'd their increased credit lines, so my boss is holding me responsible for their debts.'

'And if we asked you who these whales were, would you give us their names?' Reasoner asked.

'Only if I had to, Detective,' I said. 'My boss at the Sands wouldn't like it'

If they'd checked me out, like I thought they had, they knew who my boss was. They also knew he ran the Sands, and who he ran it for.

'Let's revisit that later,' Reasoner said. 'What do you think happened to your friend Larry, Gianelli?'

He had dropped the 'Mister,' so I said, 'Why don't you just call me Eddie, Detective?'

'Maybe we'll get friendly later, Gianelli,' Crider said. 'Why don't you just answer our questions for now?'

'From what I hear,' I said, 'I was paged in the Polo Lounge for a phone call. Larry picked it up. Then he got beat up. I'd say either a pissed off fare got to him, or somebody thought he was me.'

'Ah,' Crider said, 'and why would somebody want to put you in the hospital, Eddie?' I guessed we were friends now.

'I don't know, Detective,' I said.

'Could it have been somebody working for one of the whales you were talking about?' Reasoner asked.

'It could have been, but I haven't talked to any of them yet,' I said, 'so they don't know I'm in town.'

'And what were you doing at the Beverly Hills Hotel?' Crider asked.

'Getting a room.'

'Is that where you usually stay when you come to town?' Reasoner asked.

'No,' I said, 'but considering the caliber of people I'm here to talk to, my boss thought I should look the part.'

'So that's why you got a bungalow?' Crider asked.

'Exactly.'

'But the bungalow is registered to Lucy Johnson,' Reasoner said.

'A lady friend of mine,' I replied. 'I called ahead and asked her to get the place, and meet me there.'

'Killin' two birds with one stone, Eddie?' Reasoner asked.

'So to speak, Detective.'

'Let's go upstairs and see your friend, Eddie,' Crider said.

'Are you guys thinkin' there's an off chance that I beat Larry up?' I asked.

'I guess that's what he'll tell us,' Reasoner answered.

'If he's awake,' his partner added.

TWENTY

He was awake.

'Naw, it wasn't him,' Larry said when the cops asked him if I did it, 'it was two guys, jumped me from outta the bushes.'

'Did they say anything?' Crider asked.

'No,' Larry said, 'they just started whalin' away on me.'

'They use anything other than their fists?' Reasoner asked.

'I think they had blackjacks,' Larry said. 'One of them may have been wearin' knucks. Oh, one had a big silver ring on his, uh, right hand. Right hand?' He thought a moment. 'Yeah, right. Had, like, a snake on it.'

From the bruises on his jaw I figured he was right about the brass knuckles.

'I'm sorry this happened, Larry,' I said.

'Wasn't yer fault,' he said, then asked, 'was it?'

'Could be you got beat up because you took that phone

call for Mr Gianelli, Larry,' Crider said. 'Maybe those two guys thought you were him.'

'Jeez,' Larry said, 'I been rackin' my brains tryin' ta figure out who'd wanna work me over.'

'Any bad fares?' Reasoner asked.

'Naw,' he said, 'well, yeah, sure, but not this bad.'

'Angry boyfriends or husbands?' Crider asked.

'I wish.'

'Bookie?' Reasoner asked.

'I don't bet.'

'You got a wife that's pissed at you?' Crider asked.

'Exes,' Larry said, 'two of 'em, but if they have me put in the hospital they don't get no alimony.'

'We better talk to them, anyway,' Crider said. 'Be good if we could figure out who the real target was.'

Larry gave them the names and addresses of his ex-wives.

'OK,' Crider said, 'I guess that's it for now.'

'We'll talk to the two of you again,' Reasoner said.

'How about a ride back to the hotel?' I asked.

'Sorry,' Crider said, 'no can do.'

'Yeah,' Reasoner said, 'you'll have to take a cab.'

Not so friendly anymore.

'He can take mine,' Larry said. 'They tol' me they brought it here and put it in the parking lot. Keys are in the drawer, here.'

'That's up to you, Larry,' Reasoner said. 'That cab's your business. Up to you if you wanna let a stranger drive it.'

'We'll talk to you later,' Crider said.

They started for the door, then Crider turned and said, 'Hey, Larry. Did you know what Eddie here was doin' in the Beverly Hills Hotel?'

We all waited for the answer.

'Far as I know,' Larry said, 'he was getting' a room.'

'Yeah,' Reasoner said, 'far as you know.'

The two detectives left.

I walked to the door to make sure they weren't loitering outside the room, then returned to Larry's bedside.

'Thanks for not mentioning Ava Gardner, Larry,' I said.

'Cops,' Larry said, 'can't stand 'em. I really get beat up because I took that call?'

'I don't know, Larry,' I said, 'but I'm gonna try to find out. Meanwhile, your hotel bills here are gonna be covered, so don't worry about that.'

'I was wonderin' how I rated a private room,' he said. 'You payin'?'

'No,' I said, 'Frank Sinatra is.'

His face was bruised and scraped, one arm was in a cast, and there was a bandage on his head, but his eyes bugged out and he looked excited.

'For real?'

'For real.'

'Jeez . . .'

'That call you took for me, Larry,' I said. 'Who was it from?'

'Your boss,' he said. 'Sounded pissed off.'

'He always sounds like that.'

'He wanted you to call him when you got a chance.'

'I will. Listen, about your cab . . . you don't have to do that. I can catch—'

'What the hell, ain't doin' me no good in the parking lot.'

'I tell you what I'll do,' I said, 'when I use it I'll keep the meter running.'

His eyes bugged again.

'You gonna pay for that?'

'No,' I said.

'Not Frank Sinatra, again.'

'No, the Sands casino, in Vegas,' I said. 'That's where I work.'

'Vegas!' he said. 'I love Vegas.'

'Well, you're gonna love it even more when you get out, because you and a guest are gonna have a free week at the Sands.'

'Jesus,' he said, 'that's almost worth gettin' pounded on.'

'Larry,' I said, 'if you really did get worked over because somebody thought you were me, I'm gonna damn well make it worth your while, believe me.'

*   *   *

I left Larry's room with the keys to his cab in my pocket. I stopped at the front desk to talk to a doctor about Larry, found out he'd probably be ready to leave the hospital in about a week. The doctor said he was urinating blood on top of everything else. I told the doctor that the bills would be taken care of, to just send them to the Sands Hotel in Las Vegas, addressed to Eddie Gianelli. I also told him where I'd be and to call me if anything happened.

I left the hospital, found Larry's cab and drove it out of the parking lot. I kept checking the rearview mirror to see if anyone was on my tail, cops or not.

TWENTY-ONE

I should have thought to take a key to the bungalow with me, but I didn't, so I had to knock when I got back. When Ava opened the door, she was wearing a red wig and sunglasses.

'What's with the get-up?' I asked, stepping in and closing the door behind me.

'I didn't know who it would be,' she said. 'And just in case the police came back with you and wanted to talk to Lucy Johnson . . .' She backed away and did a quick pirouette.

'You make a good redhead, Lucy,' I said.

She took the wig off and said, 'I'll leave that to Rita Hayworth.' She ran her hand through her short black hair, and took off the sunglasses. 'How did it go?'

'Fine,' I said. 'They took me to the hospital to see Larry, the cab driver.'

'What for?'

'Well, among other things they wanted to find out from him if I was the one who beat him up.'

'Why would you do that?'

'That's what they wanted to know, but Larry cleared me.'

'Was he the driver who brought me here this morning?' she asked.

'Yeah.'

'Did he mention me?'

'No, he kept mum.'

'Is he being taken care of?' she asked.

'Yeah, I've got his bills covered.' I didn't tell her Frank was paying. I don't know why, exactly, I just didn't.

'It's gettin' late,' I said. 'Aren't you sleepy?'

'No, not yet,' she said. 'I had a nap, remember?'

'Probably the first sleep you've had in days,' I said. 'Maybe you better lay down anyway.'

'What are you going to do?'

'I'll get a room somewhere—'

'Stay here!' she said, abruptly.

'What?'

'I–I don't want to be alone,' she said. 'While you were gone I kept hearing noises, kept thinking there was some fucking creep outside trying to break in.'

'Ava, I can get a room in the hotel—'

'No,' she said, 'I don't just want you nearby. I want you close. I want you here, Eddie.'

'All right,' I said. 'I'll sleep out here on the sofa.'

'Nonsense,' she said. 'We're adults, and there's a large bed in the bedroom. We'll share it—'

'I don't know—'

'—but right now,' she went on, 'tell me what happened at the hospital.'

'All right,' I said. 'Let's sit down . . .'

TWENTY-TWO

After I told her what took place at the hospital she said, 'I don't understand why someone would want to attack you. You're only here because of me.'

'What I need to know now is, what's going on with you?

Before the cops came we were talking about your black
out.'

She averted her eyes.

'Do you think it was something medical? Or just brought
on by the booze?' I asked.

'If I say it was from alcohol I'd be admitting I'm a fucking
alcoholic,' she said.

Frank had always told me that Ava was a 'tough broad,'
so her constant profanity was no shock.

'Not necessarily,' I said. 'It could simply mean you drank
too much over a period of days and your system couldn't
handle it.'

'What's the difference?' she asked. 'I lost forty hours,
during which I ended up covered in blood.'

'What's the last thing you remember?'

'I was in a hotel in Madrid – with some men.'

Her discomfort kept me from asking what she was doing
with those men.

'And what's the next thing you remember?'

'I woke up alone in that hotel room in Chicago.'

'Where, exactly?'

'It was a room in the Drake,' she said. 'I woke up feeling
sick, staggered to the bathroom. I threw up, washed my
face and saw blood in the sink. When I looked in the
mirror I saw the blood on my clothes, and my face and
neck.'

'What else was in the room?'

'What do you mean?'

'I mean was there any luggage, yours or anyone else's?
Any room service trays, bottles, anything to indicate someone
else was in the room with you, or how many people were
in the room?'

'Well, it did look there'd been a party. Trays, plates,
bottles, overflowing ashtrays . . .'

'Anyone else's clothes?'

'No,' she said, 'only a suitcase of mine. The one I have
with me now. It just has a few clean clothes in it, and some
toiletries.'

'Did you think about calling the police then?'

'Why? Because I got so drunk I couldn't remember those two days?'

'The blood on your clothes might have given your story a bit more weight than that.'

'No,' she said, 'there'd be publicity.'

'Ava, no offense,' I said, 'but with some of the things you've pulled I never thought bad publicity was a concern of yours.'

'I was worried,' she said, 'I might have done something . . . bad.'

'So you packed up and left? You didn't check out, did you?'

'No,' she said.

'Was the room registered to you?'

'I don't know,' she said. 'I don't think so.'

Even if it was, the cops wouldn't be looking for her, not just for running out on a hotel bill. And if they were they would have gone to the studio.

The Studio.

MGM.

If somebody was after her for legal reasons the studio would know.

'I'll have to talk to someone at the studio, Ava,' I said. 'To find out if the police are looking for you.'

'I don't know how helpful that will be' she said. 'I haven't made a film for them in some years. They pretty much either released or lost all their contract players in 1960. Things have changed in Hollywood.'

'Still, if anyone – like the police – was looking for you, they'd probably go there.'

'Well, they always covered for me, including the time in Louis Mayer's office when I hit Howard Hughes with an ashtray and he dislocated my jaw.'

'Howard was begging to be my fourth husband,' she went on, 'but that was not going to happen. We were even more volatile together than Frank and I were – or are.'

That story might have been interesting at another time.

'OK,' I said, 'let's get back to you. You left the hotel in New York and did what?'

'Came here.'

'Don't you have a house here in L.A.?'

'I didn't want to go there,' she said. 'I was afraid someone would find me. I didn't go back to Spain for the same reason.'

'What did you do when you got here?'

'I sat up all night, stayed hidden all day, sat up all night again, and then the next morning – yesterday – I decided to go to Vegas to ask Frank for help. I went to the airport and got on the first flight.'

'Why not call him?'

She hesitated, then said, 'I–I wanted to see him.'

'So you walked into the Sands, saw him in the lobby—'

'With Nancy and Tina.'

'—and ran out, came back here.'

'I was lucky there happened to be another flight back to L.A. when I got to the airport.'

'And you came right back here?'

'Yes.'

'Didn't talk to anyone?'

'No,' she said, 'well, only the hotel manager, and the clerk. But no one else until you arrived.'

That meant if whoever attacked Larry was after me, they must have found out about me from the clerk, or the manager, or both.

And if they were willing to sell my name, wouldn't they be more than willing to make some money selling Ava Gardner's?

'I think it's time to get some rest,' I said.

'What are we going to do tomorrow?' she asked.

'Well, I want to go to the studio and talk to somebody – maybe Mayer himself – and then I'll come back here and get you.'

'Get me . . . to do what?'

'I want to take you someplace safe while we try to figure out what you did during those forty hours.'

'Someplace safe, like where?'

'I think I should take you back to Las Vegas with me.'

'To see Frank?' I couldn't tell if her tone was hopeful or not.

'I don't know, Ava,' I said. 'Right now I'm just thinkin' about keepin' you safe.'

'You're very sweet,' she said, stroking my cheek.

She stood up and walked to the bedroom door, then turned and said to me in her most innocent tone, 'Come to bed, Eddie.'

TWENTY-THREE

B elieve me, I was determined nothing was going to happen. After all, she was Frank's ex, and he was my friend and – even more than that – he was Frank Sinatra. He'd blown his stack at Peter Lawford one time for just being seen with Ava.

Ava's sexual appetites were legendary, awakened – so she said – by the time she spent married to Mickey Rooney. She'd been a nineteen-year-old virgin when they got married, and the first time they had sex it had awakened something inside of her. Their marriage didn't last, but her love of sex did.

Among her many conquests had been actors, singers, sports figures, bull fighters, artists . . . you name it. So what chance did a lowly pit boss have against that kind of sexuality?

I mean, it was Ava Gardner, right?

Ava had been right. The bed was king-sized and, as we went to sleep, there was a lot of space between us. Unfortunately, there was nothing she could do about the smell of sex coming from every pore of her body, which had me hard from the moment I met her. Being in bed with her – albeit with me on one end and her on the other – was painful!

When I woke up light was streaming in through the window, and I noticed two things. Ava had closed the distance between us. Her head was on my shoulder, and her body was plastered to mine. The second thing I noticed was that she was totally naked.

I looked down at her, drinking in what seemed to be acres of beautiful female flesh. Her breasts were pressed up against me, and I could feel her nipples poking into my arm. I had gone to sleep in my boxers and t-shirt, and my painful erection had worked its way out the front of my underwear. I felt like Tom Ewell in a Marilyn Monroe movie, only this was real, and it wasn't Marilyn – who I had come to think of as a little sister – but Ava Gardner, who was nothing like any relative on my family tree.

She moaned and stretched, and her eyes opened. She commented on the first thing she saw.

'Oh my, Eddie . . .'

'Ava,' I said, 'you're naked.'

'I couldn't sleep until I took everything off,' she said. 'I hope you don't mind.'

'Ava—'

'It doesn't look like you mind.'

'Ava—'

Without another word she took me in her hand and began to stroke my hard penis.

'Ava!'

'Shut up, Eddie,' she said, sliding down, 'just shut up . . .'

It seemed like hours later we were lying side-by-side, both naked now, sweating and out of breath.

'Eddie, Eddie . . .' she said, breathlessly.

I had never been with a sexual animal like Ava Gardner. All of my resolve disappeared once she had me in her mouth, and then when we were both naked all I wanted was . . . well, all of her. This was a Goddess I was in bed with, and who knew if and when I'd ever have an experience like this again. I used everything – my dick, my mouth, my hands – everything I had to enjoy her, and she was like a wild animal, whether she was on top or on the bottom.

Or on the side . . .

Or on all fours . . .

She kissed me on the shoulder and said, 'I need a shower.'

She got out of bed and padded to the bathroom. I watched

her majestic butt until she was gone, and then when the water was running I finally came to me senses.

How the hell would I ever explain this to Frank?

TWENTY-FOUR

When I came out of the shower, wearing a terrycloth robe that had been hanging on the back of the door, Ava was seated at the table with a pot of coffee, two cups, and some pastries.

'I called room service,' she said. 'I don't have anything here in the kitchen.'

'This is great,' I said.

I sat down and poured myself a cup, grabbed a Danish.

'Eddie,' she said, 'don't feel bad. I had a great time. Didn't you?'

'It was fabulous,' I said, 'but that doesn't mean I won't feel guilty.'

'Why? Because of Frank?'

'Well, yeah!'

'I've been with men since Frank, and he's certainly been with women since me. What's the problem?'

'Frank's my friend,' I said. 'I don't sleep with my friend's wives.'

'Ex-wife.'

'That, either.'

'Well,' she said, looking at me with those big green eyes and nibbling on a pastry, 'if it's any consolation, I practically raped you.'

'Yeah, you did,' I said, 'but I think I got into it, eventually.'

'Yeah, you did,' she said, with a deep-throated giggle.

I laughed, too, and then the tension seemed to break.

'What are your plans for today?' she asked.

'Well, I was going to go over to MGM.'

'And you've changed your mind?'

'I'm worried about leaving you alone, here,' I said. 'If I knew you'd be safe—'

'And how can you know that?' she asked.

'By having somebody watch you.'

'Like who?'

'That's the problem.'

I thought about Fred Otash again, the Hollywood P.I., but he lived for publicity. Bodyguarding Ava Gardner would be too tempting not to talk about it.

'I'll have to try to think of somebody,' I said.

At that point there was a knock at the door. In fact it was a pounding. I got up and walked over, gathering the robe around me.

'I'll have to make some calls, see if I can come up with—' I was saying to her as I opened the door. I stopped short when I saw who was standing on the doorstep.

'Hey, Mr G.,' Jerry Epstein said. He looked me up and down. 'How's it hangin'?'

TWENTY-FIVE

'Jerry, what the hell—' I said, shocked.

'Mr S. called me and said you need help,' the big man said. 'He got me on a red eye and told me to come here. So here I am.'

'Come on in, Jerry. It's good to see you, big guy.'

'Good to see you, too, Mr G.,' he said, pumping my hand. 'I was surprised when Mr S. said I had to come out to L.A. I thought you'd had enough of this place since Miss Monroe died.'

'Yeah, I did,' I said, 'but something came up. Did Frank tell you what's going on?'

'Nope. Just told me to get here. Said you was staying here with some broad named Lucy Johnson.'

'Well, Jerry,' I said, walking him to the table where Ava was sitting in her silk robe, 'meet Lucy Johnson.'

'Pleased ta meet ya, Miss Johnson. Jeez, you sure look a lot like that broad who was in that movie – the one in the jungle with Clark Gable?'

'*Mogambo*,' I said.

'Yeah, right,' Jerry said. 'That's it. Ya look like . . . Ava Gardner!'

'Really?' Ava asked, playfully. 'Don't you think I'm prettier than her?'

'Uh, well . . .' Jerry looked at me for help. He wasn't very good talking to women, unless they were waitresses or whores. '. . . sure, sure, you are . . . Mr G.?'

'Jerry,' I said, 'this is Ava Gardner.'

Jerry gaped at me, then at her.

'You was playin' games with me,' he said to her, finally.

'Yes, I was,' she said, 'and I'm sorry, Jerry.' She stood up and Jerry averted his eyes because the flimsy robe was clinging to her. 'Eddie, I'll go get dressed and you can talk to Jerry.'

'OK, Ava.'

We both watched her walk to the bedroom door, closing it behind her.

'Jesus, Mr G.,' Jerry said, 'are you nuts? You shackin' up with Mr S.'s wife?'

'Ex-wife,' I said, 'and it's not what you think. Frank sent me here. Frank sent me to help Ava. She's in some kind of trouble.'

'Mr S. knows you're here with her?'

'Well, he sent you here, didn't he?'

'Uh, yeah, I guess he did.'

'Sit down, Jerry,' I said. 'Let me fill you in . . .'

TWENTY-SIX

If I'd had my pick of somebody to watch over Ava I would have picked Jerry Epstein, my big leg-breaker buddy from Brooklyn. He'd had my back in most of the things I've done for Frank, Dean and Sammy. It just didn't

occur to me to call him out to L.A. for this. I was glad
Frank had thought of it. At least now I knew Ava would be
safe when I went to the studio.

'So, jeez, she can't remember forty hours?' Jerry said
when I was done.

'It might come back to her,' I said, 'but meanwhile I'd
like to find out what happened during that time. She's afraid
she might have hurt somebody.'

'Or killed 'em?'

'Yeah, that, too.'

'So whataya want me to do, Mr G.?'

'Stay with Ava, keep her safe.'

'From who?'

'From anybody,' I said. 'I don't want anyone in here,
Jerry. Not even hotel personnel.' I added to what I had
already told him that I didn't think we could trust the
manager or the desk clerk.

'One of them gave me up,' I said, 'and the cab driver
caught my beatin'.'

'So nobody in?' he asked. 'And nobody out?'

'Out? Ava won't go out. You don't have to worry about
that.'

'Can I—' he started, then stopped.

'What?'

'Can I order something from room service?' he asked.
'I'm pretty hungry.'

'Sure, Jerry,' I said. 'Order anything you want. All the
pancakes you want.'

'Thanks, Mr G. Food any good here?'

'Not great, but I've only tried the steak and hamburger
platter.'

'OK, then,' he said. 'I'll get some pancakes, maybe some
bacon. And coffee. Think Miss Gardner would want anything?'

'Ask her,' I said.

'I can . . . talk to her?'

'Sure, Jerry,' I said. 'She talks.'

'Mr G., this ain't gonna be like Miss Monroe, is it?' he
asked.

'What do you mean?'

'You know, how she got to be like . . . a sister? You pretty much ruined her for me, ya know?'

'That's not gonna be a problem this time, Jerry,' I said. 'Trust me. Ava Gardner's not your little sister.'

'Good,' he said.

'What's going on?' Ava asked, coming out of the bedroom. She was wearing a tight skirt and a chunky sweater. The combination sort of said 'look, but don't look'.

'Ava, Jerry's gonna stay with you. You can trust him like you'd trust me.'

'I just met you yesterday, Eddie,' she reminded me.

'I know,' I said, 'but Frank vouched for me, and I vouch for Jerry. He's got a big appetite, though. You gotta feed him to keep him happy.'

'He looks like he'd take some feeding.'

'Just a couple of dozen pancakes,' I said.

'Are you kidding?'

'Watch him,' I said. 'Meanwhile, I'm gonna go over to the studio and find out if anyone's lookin' for you.'

'And if they're not?'

'That'll be good news.'

'Will it?' she asked.

'It's always good news if the cops ain't lookin' for ya, Miss Gardner.'

'Just call me Ava, Jerry,' she said.

Jerry looked away and said, 'I can't do that, Miss Gardner. Mr G.'ll tell ya that.'

'Mr G?' Ava said, looking at me. 'Is he for fuckin' real?'

'Can't get him to call me Eddie,' I said. 'Been trying for a couple of years. Yep, Jerry's for real. What you see is what you get, pretty much.'

'OK,' she said, 'then call me Miss G. . . . no, you call Eddie Mr G.. It would get confusing. Call me . . . Miss Ava. OK, Jerry?'

'I could do that, Miss Gar — Miss Ava.' He smiled like a lovesick kid.

A big kid.

*   *   *

Jerry walked me out to Larry's cab. I had Ava's bloody
clothes wrapped in the towel under my arm.

'Not as good as your Caddy, Mr G,' Jerry said, looking
disappointed.

'No, but it'll get me where I want to go. I'll give it back
to Larry when he gets out.'

'When'll that be?'

'Probably a week or so. But I'll probably give it back to
him sooner. I want to get Ava to Vegas.'

'Gonna fly?'

'I don't know,' I said. 'Maybe we'll rent a car and drive.'

'I liked that drive last time,' he said.

'Yup, but that was in the Caddy,' I reminded him.

I opened the door to the cab to get in.

'Can I ask ya a question, Mr G.?'

'Sure, Jerry.'

'You said the cabbie got beat up because he picked up
a call for you?'

'Right.'

'Well, somebody musta been watchin', and heard him
pick up the call, figured he was you, right? Which meant
they was lookin' for ya?'

'Right.'

'So how'd they know you was here?' Jerry asked.

'I'm figuring either the desk clerk or manager gave me up.'

'So you told them your name when you got here?'

I thought for a moment, then looked at him and said,
'Jerry, did you know you're a genius?'

'I ain't no genius, Mr G.,' he said. 'I just sometimes know
what questions ta ask.'

TWENTY-SEVEN

Just like in the movies I had to drive through a big front
gate with Metro-Goldwyn-Mayer above it, which meant
I had to talk to a portly uniformed guard. Before going

there, though, I had found an out of the way garbage dumpster to stash the towel and clothes. There was no reason anyone would look for it there, and if anyone found it they couldn't connect it to Ava.

'Who you here to see?' the guard asked.

'Louis B. Mayer,' I said, even though I knew he had died in 1957.

'Sorry, you're out of luck,' the man said. 'He's dead.'

'So who's in charge?'

The guard must have been having a bad day – or week, or life – because he was ready to bitch to anyone who'd listen.

'You know, that's a good question,' he said. 'Right now this place has got a lot of Indians and no Chief, if you know what I mean.'

'Hard times?' I asked.

'Hard? There are more cartoons and TV shows comin' out of here than movies,' the guard said. 'MGM ain't what it used to be, pal.'

'Well, I need to talk to somebody about Ava Gardner.'

'What about Miss Gardner?'

'Frank Sinatra sent me to talk to somebody about Ava Gardner.'

The man stared at me for a minute, then asked, 'You serious?'

'I am.'

He stared some more. 'Wait here.'

'Sure.'

He stepped into his booth and made a phone call. Then leaned out the booth.

'Hey, what's your name?'

'Eddie Gianelli, from Las Vegas.'

'Where in Vegas?'

'The Sands.'

He went back inside, spoke into the phone some more, listened, then hung up and came back out.

'Pull inside and park there,' he said, pointing to some parking spots.

'OK.'

'Somebody'll be along to take you inside.'

'Thanks.'

He gave me a short salute, prepared to turn his attention to the next car.

I pulled into one of the parking spots he'd pointed to and waited. Lots of MGM's talent spent time in Las Vegas. I wondered if I'd see anybody I knew?

I had my head back and my eyes closed when somebody knocked on the window. I looked up at a grim, striking face dominated by nose and chin. I opened the door and stepped out.

'What the hell,' George C. Scott said, 'I thought that was you, Eddie.'

'George,' I said, grabbing his hand. Scott had been to the Sands more than once, and we usually took good care of him. 'How are ya?'

'Not bad. What are you doin' here?'

I shrugged.

'Gotta see a man about a debt.' It was a good enough story. 'How about you. New movie?'

'TV,' he said, a little sheepishly.

'You're kiddin'.'

'I know,' he said. 'A show called *East Side, West Side*. What are you gonna do? Everybody needs work, right? At least I get to work with a babe. She's a tall drink of water named Barbara Feldon.'

'The one that does the commercial in the tiger suit?'

'The same.'

'Yeah, not a bad gig, I guess.'

'Ah,' Scott said, 'it won't last, but it'll keep me busy for a year or so. MGM ain't what it used to be.'

'So I heard.'

'Are you Mr Gianelli?' a voice asked.

I looked at a man with a pencil thin mustache, black hair that came to a widow's peak, and piercing blue eyes. His mouth was a thin, straight line. I rolled the window down.

'That's right.'

'What are you doing driving a cab?'

'Tryin' to make some extra money?' I asked. He didn't enjoy the joke. 'I borrowed it. I needed a set of wheels.'

'I gotta go, Eddie,' Scott said. 'Nice seein' you.'

We shook hands and he moved off. The other man didn't seem impressed. Then again, he worked there.

'You got some I.D.?'

I gave him my driver's license. He looked at it then gave it back.

'OK,' he said, 'come with me.'

I rolled the window back up, got out and closed the door behind me.

'What's your name?' I asked.

'Vargas,' he said.

'What do you do, Mr Vargas?'

'I talk to strangers who want to talk to the man in charge,' he said. 'Once you talk to me, I'll decide if you get to talk to him.'

I thought that over and then said, 'That sounds fair.'

'I'm glad,' he said. 'Follow me.'

TWENTY-EIGHT

We walked across the parking lot to a two-story building with lots of doors in it. Apparently, it had been broken up into many small office spaces.

'This is where all the writers used to work when we had them under contract,' he told me. 'William Faulkner wrote in here.'

He opened a door and we stepped into a small office sparely furnished with a desk, two chairs and a file cabinet.

'You mentioned some big names to the guard,' Vargas said, seating himself behind the desk. 'Why should we believe that you have any connection to Frank Sinatra or Ava Gardner?'

'Come on, Mr Vargas,' I said. 'I had time to take a little nap in the cab. That means you spent that time checking me out.'

Vargas stared at me.

'Look, I know things are in an upheaval around here, and I'm not lookin' to take up your time. I just need to ask somebody a question.'

'What kind of question?'

'About Ava Gardner.'

'We haven't had anything to do with her since nineteen sixty.'

'But there are people who don't know that,' I said. 'If somebody was interested in talking to her they'd most likely come here.'

'What's your question, Mr Gianelli?' he asked.

I was thinking the only reason I hadn't been kicked out was because Vargas had probably talked to Jack Entratter at the Sands. Also, Vargas knew who owned the Sands. He wasn't exactly being polite to me, but he was giving me more time than he normally would have.

'Has anyone been askin' about Ava Gardner lately?' I asked.

'Asking about her . . . how?'

'Tryin' to find her, get in touch with her.'

'Who are we talking about, Gianelli?' he asked. 'The police?'

'Anybody, Mr Vargas,' I said.

Vargas studied me for a few moments.

'Look,' he said, finally, 'I'm willing to cooperate with you, but you've got to give me something.'

'Like what?'

'We're interested in getting Frank to do a picture for us,' he said.

'I don't have that kind of authority,' I told him, wondering what Jack had told him about me?

'I understand that,' Vargas said. 'All I'm asking is that you . . . talk to Frank. Put a little bug in his ear.'

'A bug in his ear,' I said.

'Yes,' Vargas said. 'We just need him to be . . . open to the possibility.'

I thought a moment, then decided Frank would probably do anything for Ava.

'OK,' I said.

'OK . . . what?' he asked.

'I think I can guarantee that Frank will be open to the possibility.'

His eyes widened and he smiled for the first time.

'That's wonderful!' he said.

'Sometimes,' I said, 'all you need to do is ask.'

'Wow,' Vargas said, 'well, OK then, exactly what do you want to know?'

'Has anybody been asking about Ava Gardner in, say, the last week or two?'

'Somebody looking to make a movie with her? Get an interview? Or are we talking legal—'

'Mr Vargas,' I said, cutting him off, 'you're makin' this harder than it has to be.'

'I'm sorry,' he said, backing off. 'I don't mean to do that.'

'Just answer the question and I can be on my way,' I said.

'As far as I know,' he said, 'nobody's been looking for Miss Gardner. She made a picture recently in Spain, but we had no involvement in that. Nobody's asked to interview her, and there have been no police here asking about her. Does that answer your question?'

'Yes,' I said, 'I think that about does it.'

'We're done?' he asked.

'I am,' I said, standing

'Very well,' he said, 'I'll walk you back to your, uh, car.'

At the cab he stood by while I opened the door.

'When can we, uh, expect a call from Mr Sinatra?' he asked.

'I suggest you get in touch with his representative,' I said. 'They'll get back to you.'

'We've been trying, but—'

'They'll get back to you this time.'

'Excellent,' he said. 'Thank you.'

I started to get in, then paused. He seemed so damned uncomfortable at that moment.

'Tough times around here, huh?' I asked.

'You don't know the half of it,' he said. 'Television! This place has made some legendary movies. It's a damn shame.'

'And nobody's runnin' the place?' I asked.

'You know, I don't even have an office,' he answered and shook his head.

As I drove through the front gate the guard said, 'You get what you wanted?'

'Pretty much,' I said 'but things sure sound grim around here.'

'Yeah,' the man said, 'I'm, thinkin' of makin' a move.'

'Sounds like a good idea,' I said.

TWENTY-NINE

D riving back to the Beverly Hills Hotel from the MGM lot I thought again about the question Jerry had asked me that morning, before I left.

I had not identified myself to the clerk or the manager before going to Ava's room. How, then, had someone managed to be in the lobby in time to hear me being paged, and see Larry pick up the call?

Had I been followed from the hotel? If so, why? Nobody knew I was in L.A., or why I was there, except Frank, Jack, Ted Silver from McCarran Airport, and Ben Hoff from LAX. I knew Frank and Jack would never talk, felt fairly sure about Ted.

That left Ben Hoff.

I'd have to go to the airport to talk to him, and I wanted to take Jerry with me.

And if the airports weren't safe – if information was being sold, or the airports were being watched – I'd have to rent a car to take Ava back to Las Vegas with me.

If somebody was looking for Ava did they have enough juice to cover airports and rent-a-car companies? Might be I'd have to borrow a car.

A better one than the cab I was driving.

*   *   *

The first time I realized I was being followed was when I heard tires screech behind me. Apparently, whoever was following me had been cut off by another car and had to swerve to miss it. That brought the dark sedan to my attention.

I made a few subtle turns, nothing obvious. I didn't want them to know I knew they were following me. But I sure couldn't drive back to the Beverly Hills Hotel. I was going to have to stop somewhere and give Jerry a call.

I spotted a likely place to stop: a hotdog stand beneath a faded Burma Shave billboard, with a pay phone alongside. I was pretty sure if I made a call, my tail wouldn't find it curious, or unusual. I was right. They pulled over, but didn't get out.

I pulled into the parking lot adjacent to the stand, walked over and ordered a hotdog with the works. Then I took it with me to the phone and dialed the Beverly Hills Hotel. I told the operator to connect me to Lucy Johnson's bungalow, number 6.

'Hello?'

'Jerry?

'Hey, Mr G. What's goin' on?'

'Looks like whoever's looking for Ava, it's not cops, or they would've gone to the studio.'

'So who are they?'

'We only know who they aren't, Jerry,' I said. 'How's Ava?'

'Gettin' antsy.'

'What is she doing?'

'We're playin' cards. Gin. I owe her like a million bucks.'

'Well, keep playing. I'm on my way. It might take me a while because I've picked up a tail.'

'You sure?'

'I'm sure.'

'You still drivin' that cab?'

'I am.'

'You think you can lose 'em?'

'I hope so.'

'Go someplace where there's lots of cabs, Mr G. Ya can lose 'em that way.'

'Jerry, that's brilliant.'

Leave it to the criminal mind.

'And what are we gonna do next, Mr G.?'

I had to take a moment to swallow the bite of hotdog I'd taken.

'Mr G.? Whataya eatin'?'

I'd forgotten who I was talking to. Jerry could hear chewing from miles away.

'Oh, I'm at a hotdog stand.'

'You went for hotdogs?' he asked, sounding hurt. 'Without me?'

His tone made me feel bad.

'Did you have your pancakes?'

'Well, yeah, but . . . hot dogs.'

'I'll bring you some.'

'Hey, Miss Ava. Ya want a hotdog?'

I heard Ava shout, 'Yes!'

'Don't forget the mustard,' Jerry told me. 'And the kraut.'

'Jerry,' I said, warning him, 'these are not Brooklyn hotdogs.'

'Then bring plenty of mustard,' he said, and hung up.

THIRTY

L ots of cabs, Jerry had said.

If I knew L.A. well enough that would've been easy. Just drive to where all the cabs are – a cab company parking lot, a lot where they keep repossessed vehicles, or . . . a big hotel with a cab line outside. Or, for that matter, the airport.

A big hotel seemed most likely. Just driving around I'd have to find one, eventually.

It didn't have to be a famous hotel. Just a big one. I

checked my gas gauge. I had half a tank. Hopefully that would be enough to find a hotel, ditch the cab, and get back to the Beverly Hills Hotel. Or it was enough to drive to the airport and then back to the hotel. But not both.

I felt bad about dumping Larry's cab, but at least I would be able to tell him where it was. Or he'd be able to get it from wherever they towed it to. I'd make sure he didn't have to pay to recover it.

On the side of his cab it said 'Horizon Cab Company.' I didn't know if Larry was just a driver, or an owner/operator. The fact that he had loaned me the cab led me to believe he owned it. I hadn't seen another Horizon cab on the street, but then I hadn't been checking out cabs. There were plenty that were yellow, but I hadn't been looking for names.

I checked the meter, which I was supposed to have kept running but had forgotten. Beneath it was a radio. It was off. I turned it on and immediately heard a voice calling out addresses for pick-ups. OK, even if Larry did own the car, he was still taking calls from the dispatcher.

A gravelly voiced guy kept calling out addresses which didn't help me. Even when he gave out the name of a hotel, he didn't give an address. Experienced cabbies were supposed to know where all the large hotels were.

After driving around for half an hour – with a bag of hotdogs in the back seat – I decided I needed help. I picked up the transmitter, pressed the button on the side, and said, 'Larry's cab to central.'

I'd heard the other cabs talking to 'Central,' whoever that was.

'Who is that?' the gravelly voice called out.

'My name's Eddie,' I said. 'I'm drivin' Larry's cab and I need some help.'

'Hey, are you the guy from Vegas?'

'That's right.'

'OK, everybody, radio silence,' he ordered. 'Ya got me. Radio silence for a few minutes while I talk ta this guy.'

The chatter on the radio suddenly went dead.

'How did you know I was from Vegas?' I asked.

'I talked to Larry at the hospital,' the guy said. 'He told me he loaned you his cab because you needed wheels. Said you were doin' something important, and for helpin' he was gonna get some free tickets for shows in Vegas. That go for anybody who helps ya?'

'It sure does, friend.'

'Well, my name is Louie, Mr Vegas,' gravelly voice said. 'Whataya need?'

'I've picked up a tail, Louie, and I wanna lose them,' I explained. 'I thought I could do that someplace where there's more cabs. A hotel, the airport, maybe a parking lot—'

'You sure could, pal,' Louie said. 'But I got a much better place for ya.'

'Where?'

'Come straight here.'

'To your garage?'

'Sure, why not? Ain't no place else got more Horizon cabs then here.'

I wasn't all that sure I should get Louie and his drivers involved. Not after what had happened to Larry.

'Look, Louie . . . I don't know exactly what these people want,' I explained. 'I don't know if they're dangerous. I mean, Larry ended up in the hospital, but I don't really know what's goin' on.'

'You think they got guns?' he asked.

'Maybe.'

'Don't worry,' he said. 'We got guns. And if these are the guys who put Larry in the hospital, we wanna piece of 'em.'

'Are you sure?'

'Whataya say, guys?' he asked the other drivers. Suddenly, there was a cacophony of voices shouting their agreement.

'See that, Mr Vegas? So you come on ahead, I'll give you the address. You ain't even gotta lose your cab. You can drive in the front and out the back. They'll never see ya.'

That sounded like a good idea.

THIRTY-ONE

Following Louie's directions I drove directly to the garage of The Horizon Cab Company. There were several doors opened in front as I arrived. Apparently, Louie had somebody watching for me, because a man appeared in the center doorway, waving me in. I drove in, up a ramp, and stopped where I saw several men standing. For a moment I wondered if I'd made a mistake. Maybe these drivers were out to get revenge for Larry . . . against me? But I was committed, so I stopped the cab and got out.

'Hey, Mr Vegas.'

I turned, saw a dark, swarthy guy about forty approaching with a big smile on his face. He had heavy black stubble that didn't make up for the thinning hair on top.

'I'm Louie,' he said, putting his hand out. 'Those guys follow you here?'

'They did. They're out front.'

'Willy, go take a look!'

'Sure, boss,' a small, wiry man said.

'We're gonna get you gassed up and out the back door in a minute, Mr Vegas,' Louie said. 'But I gotta ask ya somethin'.'

'What's that?'

'Ain't you curious about who these guys are?'

'I'm real curious,' I said. If I'd had Jerry with me I would have played it differently, stopped the cab, surprised those guys and found out who sent them. But alone I didn't have a chance especially if they were armed.

I even thought about leading them back to the Beverly Hills Hotel so Jerry and I could grill them, but I didn't want to take a chance with Ava's safety.

'So why don't I have some of the boys go out and drag them outta their car, bring 'em in here so we can find out?'

'Louie, I don't want anybody else getting' hurt—'

'I toldja, we got guns.'

'I know, but they probably do, too. You go out there and somebody's going to get hurt. Now, I appreciate your help, but all I want is the gas and the back way out.'

Willy ran back in.

'Two guys in a black Plymouth, Boss, Just sittin' there.'

Louie looked at me and I shook my head.

'OK, boys,' he said. 'Gas 'im up and let's get 'im outta here.'

With a full tank of gas I pulled out the back exit of the garage and proceeded to the Beverly Hills Hotel with no tail in sight.

'By the time they suspect anythin',' Louie the dispatcher had said, 'and come in to check, nobody here'll know nothin'.'

'If I give you a call in a few hours,' I said, 'you can let me know if they let anything slip about who they're working for.'

'Sure thing,' Louie had said. 'In fact, when they come in lookin' for you I'll have one of my drivers check out their car.'

'That'd be great,' I said.

Before I drove out Louie asked, 'You want a better car than this one, Mr Vegas?'

'No, this'll do,' I said. 'I'll leave it at the hotel after I rent another one.'

'You need to rent a car? Here.' He dug a business card out of his pocket. 'My brother's got a car lot. No questions asked. It's a cash business, though. I can get you a discount, but—'

'That's OK, Louie,' I said. 'I'm willing to pay.'

'OK, then,' he said, and we shook hands. 'Looks like we're in business.'

I pulled up in front of the hotel and grabbed the bag out of the back seat.

'They're cold,' I said, as I entered the bungalow.

'I can't eat cold hotdogs,' Ava complained.

'I can,' Jerry said, grabbing the bag.

'Then you can have them all, sweetie,' Ava told him, with a smile.

'Sweetie?' I said.

'Hey, you left us alone,' Ava said, 'so we got acquainted.'

I looked at Jerry. He blushed, bit into a hotdog and said, 'We played cards – like I told ya.'

'He owes me big,' Ava said from the sofa.

I walked over to her. She was smiling, and looked refreshed. I didn't think she had been drinking.

'What happened at the studio?' she asked.

'They're making cartoons and TV shows, now,' I said. 'They're not happy.'

'Fuck 'em,' she said.

'Nobody's been there looking for you.'

'Who told you that?'

'A man named Vargas.'

'Don't know him,' she said. 'What are we going to do now?'

'We're going to Vegas.'

'When?'

'Tomorrow.'

'Can't we go today?' she asked. 'I'm going stir crazy here.'

'Tomorrow,' I said, 'Jerry and I still have some things to do today.'

'Like what?' Ava asked. 'Something interesting, I hope?'

'Well, we have to rent a car.'

'That's not interesting,' she said, disappointed.

'We're not gonna rent it from a rental agency,' I said. I took out Louie's brother's card. 'We're gonna rent it from this guy.'

'That's interesting,' Jerry said, with – I think – the entire second hotdog in his mouth. He had mustard in the right corner of his mouth, and I didn't know how to tell him.

'Jerry, sweetie . . .' Ava said, and wiped at the corner of her mouth with her thumb.

Jerry did the same to his and said, 'Thanks, Miss Ava.'

'And after you rent a car?' she asked.

'Well, actually, probably before we rent a car we have to find out who the rat is in the hotel; the clerk or the manager.'

'And how will you do that?'

'Jerry's gonna ask them, because that's kinda what Jerry does.'

She looked at Jerry.

'This big sweet man?'

'I ask people questions they don't wanna answer,' he said. 'I can be real persuasive . . . if ya get my drift.'

I said. 'That's how it works.'

She looked at Jerry and said again, 'This big sweet man?'

Jerry blushed again, and ate the third and final hotdog.

'How were they?'

'You're right,' he said. 'Not Brooklyn.'

'So, when you go and rough up the manager, can I come?' she asked. 'I can't stand that little pipsqueak.'

THIRTY-TWO

We started with the clerk. Ava stayed in the bungalow. 'Keep the door locked,' I told her. 'We'll be right back.'

'Ya want this?' Jerry asked, holding out his forty-five.

'Ooh, yes!' she said, eyes wide.

'Oh, no,' I said. 'Put that away, Jerry.' I looked at Ava. 'Just lock the door. We won't be long.'

She pouted as we went out the door.

'Let's go to the lobby. Hopefully, the clerk is on duty.'

He was. He saw us coming, and looked like he wanted to run. The fact that he didn't had me thinking he might not be the guilty party.

'Jerry, don't hurt him, just scare him a little.'

'You don't think it's him?'

I shook my head. 'Maybe he'll give up the manager though.'

We approached the desk.

'Can I help you, sir?'

'Do you know my name?' I asked.

'Um, I'm sorry, sir,' he said. 'I know I heard it when the phone call came in, but I can't remember.'

'Try,' Jerry said, putting his big hand on the young man's chest.

'I, uh, I'm sorry—' he moved his eyes nervously between us. 'Is he gonna hurt me?'

'I'm afraid so,' I said. 'Unless . . .'

'Unless what?' he asked, leaping at what he thought might be salvation.

'Somebody made a call,' I said, 'when I got here.'

'A call?'

I nodded.

'That's why there were two men waiting to put me in the hospital when they heard me being paged,' I explained, 'only the cab driver took the call, and the beating.'

'Oh, I . . . I think I understand.'

'Did you place that call?'

'N-no, I swear.'

'Then who did?'

He looked frightened, and not only of Jerry.

'Look, if you're worried about your job, don't. Nobody will know. When I got here and asked for Lucy Johnson's room, somebody made a call. Who was it?'

The clerk didn't answer fast enough, so Jerry made a fist, gathering the kid's shirt in it.

'It was M–Mr Gentry. B–but I don't know who he called. I just know he made a phone call.'

'Where is he?'

'In his office.'

'Show us.'

The clerk nodded and Jerry released his shirt. He came out from behind the desk, walked us around the corner and pointed to a door.

'OK,' I said. 'Go back to work.'

'Sure thing.'

Jerry stopped him by putting his hand on his chest.

'Don't make no calls.'

'No sir!'

'Now get lost.'

The kid ran back to the desk.

'Do we knock?' Jerry asked.

'Why warn him?' I said. 'You go in first.' I figured Jerry's sheer size would put the manager in the right frame of mind.

'Should I kick it in?' he asked.

'Let's try the doorknob first.'

'Spoilsport,' he muttered.

He reached for the knob, turned it slowly and then nodded to me. I gestured for him to go in. He opened the door quickly and stepped inside. I followed, and closed the door behind us.

'Mr Gentry—' I said, and stopped.

Gentry was sitting behind his desk. His eyes were open, but he wasn't looked at us. In fact, he wasn't looking at anybody.

'Jerry . . .'

Jerry approached the man, examined him without touching him, then put two fingers to his neck.

'He's a stiff, Mr G.'

'How, and for how long, do you figure?'

Again, he examined the corpse as well as he could without touching it.

'I don't see no marks,' he said.

'Maybe he was strangled?'

'His tongue would be out, and swollen,' Jerry said.

I looked at the desk top. No glasses to indicate he might have been poisoned with a drink.

'His skin feels like it's coolin', Mr G..'

'So not in the past hour or so, huh?'

'Naw,' Jerry said, 'maybe this mornin'.'

'We could ask the clerk when he last saw him, but I don't want to alert him yet.'

'He's gonna give us up when he finds the body.'

'He doesn't know your name, and if he was on the level, he can't remember mine.'

'He might mention Miss Gardner.'

'You're right about that,' I said. 'We're gonna have to get out of here now. I'll call Ava and tell her to pack up—'

I was reaching for the phone when he stopped me.

'Not from this phone, Mr G.,' he said.

'Damn it, what was I thinking?' I said, snatching my hand away from the phone. 'Let's see if we can get back to the bungalow without passing the clerk.'

'If we can't, maybe we can get to a house phone.'

'If we pass him he's gonna wonder what went on,' I said. 'He might even decide to come back here to ask.'

Jerry examined the doorknob.

'We can lock this and pull it shut,' he said, 'then tell the clerk his boss don't wanna be disturbed. It might keep him out of here for a while.'

'OK,' I said, 'but let's take a quick look around first. Maybe we'll find something helpful.'

'Yeah, we can do that,' Jerry said, 'but don't touch nothin', Mr G..'

'I gotcha, Jerry.'

THIRTY-THREE

We looked the place over, mostly the desk, but didn't find anything. I was looking for a phone number scribbled on something.

'Maybe the clerk knows more than he's saying,' I said.

'I don't think so,' Jerry said, 'I don't think we can take the time to find out. We gotta get out of this hotel, Mr G . . .'

He was right. We needed to get Ava away from this murder.

'Jerry,' I said, 'any chance this man died of natural causes? Maybe a heart attack?'

'I dunno,' he said. 'There are no marks, but every heart

attack victim I've ever seen looks calm. This guy looks . . . well, surprised.'

He was right, again. With his eyes wide open Gentry looked like he'd been taken by surprise.

'OK,' I said, 'let's get out of here and lock the door. Look for a back way out to the bungalows.'

We got out of the office and pulled the door shut, locking it behind us.

'This way,' I said, and we went in the opposite direction from the front desk. After a few false starts we found another exit from the hotel. We came up to Ava's bungalow from the other side, and let ourselves in.

'What's goin' on, boys?' she asked.

'Pack up,' I said. 'we've got to get out of here.'

'Why? What's wrong?'

'The hotel manager got himself killed,' Jerry said.

'What?'

'It's probably murder,' I said. 'We've got to get you out of here before the police are called.'

'What about you two?' she asked. 'Are you in trouble?'

'The clerk saw us,' I said, 'knows that we went to see the manager.'

'He don't know our names, though,' Jerry said. 'We just need to get out of here before somebody finds the body, Miss Ava,'

'All right,' she said. 'I'll pack. But where will we go? Vegas?'

'Not tonight,' I said. 'We'll get in the cab and figure it out. We just need someplace overnight.'

'What about my house?' she asked.

'Somebody may be watching it,' I said.

'What if they're not?' she asked. 'What if whoever's looking for me has already looked there? Besides, if I was running from somebody would I go back home?'

'She's got a point, Mr G.,' Jerry said. 'I can check her place out, see if it's bein' watched.'

'All right,' I said, 'get your bag and let's get going.'

'Take me just a minute,' she promised.

Most women, no matter how little or how much they

have to pack, need a lot of time. She was true to her word
and came back out in a few minutes.

'Let's go.'

'Jerry,' I said, 'you got a bag?'

'Nope. Figured I'd get some clothes out here.'

'OK,' I said, 'we'll pick up some things for you on the way.'

Jerry played the gentleman, took Ava's bag and we left.
At the cab we looked around to see if anyone was watching
us, then we all got in with Jerry behind the wheel and Ava
in the back seat.

'Where to?' Jerry asked.

'I live on Vine Street, between Hollywood and Selma.'

'Hollywood and Vine?' Jerry asked.

'Close by.'

'Ava, tell Jerry how to get there.'

THIRTY-FOUR

With Ava's directions we drove to the neighborhood, but stopped down the block from her
house.

'OK, Jerry, take a walk and see what you can see.'

'Sure thing, Mr G.'

It was getting toward dusk as he got out of the cab and
walked down the street.

'So tell me, Eddie, how did you and Jerry meet?' Ava asked.

'He didn't tell you while you were playin' gin?' I asked.

'He doesn't like to talk about himself,' she said. 'All he
told me was that you and he were both from Brooklyn. Is
that where you became friends?'

'No,' I said, 'it was in Vegas a couple of years ago, when
Frank, Dean and the fellas were shootin' *Ocean's Eleven.*'

'Oh, that thing about Dean being threatened?' she asked.

'Yep,' I said. 'Frank brought Jerry in to help me with that.'

'You have quite a friendship,' she said.

'Well—'

'He'd do anything for you, did you know that?'

'Well—'

'And you like him. Don't try to deny it.'

'Well . . . of course I like 'im,' I told her. 'Why would I try to deny that? Plus he's saved my ass more than once.'

'He is a terrible gin player, though,' she said. 'Just awful. But he is sweet, and gentle as a lamb. Are you sure he's a torpedo?'

'He doesn't like that word,' I said, 'but yeah, he's broken an arm and a leg or two in his time. I think he's just sweet to you, the way he was to Marilyn.'

'He met Marilyn?' she asked.

'Yeah, earlier this year he helped me with something I was doing for her,' I said. 'But he was mad at me, said I ruined her for him.'

'Ruined her how?'

'He said after meeting her he couldn't help but think of her as a little sister.'

'And is that the way he thinks of me, now? As a little sister?'

'Oh, no—'

'Then what? A big sister?' I could see that neither one appealed to her.

Ava,' I said, 'believe me when I say no man could ever think of you as their sister.'

'Especially you, right?' she said, touching the back of my neck.

'Ava, that has to stay between us,' I said. 'Nobody can know what happened. Not Jerry, and especially not Frank.'

'Oh, don't worry, Eddie,' she said, 'that will be our little secret.'

Jerry appeared just then, opened the door and got in. Ava pulled her hand away from the nape of my neck.

'I didn't see nobody,' Jerry said, 'not on either side of the street.'

'OK, but I've been thinking . . .'

'What?' Jerry asked.

'Maybe we should wait until after dark.'

'And what do we do in the meantime?' Ava asked. 'Sit here in this old cab?'

'No,' I said, 'I thought we could go and buy Jerry some new clothes.'

She brightened.

'Shopping! Oh, that sounds like fun.' She clapped her hands. 'And I know just the place. Start 'er up, big guy.'

She took us to a men's clothing store right on Hollywood Blvd. and, true to her word, she had fun, especially picking shirts out that Jerry never would have picked out for himself. But he was too polite to say no.

Except when they got to the register.

'No, no, don't be silly,' she told us. 'Of course I'm going to pay.'

'No, Miss Ava,' Jerry said, 'I'm gonna pay for my own clothes.'

'I thought I could get the Sands to pay for it all,' I offered.

She slapped me on the arm and said, 'No, don't ruin my fun. Paying is part of it.' She looked at Jerry. 'Are you going to ruin all my fun?'

'No, Ma'am.'

'Then step aside.'

We both moved and allowed her to pay cash for everything. She even carried the bags.

The male clerk looked at us and said, 'You fellas notice how much she looks like Ava Gardner?'

'What?' Jerry said.

'Not so much,' I said, and we followed her out.

THIRTY-FIVE

We drove the cab back to Ava's street, still parking down the block.

'Come on,' she said, 'I know a back way.'

We had to help her over a couple of fences, but she managed to get us to the back door of her house.

She used her key and unlocked the door, and we entered through a large kitchen. She reached for the light switch but I grabbed her hand.

'No lights,' I said, 'just in case.'

'How are we going to see where we're going?' she asked.

It was dark outside, and darker still inside, but I was starting to make out shapes.

'Just wait a few moments and your eyes will adjust,' I said. 'Jerry, why don't you go and have a look out the front window?'

'Sure thing, Mr G.'

As Jerry made his way through the house to the front, Ava pulled out a kitchen chair and sat down.

'Ava, is there any chance you were back in this house during those forty hours?'

'I suppose there's a chance,' she said.

'Have a look around,' I said.

'What am I looking for?'

'Anything you might have left here during that time,' I said. 'Or maybe something you took? Anything that'll help figure this out.'

'In the dark?'

'If you have a flashlight in the house you can use that, but we wanna keep the lights off. OK?'

'OK,' she said, with a shrug. 'Is it all right if I pack a few extra things? This bag is just something I threw together in a hurry. And I've got to find some cigarettes somewhere. I'm all out.'

'Pack whatever you want,' I said. 'We don't know how long you'll be gone.'

'Oh God . . .' she said.

'It'll just be long enough to make sure you're safe.'

'Right,' she said. 'Can I take a bath?'

'Why not? We'll be here all night. In the morning we can get a car.'

'You're not going to leave me here alone, are you?' she asked.

'No,' I said, 'we'll all go get the car.'

She got up from the chair.

'Any chance there's some food in the fridge? Jerry's gonna get hungry.'

'There won't be much,' she said. 'Can you cook?'

'Not much,' I said, 'but Jerry's a whiz in the kitchen.'

She laughed.

'Now why doesn't that surprise me?'

While Ava was taking a bath I took a walk around downstairs. Everything was neat and clean, probably thanks to a maid. I wondered if she kept coming in while Ava was gone?

Jerry said there was nobody out front that he could see.

'They're gonna hafta pee,' he'd told me once, 'or hafta smoke eventually. And even if they're peeing in a bottle, you can watch for the flare of a match, or the glowing tip of a cigarette.'

So when Jerry told me nobody was there, I believed him.

'If we stay toward the back of the house, just in case, 'I said, 'we should go unseen. That means the kitchen, the diningroom, and back bedrooms.'

Ava had told me that her bedroom and master bath were in the back.

Jerry went through the fridge and the cupboard.

'There's fuck all here ta cook, Mr G. I could make an omelet, but not one big enough for the three of us.'

I could hear Jerry's stomach grumbling, and mine was close.

'I saw some places on the way here,' he said. 'In fact, there's a deli about two blocks away.'

'You remember how to get there?' I asked, unnecessarily. When it came to restaurants, Jerry had a phenomenal memory.

'Sure I do.'

'OK,' I said. 'Go back through the yards to the cab and pick up some food.'

I reached into my pocket and he said, 'I got dough, Mr G.'

'OK,' I said, 'this one's on you. I'll get the next one.'

'OK.' He headed for the back door.

'Hey, Jerry.'

'Yeah, Mr G.?'

'Did I remember to thank you for comin' out here like this?'

'Hey,' he said, 'when Mr S. told me you needed help, I dropped everythin' I was doin' and hopped the first flight. Why wouldn't I?'

'In any case, thanks, big buy.'

''Course, I wasn't doin' much of anythin', anyway . . .' he added.

'Fuck you . . .'

He was laughing and shaking his head when he went out the door.

'What's going on?' Ava asked.

I watched her walk into the room fresh from the bath. She was wearing a simple terrycloth robe this time, and was vigorously drying her hair with a towel. She wore no make-up, and was still the sexiest, most beautiful thing I'd ever seen in my life – and remember, I live and work in Vegas. There wasn't a showgirl I knew who could hold a candle to Ava Gardner straight from a bath.

'Jerry went to get some food.'

'What's he getting?'

'Deli.'

'Oh, good,' she said. 'I love those big pickles. I hope he brings some.'

'Yeah,' I said, 'he'll come back with a little bit of everything, if I know him.'

'There's some booze in the house,' she said. 'Do you want a drink?'

'No. I want to stay alert.'

'Do you mind if I have one?'

'Go ahead, but remember,' I said, 'no lights, and stay away from the windows.'

'Luckily,' she said, 'I know where everything is. I could get around this house with my eyes closed.'

'I hope so.'

She turned and left the kitchen. A moment later I heard her walk into something and snap, 'Ouch! Fuck!'

I shook my head, got myself as glass of water from the tap. I knew I could count on Big Jerry to come back with coffee.

THIRTY-SIX

When Jerry got back he had half-a-dozen brown bags with him. Ava had found a flashlight in the house, a pretty good one, so we set it on the table and started emptying bags. There were sandwiches, knishes, fries, potato salad, pickles, containers of coffee and a few cans of Dr Brown's soda, which I hadn't seen since I left New York.

'Wouldja believe it?' he asked. 'I found a Jewish deli in L.A. that sells Dr Brown's.' He was ecstatic. He'd brought Cream, Black Cherry and Cel-ray.

'What's this?' Ava asked, picking up a bottle of the Cel-ray.

'Celery flavored soda,' I said, 'from New York.'

'Yuch.' She was still working on the large highball she'd built.

Jerry got some plates from the cupboard – he already knew where everything was – and set them out, and we doled out the food.

The sandwiches were pastrami or brisket, and we managed almost equally to divide up the food: half for Jerry, and half for me and Ava.

'Oh, I can see hanging around with you two characters is going to have a real effect on my figure.'

'Nothin' wrong with your figure that I can see, Miss Ava,' Jerry said.

'Thank you, Jerry,' she said. 'You're very sweet.'

After we ate we finished our coffee and played some three-handed gin at the kitchen table by flashlight until Ava's eyelids started to droop.

'That's it for me, boys,' she said. 'I've got to get some

sleep. You figure out how much you both owe me and let me know tomorrow.'

She stood up, walked to the doorway, then turned and looked over her shoulder at us.

'Pick any bedroom you want,' she said.

'One of us will be up all night, Ava,' I said. 'In case you hear something, or want something.'

'I feel safer already,' she said, 'but I hope you guys are better at bodyguarding than you are at cards.'

When she left the room Jerry said, 'Hey, Mr G., you notice how much she's like that broad she plays in *Mogambo*?'

'Honey Bear.'

'Yeah, that's her,' he said. 'Geez, I can see why Mr S. is so gone on her.'

'You wanna keep playin' for a while, Jerry?' I asked. 'Maybe one of us can get back some of what we lost to her.'

'Sure, why not?'

Playing Jerry heads up wasn't such a good idea. Not only did I lose but he frustrated me. He didn't play well – at least he didn't play the way I was taught. He seemed to pick up cards only to discard them a few rounds later. He fed me two cards in a row, didn't seem to make any attempt to remember what he gave me, and in the end he won anyway.

He had me shaking my head.

'You play this game a lot, Mr G.?' he asked.

'I've been playing cards since I was a kid, Jerry,' I said.

'You ain't doin' so hot.'

'You ain't playin' right,' I said.

He shuffled the cards and muttered, 'Yeah, but I'm winnin'.'

'Just shut up and deal.'

THIRTY-SEVEN

Later, while we were still playing, Jerry said, 'Funny thing.'

'What's funny?'

Jerry looked up from his cards. Before answering he discarded an Ace he had just picked up two rounds before. I shook my head.

'You and me, Mr G.,' he said. 'The way we stumble on bodies.'

He looked and sounded like he was reminiscing fondly about his past.

'That's not something I think about, Jerry,' I said. 'Not something I look forward to either.'

'Oh, no, I didn't mean that,' he said. 'I just meant it's like . . . something chemical. You and me end up in the same place, and bodies start to show up.'

'Well, let's hope this body's got nothin' to do with us,' I said. 'Maybe the manager pissed off some other guest.'

'I wonder if Miss Ava has a radio around here some-place,' he said. 'Or we could turn on the TV, see if there's anything on the news.'

'There's a television in the living room, but it would throw shadows,' I said. 'But a radio is not a bad idea.'

'It's only taken me a couple of years to get you thinkin' like a criminal.'

I didn't know what to say to that. We finished the hands – he made gin – I tallied up what I owed him and then we looked for a radio. We didn't have to look far. There was one on a shelf in the kitchen. It was plugged in so we turned it on, found a news station, and kept the volume low. We were back to playing gin when the first mention came on.

It said the body of the manger of the Beverly Hills Hotel

was found in his office. The cause of death was as yet unknown, but the man was believed to have been murdered. A witness – a desk clerk – had described two men who were looking for the manager, and were believed to be the last to see him alive. They described us as two white males, one six feet tall and the other six and a half. Thankfully, there was no mention of Ava Gardner or 'Lucy Johnson.'

In a possibly related story – it went on – a cab driver had been beaten up outside the Beverly Hills Hotel the night before and was in the hospital. The police are investigating the possibility of a connection.

'Hey, at least your buddy Larry's got an alibi,' Jerry said.

'It's a good thing we have a safe place to go to rent a car tomorrow,' I said.

'Maybe I shouldn't go in with you,' Jerry said.

'Why?'

'There are lots of fellas six feet tall,' he said 'but six and a half?'

He was right. Louie the dispatcher and his brother might not have minded helping me because Larry said so, but if Jerry came along and they'd been listening to the news they might not be so helpful. As it was, the mention of Larry being beaten up in connection with the manager's murder might cause a problem. But I wouldn't know that until I got to the car lot the next morning.

'I could steal a car, Mr G.,' Jerry said. 'Ain't done it since I was a kid, so I'd be a little rusty, but—'

'No, no,' I said, 'forget that. I don't want you gettin' pinched for stealing a car.'

'What about Miss Ava?' he asked.

'What about her?'

'She must have a car, maybe two. Them Hollywood types always got more than one.'

'Hey,' I said, 'there is a garage out back, isn't there?'

He smiled, nodded and said, 'A two-car garage.'

'Why wouldn't she have mentioned that when we started talkin' about renting a car?' I wondered.

'She ain't used to takin' it on the lam, Mr G.,' he said. 'Could be she just didn't think of it.'

'Why don't we take a look?'

'Let's finish this hand,' he suggested.

We did.

He made gin.

'I'm not playin' with you anymore,' I said, throwing down my cards.

It didn't work out.

We went to the garage, entered through an open side door. We took the flashlight with us, and by its light saw that Ava had two roadsters – two seaters, both of them.

'We could take both of 'em,' Jerry said, hopefully. 'I drive one, you drive the other.'

'No,' I said, 'we'll stick to the original plan. We'll go rent a car from Louie's brother in the morning.'

Jerry shined the flashlight over the cars again, gave them a long, loving look, and then followed me back to the house.

'You tired?' I asked.

'Naw,' he said, 'I got first watch. I'm gonna eat some leftovers.'

'They're all yours,' I said. 'I'm gonna lie down on that big sofa in the living room.'

'Don't wanna sleep in one of the beds?'

'I don't want to get too comfortable,' I said. 'Wake me in three hours.'

'Not four?'

'I wanna shower and change into some fresh clothes, then I'll take watch and you can sleep till morning.'

'I gotta sleep on the sofa, too?'

'No,' I said, 'it's not big enough. You can take a bed.'

'Thanks, Mr G.'

He grabbed the leftover deli sandwiches from the frig.

'Enjoy,' I said, and went to lie down. I didn't realize how tired I was until I hit the sofa.

THIRTY-EIGHT

Surprising what living in a town that never sleeps can do for you. I'd learned a long time ago to get by on naps. After three hours on that sofa, a shower in the second bathroom, and a change of clothes, I felt refreshed.

I sent Jerry to bed in one of the bedrooms, told him I'd wake him at eight a.m. That was four hours. He told me he'd made a pot of coffee, and left me a sandwich. I was surprised to find I was hungry.

I went to the kitchen, unwrapped the sandwich – brisket on a Kaiser roll – and started eating. Poured myself a cup of coffee and carried both into the living room with me. I took a peek out the front window, didn't see anything.

I sat on the sofa with my sandwich and coffee and went through my options. I could have sent Jerry and Ava to Vegas in one of the roadsters, but I really didn't know what I'd do in L.A. I wasn't a detective. I was a pit boss who was also a fixer. But most of my fixing was done in Vegas, which was my backyard. So we'd all go to Vegas, make sure Ava was safe, and then figure out what to do.

As it turned out I really only had one option. Get a car, get to Vegas.

I finished the sandwich, went to the kitchen to refill my coffee cup. I don't know how Jerry did it, but he made the best damn coffee I'd ever tasted.

I turned the radio on. There were no more reports about the manager's death. I turned it off. I thought about watching TV, but I was the one who had mentioned the shadows that could be seen from outside.

After about two hours I got hungry again. Jerry was a bad influence on me. I looked in the refrigerator and found a knish. I wondered if Jerry had been saving it for breakfast. I ate it cold. I figured if he got upset I'd make it up to him. We'd go out for breakfast after we picked up a car.

I took out the card Louie had given me. It read: USED CARS and at the bottom had an address and phone number. On the back Louie had written 'Freddy.' That was it. From Louie's body language I assumed that everything Freddy did at his car lot was not on the up-and-up. That was fine with me. It would work to our advantage if nobody asked any questions.

I sat at the kitchen table and played solitaire by the light of the flashlight.

At seven-thirty a.m. Ava came down. She was once again wearing her terrycloth robe. She ran her hands through her hair as she entered the room.

'How old is that coffee?' she asked.

'Almost four hours.'

'Good enough.'

She waved me away as I started to get up, got a cup and poured herself some coffee. Then she joined me at the table. She smelled great.

'Jerry's sleeping peacefully,' she said. 'I passed his room.'

'I'm gonna wake him at eight,' I said. 'I was gonna wake you at the same time.'

'Then what?'

'You guys get dressed, we go and rent a car and head for Vegas.'

'And then what?'

'Once I'm sure you're safe,' I said, 'I'll try to find out what happened during those missing forty hours.'

'How are you going to do that?' she asked. 'Are you a detective?'

'No, but I have a friend who is. He's a private eye named Danny Bardini, lives and works in Vegas. I'll put him on it. If anybody can find out what happened, it's him.'

That seemed to satisfy her for the moment.

'Red Six on black seven,' she said. 'I'll go get dressed. You want me to wake Jerry?'

'No. I'll do it. You gotta do it carefully with the big guy. He sleeps with his .45.'

She stood up with her coffee cup.

'Very happy to leave that to you, then,' she said. 'On top of everything else that's gone wrong in my life, I don't want to get shot.'

I didn't blame her.

I crept into Jerry's room, stood back from the bed and called out to him, trying to wake him as gently as I could.

'Fresh coffee,' I said to him.

He jerked his head up, but didn't go for his gun.

'Hey, Mr G. That time already?'

'Yep,' I said. 'We've got coffee, but that's all. We'll get something when we go out.'

'OK.' He sat up, put his feet on the floor.

'Get showered and change into some of those nice clothes Ava bought you.'

He made a face.

'They ain't my style,' he confided, 'but I didn't wanna hurt her feelings.'

'I don't blame you,' I said. 'See you downstairs.'

In the morning light we were able to move about the house more normally, but continued to stay away from the windows.

Jerry came down and had some coffee. We were both sitting at the kitchen table when Ava entered, holding a gun.

'Ava . . .' I said, warily.

'What do you think of this, Jerry?' she asked, and handed it to him.

It was a pearl handled automatic. That was all I knew. It looked tiny in Jerry's hands.

He ejected the clip, smelled the gun, worked the slide, put the clip back.

'Could use a cleanin', Miss Ava, but it should work.' He handed it back to her. 'Kinda small for my taste, but it's a lady's gun.'

'And I'm a lady,' she said. 'It's been here in the house for a long time, since Frank first bought it for me.' She dropped it in her purse. 'I think I'll take it with me.'

'That's fine, Ava,' I said, 'but do me a favor, don't take it out unless Jerry takes out his. OK?'

'OK,' she said, 'I won't show him mine until he shows me his.'

I was shocked to see Jerry blush.

THIRTY-NINE

When Ava saw the address for the car lot we were going to she said, 'That's not a really good neighborhood. I'm glad I have you guys – and that I'm packin' heat.' She laughed.

She directed Jerry as he drove the cab. We drove past burnt-out buildings and a collection of bums and derelicts who found us very interesting. There was also a lot of graffiti, some of which Jerry said wasn't there just for decoration.

'Gang signs,' he said. 'We better get done what we gotta get done, Mr G., and haul ass outta here.'

'Agreed.'

We pulled up in front of the lot. It looked more like a junk yard than anything else.

'Have you got money?' Ava asked me.

'Some.'

'Any idea how much this car's going to be?'

'I hope it's reasonable,' I said. 'I'm looking to rent, not buy.'

'Here,' she said, and handed a sheaf of bills over the back of the seat. 'Take this.'

'How much is there?'

'I don't know,' she said. 'I grabbed it from my dresser as a last thought. Thousands.'

'I better go in with ya, Mr G.,' Jerry said, eyeing the money.

I was wearing a windbreaker with an inner pocket, so I stuffed the cash inside.

'You have to stay out here with Ava, Jerry,' I said.

'Then take this with ya.' Jerry held out his .45.

'I haven't gotten any better with that, Jerry,' I said. 'I'll probably shoot my foot off.'

'How about mine?' Ava asked, digging into her purse.

'I'll shoot off my toe,' I said. 'Don't worry, I'll be right back.'

'Don't worry, he says,' I heard Ava mutter as I got out of the car.

I went through the front gates, wondering if I was going to be chased by a couple of junkyard dogs. When none appeared I kept walking. There were aisles of discarded and junked automobile parts, with a hollowed out car carcass here and there. I reached the center of one row when a man stepped out from nowhere and stopped in front of me.

'You lookin' for somethin'?' he asked.

He was taller, thinner and about ten years younger than Louie the Dispatcher, and while Louie's hair was thinning, the guy had a mop of unruly black hair. But I could see by his features and heavy stubble that he was Louie's brother.

'I'm lookin' for Freddy.'

'I'm Freddy,' he said. 'You Mr Vegas?'

'That's me.'

'Come on through,' he said. 'Got a garage in the back.'

I looked around, didn't see anyone else, so I decided to follow him. We walked the rest of the aisle and came to a garage that looked like it had been made from corrugated metal. There were two large white doors that could swing out to open.

As we approached, the garage doors did open and one man appeared at each one.

Freddy kept walking, so I followed him into the garage. In the center was a vehicle completely covered by a tarp. Off to each side were similarly covered vehicles. The two men on the doors pulled them closed, and someone turned on overhead lights that bathed us in yellow. I made it four men.

'My brother said you need a car with some kick,' Freddy said.

'I need a car that'll get me where I'm goin',' I said. 'It doesn't have to break any speed records.'

'This baby will do both,' he said.

He grabbed the end of the tarp and pulled it off. I was surprised to see a red Chrysler C-300. I remembered when the car was first introduced; Chrysler called it 'America's most powerful car.' It only had two doors, but there was a back seat.

'Whataya think?' Freddy asked.

'It's a beautiful machine,' I said. 'But it's not what I need.'

'It's what every man needs, man,' Freddy said.

The other three men closed in, standing with me in the middle. They were similar in age and build to each other – thirties to forties, with hard, round bellies pushing against their t-shirts. Freddy was the only one without that bowling ball belly, and he looked almost emaciated. There wasn't a friendly face among them.

'Let's talk price.'

'What are those?' I asked, waving at the other covered cars.

'They ain't for you,' he said. 'Twenty-five hundred, and that's a deal because my brother sentcha.'

'I'm lookin' to rent, Freddy, not buy.'

'Rent? How do I know where you're goin' or if you'll bring it back?'

'Well, I thought since your brother sent me—'

'Fuck that, man,' Freddy said. 'I ain't in business for my health.'

'I don't think we can do business, Freddy,' I said.

'You got cash on ya?'

I didn't answer.

'Yeah, you got cash on ya.'

I stayed quiet, but my pulse was racing. Shoulda went to Hertz, I thought. Shoulda taken Jerry's gun, or even Ava's.

'Freddy—'

'You're on the run from somebody, man,' Freddy said, cutting me off. 'Maybe the cops, maybe not. You can't be fussy. But if you don't want my car we can just take your cash and dump you someplace for somebody to find.'

'Or not,' one of the other men said, and suddenly he had a crowbar in his hand. I turned. Another man had a wrench, and a third was holding a pry bar.

When I looked back at Freddy, he was holding a gun, a long barreled revolver.

'Just in case you're heeled,' he said.

'I'm not.'

'That's good,' he said. 'That might be the thing that lets you come out of this alive.'

'Guys,' I said, 'there's no need for this. What would your brother say, Freddy?'

'My big brother's an idiot,' Freddy said. 'Why do you think he's a fuckin' dispatcher?'

And what are you, I thought, but I didn't say it. Instead, I started looking for a place to run, or something to use as a weapon.

'Let's start with the cash, man,' he said, 'and then we'll get to the pain.'

I started to sweat.

FORTY

I'd been in some tight spots before, even been shot at a time or two, but it occurred to me that this time I could really get busted up.

'Freddy, take it easy . . .' I said.

'Shut up, man!' Freddy said. 'Just take out the cash!'

'I'd take his advice if I was you,' Jerry said from behind Freddy.

I had no idea where he had come from, but was more than relieved to see the big guy step out.

'Take it easy.'

Freddy froze, then turned. He saw Big Jerry standing there with that cannon in his hand.

'Hey, man, what's the idea?' he said, as if he was accusing me of something. 'We were just supposed to do business.'

'Sounded to me like you were about to hurt our Eddie,' Ava said, from behind me.

I turned and saw her standing there, overdressed for her surroundings in a jacket and pants that cost more than most of the cars around us. She was standing hipshot, holding her gun out like she was posing for a movie still.

'What the hell—' Freddy said.

'Hey!' Jerry snapped. 'That's no way to talk to a lady.'

He walked up to Freddy, who was still holding his gun, although loosely now. Still, Jerry grabbed his hand and, without removing the weapon, broke his wrist. We all heard the bone snap, and then Freddy screamed and the gun hit the dirt floor.

'Jesus!' one of the other men said.

'Here comes the pain,' Jerry said.

The other three men exchanged a glance, then dropped their iron and ran for the door. Freddy sat on the ground, cradling his damaged wrist, whimpering.

'Should I shoot 'em?' Ava yelled.

'Let 'em go!' Jerry called back.

'I don't know how you two got in here,' I said, 'but I'm glad you did.'

'Hey, Mr G.,' Jerry said, 'you had 'em right where you wanted 'em.'

'The hell I did,' I said. 'I was about to get my ass handed to me. I can't thank you two enough.'

'So the next time I offer you my gun . . .?' Jerry said.

'I'll take it!'

We pulled Freddy over to one side and tied him up, just to keep him out of the way. He cried when Jerry pulled his hands behind him, but Jerry ignored it.

'What have we got here, Mr G.?' he asked, then, looking at the Chrysler.

'Forget it, Jerry,' I said. 'That's too much car for what we want.'

'Lemme just look under the hood,' he pleaded.

'We don't have time,' I said. 'Let's see what's under these other tarps.'

It must have been Chrysler day at Freddy's Car Lot. We pulled the tarps off two more. One of them had been painted dark green, the other was covered with primer, ready to be painted.

The green one was a 1960 model and if the key was in it, we'd found our car – if it had an engine.

'Look under the hood of this one, Jerry,' I said.

'These cars have all been boosted, Mr G.,' he said, raising the hood.

'I'm sure this one's had more done to it than a fresh paint job,' I said.

'You're right,' he said. 'The VIN number's been changed. Nice job, too.'

I looked inside and saw the keys in the ignition.

'How's the engine?' I asked.

'Ain't been souped,' he said, 'but it's had some work.' He stood up straight and looked at me. 'It'll get us where we're goin'.'

'This is our ride, then.'

Jerry looked over at Freddy.

'Should we give him some money?' Jerry asked.

'Are you serious?' Ava asked. 'He was going to kill Eddie.'

I remembered Ava saying my name in front of Freddy. That wasn't good, but I didn't mention it.

'Here,' I said, peeling a hundred dollar bill from the sheath of cash Ava had given me, 'give him this for the emergency room.'

Jerry took the bill, walked over to Freddy and shoved it into his mouth. Freddy looked up at Jerry, too afraid to spit it out.

'Let's go!' I said.

Ava helped me open the garage doors while Jerry got behind the wheel. He drove it through the doors and we got in. He continued through the lot to the entrance, where we moved our bags from the cab to the Chrysler.

'We gonna leave the cab here?' he asked.

'Yeah,' I said, 'Larry works for Freddy's brother, Louie. Let them work it out.'

We got back in the car.

'You looked pretty good in there, Ava,' I said. 'Like you were made for that part.'

'That wasn't acting,' she said, 'that was real life – and you know what? I liked it.'

'Well, I gotta thank the two of you again. You saved my ass.'

'And what a cute ass,' Ava said.

'Here,' I said, holding the money out to her and ignoring the comment, 'take your money back.'

'Keep it,' she said.

'I'm not doin' this for money, Ava.'

'I know that, Eddie. Keep it for expenses. I don't want Frank footing the bill for you helping me. Or the Sands. I pay my own way.'

'Where we goin', Mr G.?' Jerry asked. 'I'd like to get outta this neighborhood.'

'Head for the highway, Big Jerry,' I said, tucking the cash back into my pocket, 'we're goin' to Vegas.'

'Now you're talkin'.'

FORTY-ONE

The main run from L.A. to Las Vegas was Highway 15 and that was where Jerry decided to let the car out.

'Hey,' he said, 'this thing runs pretty good.'

'Just remember it's got phony plates and an altered VIN,' I said. 'Don't get stopped.'

'Gotcha, Mr G.'

The place to stop to eat during that journey always seemed to be Barstow. True to form, that's where Jerry got hungry.

'I could eat, too,' Ava admitted.

'OK,' I said. 'Get off at Barstow. Plenty of places to eat right by the highway.'

'A diner's good enough for me,' Jerry said.

'Me too,' Ava agreed.

'I still owe you guys for saving my bacon,' I said. 'I'm gonna buy you lunch.' I looked at Ava. 'With your money, of course.'

She laughed throatily and said, 'Suits me.' She looked better than she had in days. Holding a gun on some hoods seemed to agree with her.

Right off the highway Jerry spotted a diner and pulled into the parking lot.

'Hang on a minute, Mr G.,' he said, as he put the car in park. 'I wanna have a look around.'

'Good idea.'

He got out of the car and slammed the door.

'Does he think we're being followed?' she asked. 'Or that somebody got here ahead of us?'

'Jerry's just bein' careful.'

'But how could anybody have gotten here ahead of us?' she asked. 'We didn't even know we were coming here.'

'I know,' I said, and then repeated, 'Jerry's just bein' careful.'

'I guess that's wise.'

We waited until Jerry took a turn around the parking lot and peered in the window of the diner, then returned to the car. He opened the back door for Ava.

'It's OK,' he said.

'Good,' Ava said. 'I'm starving. I don't think I've ever eaten as much as I have with you guys.'

'Yeah,' I said, 'that's what happens when you're around Jerry.'

We went into the diner and got a booth away from the window. Jerry sat on one side, Ava and I the other. The middle-aged waitress came over, gave us menus, stared at Ava for a few moments, then went off to get coffee.

When she came back with a pot and three cups she filled them slowly, still staring at Ava.

'Honey, I swear,' she said, finally. 'You look like that movie actress? What's her name?'

'I get that a lot,' Ava said. 'I don't see it myself.'

'Joan Crawford, right?' I said to the waitress.

'No, no, that's not it,' she said. 'I'll think of it before you leave, though. What'll ya'll have?'

Jerry ordered two stacks of pancakes, an order of bacon, four pieces of toast and a large glass of orange juice. Ava and I both ordered burgers and fries.

'What's with you and the pancakes?' she asked Jerry.

'What? I like pancakes.'

'And he makes really good pancakes, too,' I said.

'He's cooked for you?' Ava asked.

'Sure I did,' Jerry said. 'Mr G. stayed at my place for a few days earlier this year.'

'In Brooklyn?'

'Yeah,' Jerry said, 'he had to go back there for . . . somethin'.'

He caught himself before saying I had gone back to Brooklyn for my mother's funeral, and one last meeting with my dysfunctional family.

She looked from his face to mine, back to his, and then said, 'Not something we want to talk about?'

'No,' I said.

'Fair enough. Listen, I've had a thought about you taking me to Vegas.'

'What's that?' I asked.

'I don't want Frank to know where I am.'

'Why not?'

'We don't know what's going on,' she said. 'What happened during those forty hours. If it's bad, if I'm involved in something really bad, I don't want him involved. Frank gets enough bad press as it is.'

'Makes sense to me,' Jerry said.

'I don't know,' I said. 'I'm supposed to be keeping you safe for Frank.'

'You can do that,' she said, 'and you can keep Frank safe for me – and from me – until we find out what's going on.'

'OK,' I said, 'OK, let's say I agree to that, for now.'

The waitress came with the food, setting the plates down while staring at Ava's face.

'Rita Hayworth, right?' Jerry asked.

'No, no, that ain't it,' she said. 'I'll get it.'

'Have I been out of films that long?' Ava asked.

'A couple of years,' Jerry said. 'When does your new movie come out?'

'I don't know,' she said. 'Maybe never.'

'Why do ya say that?' he asked.

'Because I was awful in it,' she said. 'I look awful and I performed awfully.'

'You can't look awful, Miss Ava,' Jerry told her.

'I agree with Jerry.'

'You two are sweet,' she said. She picked up her burger and bit into it. There's nothing like a good, big diner burger. And they make the best fries. I covered mine with ketchup.

We devoured our food and when the waitress came with the check she said, 'I think I got it!'

Ava looked at her, smiled and said, 'Kathryn Grayson.'

'I knew it!' the waitress said. 'That's what I was gonna say!'

As we walked to the car I said, 'Kathryn Grayson?'

'I didn't think you wanted her broadcasting that she'd served Ava Gardner in her diner,' she explained. 'Katy's a good friend of mine, and she's beautiful.'

'You did *Show Boat* together,' Jerry said.

'That's right.'

'She ain't as beautiful as you.'

I nodded. 'He's right.'

'You two are so good for my ego.'

We got to the car and got in. Across the street was a gas station.

'Let's gas up, Jerry,' I said.

'Right, Mr G.'

He pulled out of the parking lot and right into the gas station. He told the attendant to fill it up.

'Check under the hood for ya?' the man asked.

'No, it's fine.'

Ava sat back and kept her face averted so the attendant couldn't see her while he cleaned the windshield.

He came to the window and Jerry paid him.

'Think he saw me?' she asked.

'No,' Jerry said, starting the engine.

'Next stop, Vegas,' I said.

FORTY-TWO

I had the length of the drive from L.A. and Vegas to decide where to put Ava. In the end, it was Jerry who came up with the answer. More than once Jerry had proven to be not just muscle, and it was usually when he came up with the simplest of answers.

'Take her to your house,' he said. 'Nobody's gonna look for her there.'

'And you'll be there with her.'

'Right.'

I turned my head and looked at Ava.

'I'd love to see your house,' she said.

'It would fit into one room of yours,' I said.

She shrugged.

'And my house would fit into one room of my villa in Spain,' she said. 'It's all relative.'

I turned back and looked at the road.

'How come I can't sit in the front?' Ava asked.

'Because I called shotgun,' I said.

'Boys and their stupid games.'

As we approached Vegas Jerry said, 'You callin' yer buddy Bardini into this?'

'Yeah,' I said. 'I need a P.I.'

'And he's the one?' Ava asked from the back seat.

'He's a good one,' I said.

'And a pretty good guy,' Jerry said.

'Really?' I asked.

'You never noticed?' Jerry asked.

'You know,' I said, 'Danny says the same thing about you.'

'That's nice.'

'What are you going to have your friend do?' Ava asked.

'He's gonna find out what happened during your missing hours, Ava,' I said.

'Will he be discreet?' she asked. 'My experience with detectives—'

'He's not only good at his job,' I said, 'he's also my friend. And he's a movie buff. As long as he gets to meet you he'll be fine.'

'He'll expect you to fall for him,' Jerry warned her.

'Oh, one of those men?' Ava asked. 'I can handle him.'

'This should be real interesting,' I said.

'Hey, Mr G.,' Jerry said, 'think we can get to a book? I wanna make a bet on the Liston-Patterson fight. I think Liston's gonna flatten him.'

'No way,' Ava said. 'Patterson will box his ears off.'

'No chance, Jerry,' I said. 'But bet with Ava. Maybe you can make back some of your gin losses.'

They started discussing terms.

Jerry drove directly to my house without asking me for directions.

'Cute,' Ava said, as we got out.

Jerry got the bags out of the trunk while I unlocked the front door.

'Gotta open the windows and let some air in, Mr G.,' Jerry said.

'Do it.'

Since meeting Frank, Dean and the rest of the guys I'd been beaten up in my house, Frank had make coffee in my kitchen, and Sammy Davis had shot a man in my living room.

Now Ava Gardner was in my house.

'My room is your room,' I said to Ava.

'That's very kind,' she said. 'Where will you sleep?'

'I probably won't be here very much,' I said. 'Jerry will sleep on the couch. He's done it before.'

'Will you go and see Frank now?' she asked.

'Later tonight.'

We'd gotten an early start that morning. Even with the 300 mile drive it was still pretty early for Vegas.

Jerry looked at me and asked, 'Can we eat first?'

FORTY-THREE

I went out, got some food and brought it back to the house. I had a bite and left Ava and Jerry still digging in. When she was hungry she had quite an appetite, almost but not quite matching his.

I left the house, drove the car directly to a gas station to gas up. While I was waiting I thought about what I was going to say to Frank. How would I explain that I couldn't tell him where Ava was? I was going to need Jack Entratter's help for that.

As I drove down the strip toward the Sands I got my usual kick out of reading the various marquees. Alan King at the Riv, Buddy Hackett at the Sahara, Louis Prima and Keely Smith at the Desert Inn. After almost 14 years in Vegas I still got a kick out of it like no other town, not even New York.

I parked at the Sands and entered by the back way. The Sands was a special place to me. I couldn't walk ten feet without bumping into somebody I knew, exchanging a friendly greeting. The amazing thing about my time there was that there was no one employee I actively disliked. Think about all the jobs you've held? How many times can you say that?

OK, there was Jack's girl, but she had a chip on her shoulder. I didn't dislike her.

I entered the office and asked her. 'Is he in?'

She looked surprised that I'd even asked.

'Yes, he's in.'

I went into his office without another word.

'Why don't you ever let her announce you?' Jack asked from behind his desk.

'That would just disappoint her,' I said, sitting across from him

'OK, so you're back from L.A.,' Jack said. 'What's goin' on?'

'Have you talked to Frank?'

'Only to find out that he sent Jerry to L.A. to help you. Is he with you?'

'Yes.'

'And Ava?'

'She's with me too.'

'Good,' Jack said. 'Where are they?'

'I don't know if I can tell you that.'

He glared at me. 'What?'

'Before I tell you where she is I need some assurances from you.'

'What?' he asked, again.

I started to talk and he said, 'Wait a minute.'

He opened a drawer, took out a bottle of bourbon and two glasses. He poured two fingers into each glass, pushed one over to my side of the desk. He downed his, so I picked mine up and did the same.

'OK,' he said, 'I thought I needed a drink before I heard this. Go ahead.'

'If I tell you where Ava is,' I said, 'I don't want you to tell Frank.'

'Why the hell not?'

'Because something happened to Ava that she doesn't remember,' I said. I explained about the missing forty hours.

'Somebody may be after her, and you don't want me to tell Frank?'

'Exactly.'

'Are you nuts?'

'That's what Ava wants,' I said. 'She doesn't want her trouble spillin' over on to Frank. She's tryin' to protect him, Jack.'

'Well . . .'

'Is Frank still in town?'

'He's in Tahoe, at the Cal-Neva, in a lodge,' Entratter said. 'He finished his engagement here and his family went home. So he went to Tahoe, and he wants me to call him, or you to call him, there.'

Well, at least I wouldn't have to face Frank. That was something.

'I don't know about this, Eddie,' Jack said. 'Frank's not gonna stand for it.'

'We have to convince him, Jack.'

'We?'

'I need your help on this,' I said. 'We either have to convince him, or lie to him.'

'You want me to lie to Frank Sinatra?'

I didn't blame him. It's not something I wanted to do, either. Then I got an idea.

'Is Dean still in town?'

'Yeah,' Jack said. 'He wants to get in some more golf. He's stayin' in his suite.'

'OK,' I said, 'let's get him to help.'

'So you want Dean Martin to lie to Frank.'

'Dean won't have to lie,' I said. 'He'll be able to convince Frank that we're doin' the right thing in not tellin' him. I think if Frank will listen to anyone, it's Dean.'

Jack Entratter thought that over, then said, 'You might have a point there.'

FORTY-FOUR

Dean was on the golf course, and since it was late in the day I didn't want to bother him. I figured I'd let him finish his round and then catch him when he came back. Instead, I went down to the lobby and used one of the desk phones to call Danny Bardini.

'How's your case load these days?' I asked when he picked up.

'I answered my own phone, didn't I?' he asked.

'I noticed that. Where's Penny?'

'Gone for the day. Not enough for her to do.'

'Well, I got a job for you, but it might involve some traveling?'

'All expenses paid?' he asked.

'Of course.'

'Where to?'

'Well, L.A., New York . . . and probably Spain.'

'Spain? Are you serious?'

'I am.'

Danny hesitated, then said, 'This has got somethin' to do with them, ain't it?'

'It kinda does.'

'What does "kinda" mean, Eddie?'

'I'm sort of doin' a favor for a friend of a friend.'

'Like with Marilyn Monroe?'

'Like that, yeah.'

'OK,' he said. 'Who's the client?'

Now it was my turn to hesitate before I said, 'Ava Gardner.'

'You better not be kiddin', bud.'

'I'm not kiddin', Danny.'

'Where do I sign up?'

'Silver Queen Lounge, half an hour.'

'Make it the Garden Room and a meal and you got a deal,' he said.

'Be there,' I said.

Half an hour later we were sitting in the Garden Room Restaurant of the Sands, Danny with a burger and fries in front of him, me with coffee. Danny was a man of simple tastes.

'You're not eatin'?' he asked.

'I've been eating too much lately.'

He stopped chewing for a moment, then smiled and said, 'Damn, Jerry's in on this, ain't he?'

'He is.'

'Is he in town?'

'He is.'

He leaned forward and lowered his voice.

'And is she in town?'

I lowered my voice and said, 'She is.'

He popped a fry in his mouth and said, 'OK, I'm gonna eat now and listen. Go.'

I told him the story from the start, and I didn't leave anything out. Danny was my oldest friend in the world – my big brother's best friend when we were kids – and I trusted him like I trusted nobody else.

He listened intently and didn't stop me with any questions. He had one of the sharpest minds I'd ever encountered, hid it behind what some people called 'childish bravado.'

When I was done he shook his head and said, 'Ava Gardner. Hot damn. Do I get to meet her?'

'Of course.'

'Is she like they say?'

'She's exactly like they say,' I answered, 'and much more.'

He ate his last fry and asked, 'She's at your place, isn't she? With Jerry?'

'Now how'd you know that?'

He smiled.

'Last place anybody's gonna think you'd put her, my friend,' he said. 'It would be too dumb.'

'Yes, it would.'

'Another foolhardy idea would be to try lying to Frank Sinatra.'

'That's why I'm gonna enlist Dean's help to get Frank to go along with Ava's idea.'

'And you think he will?'

'I don't know,' I said, 'but he always listens to Dean.'

'I'd tend to agree with that. When are you gonna talk to Dean?'

'Right after I finish feeding your cheap ass,' I said.

'I am not cheap,' he said, 'I'm broke.'

'You been payin' Penny?'

'She insists on it. I've been writin' her pay checks every week.'

'She been tearin' up the checks?'

'Yes,' he said, smiling. 'She insists on it.' He sat back in his chair and sighed. 'OK, tell me what you want me to do.'

FORTY-FIVE

I left a message for Dean. I also told the front desk where I'd be: on the casino floor, even though I was technically off duty.

I strolled through the casino, talking to some of my regulars, patting the butts of some of the waitresses – which was allowed back then – exchanging greetings with a celebrity or two; Nat King Cole, for one, who had come in right after Frank and Dean.

We talked a few minutes and he said, 'Hey, I understand Tony LaBella's going to be in the lounge. Now, there's a cat with some pipes.'

'I bet he'd love for you to come and see him, Nat.'

'You know what, Eddie? I'll do that.'

It was because of Frank and Dean that Sammy Davis, Nat Cole and other black performers were being allowed to stay in the same hotels they played. Just one way they had changed Las Vegas.

I had just finished talking with Nat when one of the desk clerks came up to me and said, 'Mr Martin picked up his messages, Eddie. Says you should come on up.'

'Thanks, Harry.'

I walked back to the lobby with him, then took the elevator up to Dean's suite.

Mack opened the door and said, 'Come on in, Eddie. He'll be right out.'

He walked to the bar.

'Bourbon?' he asked.

'Sure,' I said, 'rocks.'

He poured a bourbon for me and a ginger ale for Dean. The ever-present comic books were on the coffee table in front of the sofa – Dean's, not Mack's.

As he passed me the drink Dean came out, his black hair wet from a shower.

'Hey, Pally,' he said. 'Good to see ya.'

He sat on the sofa. Mack walked over and handed him the ginger ale.

'Thanks, Mack.' Dean moved the comic books on the table around so he could see the covers. That led me to believe Mack had bought them and put them there for him. I could see a lot of color, but not what the books were. Or maybe I just wasn't that interested.

'Why don't you go on to your room, Mack,' Dean said. 'I'll see you in the mornin'.'

'Call me if ya need me.'

'I will.'

Dean waited until the door closed behind Mack's hulking form.

'What's on your mind, Eddie?'

I sat down on one of the stools at the bar.

'It's about Ava, Dean. And Frank.'

'I had a feelin',' he said. 'What's goin' on?'

'I'm really not sure yet, Dean,' I said. 'I'm tryin' to find out, but I've got a problem that only you can help me with.'

He looked up from the comic books and said. 'What's that?'

'I've got Ava stashed away someplace safe—' I started.

'She needs to be stashed?' he asked.

'Yeah, we think so.'

'We?'

'Me, Jerry and Ava.'

'Ah, Jerry,' he said. 'I shoulda figured he'd be involved, too. OK, go ahead. Sorry I interrupted.'

'Well, the simple fact of the matter is, I've got her hidden away someplace safe and she doesn't want Frank to know where that is.'

Dean sat back on the sofa, sipped his ginger ale and said, 'Oh.'

I put my drink down on the bar.

'Dean, Ava doesn't want her troubles to spill over on Frank.'

'What exactly are her troubles, Eddie?'

I explained about the lost hours, about the cab driver getting beat up by somebody who thought he was me, about being followed.

'She's afraid she's done something . . . bad, something that would bring her terrible publicity . . . or worse, something she couldn't live with. If there is bad publicity it might affect Frank. She doesn't want that.'

'Can't say I blame her.'

'I don't want to lie to Frank,' I said.

'So you want me to lie to him?'

'No, sir,' I said. 'I want you to tell Frank the truth, and get him to accept it.'

Dean crossed his leg, drank some more ginger ale and considered my request.

'I tell you what I'll do, Pally,' he said, finally. '*You* tell Frank the truth, and then I'll try to get him to accept it.'

I picked up my drink, finished it, put the glass down and said, 'I guess that's fair.'

FORTY-SIX

Earlier in the year I'd been flying back and forth from Vegas to Tahoe because Marilyn was there, staying in one of the Cal-Neva lodges. Frank had developed the Cal-Neva into a year round resort that the likes of Dean and Sammy and Nat King Cole and others had started playing on a regular basis.

The Sands had a helicopter at its disposal for the use of its high-stakes clientele, and as had been the case earlier in the year, that's what Dean and I used to fly to Tahoe to see Frank.

Frank had told us to meet him in the Lakeview Dining Room for a late dinner. We got there first and were seated close to the window. The moon was reflecting off the water and made me wish I was there with a lady instead of Dino.

Dean was staring out the window and said, 'Makes me wish I was here with Jeannie and not you – no offense, Eddie.'

'None taken.'

I had a bourbon in front of me and Dean a ginger ale when Frank walked into the room. He was glad-handed from the door to our table.

'Ain't this place great?' he asked, as he sat across from us. 'Dino, you shouldn't have sold your interest.'

Dean had sold his small interest in the Cal-Neva because he didn't want to be in business with the boys. Frank knew that. Dean didn't respond to Frank's remark.

'Ah, never mind,' he said. 'It's good to see you guys. Lemme get a drink and then we can talk.'

He turned, flagged down a waiter and ordered a glass of Jack Daniels. I was drinking Jim Beam.

'Need some gas,' Frank said to us. To Frank his Jack Daniels was always 'gasoline'.

'OK, what brings you two jokers here? Eddie, you're supposed to be lookin' out for Ava.'

'That's why I'm here, Frank,' I said. 'To give you a progress report.'

'Good man! Let's have it.'

I told Frank everything that had happened since I started looking for Ava, even though he knew some of it. I started at the beginning so I'd have time to work my way up to what I really had to tell him.

Of course, I didn't tell him everything, just what he needed to know.

When I was done he said, 'This don't sound too good. I'm glad I had Jerry come out to help you. I don't want you gettin' pounded on account of this, Eddie.'

'I'm doin' my best not to, Frank.'

'Jesus,' he said, laughing, 'I wish I coulda seen Ava holding a gun on those four Clydes. That woulda been a hoot.'

The waiter came with his drink and Frank took a long sip before asking the question I was dreading.

'OK, Eddie, so where's Ava now?'

'She's safe, Frank.'

'Whataya mean, she's safe?' He looked directly at me and the expression on his face wasn't friendly. Frank had a rep for having a bad temper and I'd only seen it once or twice, but I didn't want to see it again. 'Where is she?'

'Frank,' I said, 'Ava doesn't want you to know where she is.'

He put his glass down so hard some bourbon slopped on to the table.

'Whataya talkin' about, Eddie? She came lookin' for me for help, remember?'

'She did that without thinking, Frank,' I said. 'Now that she's had time she doesn't want you involved. Just in case there's some bad publicity.'

'Bad publicity?' Frank said. 'What other kind do I get?' He looked at Dino. 'Dag, get a load of this guy.' 'Dag' was Frank's nickname for Dean, stemming from 'Dago.' Nobody else ever called him that.

'I don't think it's such a bad idea, Frank,' Dean said, looking down at his cigarette.

'What? Not you, too.'

'Hear Eddie out, Frank,' Dean suggested, quietly.

I had seen Dean's brand of 'quiet cool' calm Frank down before, and it was having that effect now.

'OK, kid,' he said to me, making a show of sitting back in his chair, 'pitch.'

As I started talking I was aware that my mouth was going a mile a minute. I had to make a good case for this or it just wasn't going to work.

'You wanted me to help Ava, Frank. That's what I'm doin'. I've got Danny Bardini on it and we're gonna find out what happened during those forty hours. If it's something bad and she needs a lawyer, you're the first guy we're gonna call. But if it's not somethin' you can help with, then Ava doesn't want any mud gettin' slung on to you.' I took a quick breath and went on before he could speak. 'If you want me to help Ava I've got to do it her way. You know what'll happen if I don't.'

He stared at me for a few seconds, then grinned and said, 'Yeah, she'll go off like a Roman candle.'

'You got it!'

He looked at Dean.

'So you go along with this?'

'I do,' Dean said. 'You asked Eddie to handle it, and you know you can trust him. Let him do what he does.'

Frank looked at me, pointed his index finger and said, 'You got a lotta balls.'

'Well . . .'

'But you were also smart enough to bring the right back up,' he finished. 'So OK, don't tell me where she is. I'm gonna assume since you're here, Jerry's with her?'

'That's right, Frank.'

'I do trust you, Eddie,' he said, 'and I trust Big Jerry, but you're the one I'm gonna hold responsible if anythin' happens to Ava. Got it?'

I swallowed and said, 'I got it, Frank.'

'All right,' he said, 'so we got that settled. Now how about we get some steaks, huh?'

FORTY-SEVEN

D ean and I got back to Vegas late. After drinking all night with Frank, Dean had to get me from the airport to the Sands. He pushed me into the limo and sat back.

'You did it, kid,' he said.

'Me? You did it. All you hadda do was say "hear him out Frank," in that cool way you talk, and that was it. How do you do that? Get him to listen to you?'

'Oh, he doesn't always listen to me, but Frank knows I have his best interest at heart.'

'When *don't* he listen to you?'

'Like when I advised him to dump his holdings in the Cal-Neva,' he said. 'I still think it's gonna come back and bite his ass. Also, the whole JFK thing. I knew he was gonna end up gettin' hurt. There's more. You wanna hear it?'

'No,' I said, 'I'm too drunk and I'll forget it all by mornin'. But I getcha, Dean. I getcha.'

'You're gonna have to keep a tight rein on Frank yourself from now on. I gotta get back home. I got some meetings, and dates to play. And I wanna spend some time with my family.'

'I'll take care of 'im,' I slurred. ''s'no problem, Pally.'

At least I wasn't drunk enough to try calling him 'Dag.'

It was almost midnight when we got back to the Sands. Way past Dean's bedtime, so he went right to his suite after I thanked him for his help.

'Don't mention it, Pally. You gonna be all right?'

'Oh sure,' I said. 'The fresh air helped me, and I'm gonna go and have some coffee in the Garden Room.'

'I'm headin' home in the mornin',' he said. 'You've got my number.'

'Yup. I've got it. Thanks.'

Sometimes I still had to pinch myself that I had Dean Martin's home phone number.

I went to the Garden Room, sat in a booth and had several cups of coffee. I knew Entratter wasn't in his office now, and I could have called his suite, but I decided to wait until the next day.

I was almost done with my coffee when I saw Tony LaBella walk into the room. Tony was an old time crooner, an early influence of Frank's, as a matter of fact, who had fallen on hard times of late. Jack Entratter booked him into the Silver Queen lounge whenever Tony needed work. I thought the guy could still sing, myself, but I was surprised to see him up this late. He was approaching sixty, and usually asleep at this time. I waved to him and he came over.

'What's doin', Tony?' I asked. 'Kinda late for you, ain't it?'

'Couldn't sleep, Eddie,' he said. 'Mind if I sit?'

'Sure, go ahead. You want some coffee?'

The waitress came over when she saw Tony join me. He looked at her and said, 'Tea, please, with honey.' He looked at me. 'Good for the throat.'

'You feelin' OK?'

'Oh, yeah,' he said, 'just a little insomnia.'

'I didn't know you suffered from that.'

He rubbed his hands over his face. His hair was thinning, once brown, now mostly grey, his face a map of well-earned lines.

'Only when unwanted memories come flooding back in the dark,' he said. 'Then I need some tea, some light . . .'

'And somebody to talk with?'

He smiled and said, 'That wouldn't hurt.'

'What the hell,' I said. 'I could use a little more coffee.'

I stayed with Tony for about half an hour, letting him talk about whatever he wanted. He talked about a hideaway he had in Lake Mead, went on about past hit songs for a while, then started to talk about the future.

'I'd really like to get myself a hit, and I think I've got the song,' he said.

'Oh? Which one?'

'Frank's song, the one he wrote for Ava after they broke up,' he said. '*I'm A Fool To Want You.*'

'That's a great song.'

'Yeah, it is. I'm gonna ask him, but I'm building up the nerve.'

'Hey, Tony,' I said, 'you know Frank looks up to you, right?'

'Well . . .'

'He always says he based his early style on you and Bing.'

'That's nice to hear . . .'

'No bullshit, Tony,' I said. 'I really think you should ask him.'

'Hey, thanks Eddie,' he said. 'I'm gonna do it.'

I checked my watch.

'I gotta go,' I said. 'It was great talking to you.'

'Thanks again, Eddie.'

We shook hands and I walked out, hoping he would call Frank in the morning and ask him.

FORTY-EIGHT

Since my house only had one bedroom, and Ava was using that – with Jerry on the couch – I spent the night in a room at the Sands. I woke up with only a slight hangover, called the house and told Jerry to get Ava ready to go out for breakfast.

'Where we goin'?' he asked. 'The Horseshoe?'

'Yes,' I said, 'I want Ava to meet Danny before he starts working.'

'Great pancakes there.'

'I remember,' I said. 'I'll see you both there in an hour. And tell Ava it's time for her dark glasses.'

'You got it, Mr G.'

As I headed for the door he said, 'Hey, Mr G.!'

I turned.

'The radio says Liston KO'd Patterson in the first round.'

'That get you even with Ava?'

'Almost.'

Before I went to the Horseshoe I stopped by Entratter's office to fill him in. It was early and his girl wasn't there, which suited me.

He had a mug of coffee in his hand when I walked in.

'Had to get this from the Garden Room,' he complained. 'I don't know where that girl of mine is.'

'I gotta go, Jack. I just wanted to let you know that Frank's on board.'

He looked surprised.

'He went along with it?'

'Dean and I were able to convince him.'

'Well . . . good for you. Now what?'

'I'm introducing Ava to Danny and he's gonna start workin' on those missing hours.'

'You better not leave that guy alone with her,' Jack said.

'You know, if I did I wonder who'd be in more danger?' I asked.

'You got a point there,' Jack said. 'How about you?'

'What about me?'

'Are you safe from Ava's feminine wiles?'

I hesitated, then said, 'What man is, Jack? I'm doin' the best I can.'

'Yeah, OK. Oh, there she is,' he said, spotting his secretary. 'If she thinks she's gonna sneak in on me she's mistaken.'

'Let me get out of here before you tear into her,' I said. 'She'll find a way to blame me.'

'Yeah, why *does* she hate you?' he asked. 'What's that about?'

'Beats me, but I don't have the time to find out. I'll see you later.'

Benny Binion had the best coffee shop in Vegas in the bowels of the Horseshoe. I got there first, ordered coffee and waited. Danny was next. His office was nearby. He slid into the booth next to me.

'I wanted to make sure I was here when she walks in,' he said.

'You gonna rein in your libido and be serious?' I asked.

'Is she?' he asked, with a wry grin.

'I guess we're gonna see, aren't we?'

'You don't look so good,' he said, 'and I know that look. Who were you up late drinkin' with?'

'I was drinkin' in Tahoe with Frank, and then up late havin' coffee with Tony LaBella.'

'He ain't dead?'

'He's only sixty, and he's playin' the lounge at the Sands.'

'He had a helluva voice once.'

'Yeah . . . it's still pretty good.'

I couldn't remember much of what we talked about. I thought I recalled Tony telling me something about a cabin he had by Lake Mead, where he sometimes stayed between shows. I remember thinking he must not have been so hard up if he had a place in that area. Just because he'd been out of the limelight for a while apparently didn't mean he was broke.

At that point Jerry came down the stairs. Ava was behind him, hidden from view. Jerry looked quickly around the room, making sure everything was OK for Ava to enter. Satisfied, he turned, said something to her and let her enter ahead of him. She was wearing the dark glasses and a scarf but, thankfully, no blonde wig. She was also wearing a loose sweater, but tight fitting jeans and flat shoes. She wasn't Ava Gardner, the screen Goddess, but the men in the room still watched her walk to our booth.

'Good morning, Eddie,' she said, in that sultry voice of her. 'Who's your handsome friend?'

'Have a seat, Ava, and I'll introduce you.'

Jerry stood by the booth. Ava sat then slid over to make room for him.

'No way, Miss Ava,' he said. 'I ain't built for booths. I'll sit at the counter. Hey Gumshoe.'

'Hey Gunsel.'

Jerry grunted and went to the counter, where he'd order at least a dozen pancakes – to start.

Ava slid to the center of her seat and removed her dark glasses. I knew Danny was feeling at least what I was, like a slug to the stomach. Ava took your breath away.

'Ava, this is Danny Bardini. He's the best private eye I know.'

'Yeah, but ask him how many he knows,' Danny said. He put his hand out and Ava slid hers into it. 'It's a pleasure to meet you, Miss Gardner.'

'Ava, please, Danny,' she said. 'It's nice to meet you too.' She looked at me. 'Did you see Frank?'

'I did,' I said. 'He's goin' along with us.'

'What did he sa—'

'Let's order,' I said, waving at the waitress, 'and then I'll tell you all about it.'

FORTY-NINE

Over breakfast I filled both Danny and Ava in on my meeting with Frank.

'Sounds to me like Dean swung it for ya,' Danny said.

'Dean can usually calm Frank down,' Ava said. 'Well, this makes me feel better. Now what?'

'Danny's gonna start workin',' I said. 'You need to tell him everything you can remember, from Spain to New York to L.A. and anything else.'

'Now?'

'Right now.'

She continued to work on her omelet while she talked. I ate my scrambled eggs, but Danny couldn't take his eyes off Ava's face the whole time and his eggs were getting cold. The only time he did look away from her was to make some notes in a little book he carried.

'OK,' Danny said, taking a bite of his toast, 'is that it?'

'I know it's not much,' she said, 'but it's all I can remember.'

Danny looked at me. She hadn't given him any more than she'd told me. It seemed to me Danny was going to have to start in New York, where she woke up with blood on her.

'OK,' he said. 'I guess I have all I'm gonna get. Time to get to work.'

He started to slide out of the booth but Ava put her hand on his arm to stop him.

'Thank you so much, Danny.'

He smiled and patted her hand.

'You do everything Eddie tells you to do, Ava, and we'll figure this out. OK?'

'OK.'

Danny stood up and headed for the door, pausing only

to slap Jerry on the back. The waitress came by and refilled our coffee cups.

'Is Danny done?' she asked, pointing to Danny's plate.

'Yeah, you can take it away.'

She grabbed the plate and carried it away. I saw her sneaking glances at Ava, but she'd been working in Vegas too long to make a fuss.

'He's very good-looking,' she said.

'And he knows it.'

'Is he good at his job?'

'Very good. I've known him since we were kids. We can trust him.'

'I trust you,' she said. 'If you trust him, that's fine with me.'

She toyed with her omelet. Something was obviously on her mind.

'Ava?'

She looked at me.

'I want to call my sister, Bappie.'

'Bappie?'

'Her name's Beatrice, but I call her Bappie. She needs to know where I am.'

'I don't think so.'

'Eddie—' For a moment she worried, or was she feeling guilty? Or just upset that I wouldn't let her call her sister.

'You can call her,' I said, 'tell her how you are, but don't tell her where you are, Ava. We need to keep that to ourselves.'

She bit her lower lip.

'All right,' she said, 'but can't we find someplace else to stay?'

'You don't like my house?'

'It's a nice house, Eddie, but it's your house. It's too small. Where did you sleep last night?'

'At the Sands.'

'You need to be able to sleep in your own bed.'

I hesitated, then said, 'I guess I could find another place – but give me a day or two.'

'Sure.'

I looked over at Jerry. He was working on another stack

of pancakes, but keeping his eyes on us, and all over the room at the same time.

I had wondered briefly if Ava's voracious appetite for sex would end up consuming Jerry, but he never would have been able to look me in the eye if that had happened. In fact, I'm not even sure he would have gone for it. Jerry's got his own code that he lives by, and it's based on the word 'loyalty.' I say this because it occurred to me at that moment to ask Ava about it, but I quickly decided not to bring it up.

'What are we going to do now?' she asked.

'We can't interrupt Jerry during his meal,' I warned. 'When he's done we'll go back to the house. I'm going to pack a few things to take to the hotel with me, just for a day or two, until I find you a new place.'

'OK.'

'Ava,' I said, 'you know the Cal-Neva wouldn't be a bad place for you to go, but . . .'

'. . . we'd have to tell Frank, and I don't want to do that. But you know, I think Howard owns some homes in Tahoe, and here.'

'Howard?'

'Hughes,' she said. 'I know you don't want to tell anyone where I am, but I mean, who knows more about privacy than him?'

'Why don't we put that idea on the back burner, 'I suggested. 'Let me look around first.'

'OK, Eddie,' she said. 'Whatever you say.'

I doubted she would be this cooperative all the time, but for the moment I appreciated it.

'You know,' she said, 'you could come home, spend the night in your own bed . . . with me.'

'Not with Jerry on the couch,' I said.

'You don't think he'd actually tell anyone, do you?'

'I wouldn't want to test Jerry's loyalties,' I said. 'I wouldn't want him to have to make that decision.'

'No,' she said, thoughtfully, 'no, neither would I. That would kill him.'

I was impressed that she already knew that much about him.

Jerry came over at that point, carrying a cup of coffee. He sat across from us. He was right about him and booths. Ava and I had to move our legs closer together for him to fit. She also rested her hand in my lap.

'Everythin' OK?' he asked.

'You done?' I asked.

'Yup.'

'Will that hold you?' Ava asked.

He grinned at her and said, 'For a while.' Then he looked at me. 'Where to, Boss?'

'Back to the house,' I said. 'Then I'm going to the Sands.'

'You takin' the Caddy again?'

'Yes,' I said. 'You and Ava aren't goin' out, remember?'

He looked at Ava.

'We better buy some more cards,' he told her. 'The ones we're usin' are soggy.'

'Well,' she said, with a smile, 'this is the town for cards, right?'

Jerry laughed. I tried not to jump when she gave me a not so gentle squeeze through my trousers. Having sex with Ava had been a mistake – and I knew I'd do it again in a second.

FIFTY

'We got a tail,' Jerry said.

He was driving, and if he said we had a tail we did. But I still said, 'We can't.'

'We do.'

'What now?' Ava asked.

'This time,' I said, 'I think we'll find out who they are.'

'They musta picked us up at the Horseshoe,' Jerry said. 'There was nobody following our cab on the way there.'

'Maybe they picked me up at the Sands,' I said. 'I'm not as good at spotting a tail as you are.'

'I doubt it,' Jerry said. 'I think you woulda noticed.'

I smiled. 'It's nice that you have all that faith in me, Jerry.'

'Why wouldn't I?'

'You guys are something,' Ava said, with a smile.

Jerry and I exchanged a glance, and shrugged.

'Where to, Mr G.?' he asked.

'Remember that time we found the body in the dumpster?'

'Yep.'

'Remember how to get there?'

'Industrial Road, right?'

'That's right.'

'Hold on,' he said, pressing down on the gas petal.

'Don't lose 'em.'

'I'll just scare 'em a little.'

I would have preferred to do this without Ava in the car, but we didn't have a choice. If we wanted answers we'd have to get them now.

'Jerry, you got your .45, right?'

'Mr G.,' he said, as if I'd just asked him if he had both arms.

'Ava, you got that little popgun of yours?'

'I don't think I'll go anywhere without it for a while.'

'Pass it to me, will you?'

'Why can't I hold it?' she asked.

'You're gonna stay in the car when Jerry and I get out.'

'But . . . wasn't I good at that junkyard?'

'You saved my ass at that junkyard,' I said, 'but the point of this whole exercise is for me to save your magnificent ass, right?'

She sighed and said, 'Right.'

As she handed the gun over the back of my seat I noticed Jerry giving me an odd look. I was going to have to remember not to be so informal with Ava in the future. I didn't want him getting any ideas. They might be right.

FIFTY-ONE

Jerry drove us to the warehouse building where we had found a body in the dumpster during the *Ocean's 11* – what should I call it? Caper? Case? How about . . . adventure?

He pulled into the abandoned parking lot, and I wondered if the other car would be so obvious as to follow us. They did. Apparently they didn't care if we knew they were following.

'What now?' Ava asked. 'We drive around the parking lot?'

'No,' I said, 'just around the building.'

'Gotcha, Mr G.'

Jerry accelerated around the side of the building, the other car following. Jerry kept going, turned around the back wall, then braked and put the car into reverse. The tires had squealed as we drove around the building. When they came around the back wall we were coming at them, backwards.

I watched through the back windshield as Ava covered her head. The other car's driver's eye went wide and he slammed on his brakes. Jerry did the same, but he tapped ours. He wanted there to be contact, and there was . . . just enough to jar the two men in the other car.

The three of us had braced ourselves, so damage from the impact was negligible.

'Stay in the car!' I shouted to Ava.

Jerry was out, and I got out a split second later. The men in the other car threw a monkey wrench into our plans by recovering more quickly than they should have. They weren't out of the car but had guns in their hands – big ones.

'Get down, Mr G.!' Jerry yelled.

If I got down that would have left Jerry to face the two armed men alone. I remained on my feet.

The man in the driver's seat aimed at Jerry without even

opening his door. He was going to fire through the windshield. Same with the second man, only he was aiming at me. We weren't going to get a chance to ask these assholes anything.

I raised my little gun to fire, but Jerry was much quicker on the trigger.

Jerry fired four times. There was no point in doing less, not when two men were intent on killing you. I'd learned that much from him.

The windshield starred, the cracks traveled to both ends, but it remained in place.

Jerry ran to the driver's door, yanked it open and pointed his gun. I did the same on the passenger side. Both men were dead.

'Sorry, Mr G.,' Jerry said.

'For what?' We looked at each other through the car.

'Killin' 'em before we could talk to them,' he said. 'But they were pros . . . sort of. They had their guns out already.'

'Sort of pros?'

He straightened and we looked at each other over the car.

'If they were real good they wouldn't have followed us into the parking lot,' he said. 'They woulda known somethin' was up by then.'

I leaned on the car. Jerry reached in and took out their guns, just in case. He set them on top of the car. .45's, like his.

'We gotta go through their pockets,' he said.

'I know.'

'I'll do it if—'

'No,' I said. 'I've got mine.'

We both leaned back into the car and relieved the bodies of their wallets and whatever else was in their pockets. We left the change. We'd look the stuff over later. I was about to withdraw from the car when I noticed the right hand of the passenger. He wore a silver ring with a snake on it.

'Jerry.'

'Yeah?'

'His hand. The ring.'

'Yeah?'

'These are the two guys who put the cab driver in the hospital.'

'That's not good,' he said.

He walked away from the car. I started to, but at the last minute took the ring from the dead guy's hand and put it in my pocket.

'What about the trunk?' I asked.

'It's a rental, but there's no harm,' he said.

He pushed the driver's wallet and things across the top of the car toward me, then grabbed the keys from the ignition and we opened the trunk. It was empty as a rental car's trunk should be. No luggage, no nothing, just a spare and a jack.

Jerry slammed the trunk.

'I'll check the back and then we gotta get out of here,' he said.

'Right.'

He opened the back door and searched the back seat, sliding his hands into the cushions. Nothing.

'That's it,' he said.

We turned back to the Caddy, and Jerry looked down at where it had come in contact with the other car.

'Sorry, Mr G.'

'We can get it fixed.'

'Then let's get out of here.'

As we walked back to the car Ava opened the back window and asked, 'Can I get out now?'

'No!' we both shouted.

FIFTY-TWO

We didn't talk on the way back to the house. Jerry pulled into the driveway and turned the engine off. 'Still think you oughtta build a garage, Mr G.,' he said. 'You got a driveway, but no garage. What's that about?'

'I'll give it some thought.'

At that point Jerry looked in his rear view mirror and said, 'Mr G.'

'What?'

He was still looking in the mirror so I turned in my seat and looked. Ava was sitting there, just staring straight ahead. I wasn't even sure she was breathing.

'Ava.'

No answer.

'Ava!'

Still no answer. Her face was white as a sheet, her eyes slightly unfocused.

'She's in shock, Jerry.'

'Whatta we do?' Jerry asked. 'Take her to the hospital?'

'There would be publicity.'

'We could give a phony name.'

'She's Ava Gardner, Jerry,' I said. 'Somebody's gonna recognize her.'

'So then what?' he asked.

'Let's get her inside.'

'Should I carry her?'

'I think she'll walk.'

We got her out of the car and walked her inside; Jerry really impressed me. He spoke to her the whole way. 'Don't worry, Miss Ava, everythin's gonna be OK. You're gonna be fine.'

Obviously, Ava had never seen a shooting before. I knew how she felt. After my first I shook for days. We got her inside and wrapped her in a blanket to keep her warm. Then I got a bottle of bourbon out, poured her a small drink and both me and Jerry a big one. Jerry fed her the booze like she was a child, and immediately the color began to come back into her face.

'Ava? Sweetie?' I said. I slapped her face lightly and her eyes fluttered. 'Ava!' I snapped.

'What the hell—' she said, and pulled the blanket tighter around herself. 'I need another drink.'

I poured her another but this time I let her hold it and drink it herself.

'What the hell happened?' she demanded. 'What the fuck happened back there? All I know is there was a lot of shooting.'

'Don't worry about it, Ava,' I said. 'It's over.'

'Did you kill them?' she asked. 'Did you actually fucking kill them?'

'Yeah, Miss Ava, I killed 'em,' Jerry told her. 'They went for their guns. I had no choice.'

'This is crazy,' she said. 'What if they weren't really following us? What if they were fucking innocent?'

'Ava,' I said, getting right in her face, 'they followed us to an abandoned parking lot and pulled their guns. Believe me, they weren't innocent.'

'Oh God . . . this is my fault.'

'I think you need some sleep,' I said.

'Sleep? It's early. It's fucking day time, for Chrissake.'

'You need a nap,' I said. 'Have some more.' She finished the drink she held in her hand and I took the glass away. Then I walked her into the bedroom, laid her down on the bed, still wrapped in the blanket. In minutes she was asleep.

I walked back to the living room, where Jerry was having another drink.

'This sucks, Mr G.,' he said.

'I know it, Jerry.'

'How the hell did they get on to us so fast?' he asked. 'Somebody's talkin'.'

'Who?' I asked. 'Not you, not me. Not Ava. Not Jack Entratter.'

'Not Mr S.'

'Not Dean.'

We stared at each other.

'Too many damn people already know what's goin' on,' I said. 'What if one of them just . . . slipped?'

'But . . . who?'

I thought for a moment, had another drink, then closed my eyes and said, 'Shit.'

'What?'

'Ava asked me if she could call her sister.'

'You said no, right?'

'Right, but the look on her face . . .'

'What about it?'

'Damn it, Jerry,' I said, 'what if she already did call her?'

FIFTY-THREE

'We need to get out of here,' I said.

Jerry and I were sitting in the kitchen. We had the items we had taken from the dead guys spread out on the table in front of us, and we had coffee cups.

We went through the wallets, found Chicago driver's licenses for each man – Aldo Camanitti and Tony Del Grosso – but there was no guarantee that these were their real names. They each had over two hundred dollars and several books of matches in their pockets from local strip clubs. One of them had a hotel key, but there was no telling which hotel. But since only one of them had a key they must have been sharing a room.

They each had plane tickets from Chicago to Las Vegas. They arrived the night before on a red-eye. Somebody had sent those two jokers to Vegas in a hurry.

'Two guns from Chicago on a red-eye,' I said. 'We gotta get out of here, Jerry, before somebody comes lookin' for these guys, or sends replacements.'

'Hold up, Mr G.,' he said. 'Nobody's gonna replace 'em until they're found. We're OK for now, but I agree we gotta get Miss Ava outta here soon.'

'Yeah,' I said, 'soon, like tomorrow. But first we gotta find out if she did call her sister.'

'She was still asleep last time I checked.'

It was later in the afternoon, and I could hear Jerry's stomach growling.

'That diner down the block still open?' he asked.

'Yeah.'

'How about I go grab us some food?' he asked. 'I think better on a full stomach.'

'Fine.' I gave him some of the money Ava had given me. 'Get whatever you want, bring me and Ava some burgers and fries.'

'High class lady like her must be useta eatin' better than we been givin' her,' he said.

'She hasn't complained about the food yet, Jerry.'

'Maybe I'll bring her a club sandwich,' he said. 'Classy people like club sandwiches.'

'Whatever you think, pal.'

He grabbed my car keys. The Caddy had driven fine on the way home, betraying no damage other than some scratches to the back.

As the front door closed I thought I heard Ava stirring in the bedroom. She had been asleep for about three hours. I got up and walked to the doorway. She was moving around, then suddenly the blanket spread open and she rose up into a seated position.

'What the hell happened?' she asked.

I entered the room and approached the bed. She looked better, more color in her face and focus to her eyes.

'You went into shock after the shooting,' I said. 'What do you remember?'

'I remember Jerry shooting the shit out of those two bastards,' she said. 'Did you fire my gun?'

'I didn't have time,' I said. 'Jerry was too fast.'

I had the distinct feeling that she was happy her gun hadn't killed anybody.

'Don't look at me,' she said, suddenly. 'I must look like shit.' She leaped from the bed, ran to the bathroom and slammed the door.

I walked to the door and said, 'Jerry went for some food.'

'Good,' her muffled voice said, 'I'm starving.'

That, at least, was a good sign.

'I'll see you in the kitchen.'

No answer, so I left the room.

*   *   *

When she came into the kitchen she had applied her make-up and combed her hair, was still wearing the sweater and jeans from that afternoon but was barefoot. I couldn't help thinking, the Barefoot Contessa is barefoot in my kitchen.

But I had to put aside all my feelings for Ava – lust, affection, awe – and be kind of tough with her, because I needed to know.

'Ava, some coffee?'

'Sure. Where's Jerry with that food?'

'Any minute.' I poured a cup of coffee and she sat at the kitchen table.

As I slid it over to her I said, 'I have to ask you a question.'

'Go ahead.'

'You told me this morning you wanted to call your sister,' I said. No comment. I went on. 'I have a feeling you already called her.'

She stared at me, then lifted her chin and asked haughtily, 'What if I did?'

'Then you may have almost got us killed today.'

She tried to hold my eyes, but in the end she looked away and bit her lip. I gave her a minute. Yeah, I know. Real tough guy.

'OK,' she said, looking at me, 'OK, I called her yesterday.'

'Did you tell her where you were?'

She hesitated, then said, 'I didn't tell her I was in your house.'

'But you did mention Vegas.'

'Yes.'

I shook my head.

'She wouldn't have told anyone,' she said. 'I swear!'

'She might not have to, Ava. If someone is lookin' for you bad enough, they may have bugged her phone, or her house.'

'Jesus,' she said, as that realization set in. 'So it might be my fault those two men are dead?'

I was afraid she might get upset again. If she went into shock this time we might have to take her to the hospital.

'Ava, those men got themselves killed,' I said. 'Anybody who pulls a gun on Jerry is an idiot.'

'Eddie . . . I'm sorry,' she said, sincerely.

'I know, Ava.'

'So now what?' she asked.

'Tomorrow we'll find someplace else for you.' At that moment I heard Jerry come in the front door. 'Right now, we eat.'

FIFTY-FOUR

'Should we warn Bappie?' Ava asked while we were eating.

'I don't think so, Ava,' I said. 'She's probably not in any danger. If they bugged her, they know everything she knows, and they realize she doesn't know much.'

Ava looked at Jerry for reinforcement. He looked at me for permission. I nodded.

'Mr G. is right,' he said. 'She's OK. Just don't call her again.'

'I won't,' Ava said. 'I just . . . I didn't want her to worry.'

'It's OK,' I said.

Ava bit into her club sandwich and said to Jerry, 'This is perfect, Jerry. Thanks for thinking of it.'

Jerry gave me a self-satisfied look as I bit into my burger.

I decided to stay in the house that night, so I got some blankets and a pillow and made myself a bed on the living room floor. Me and Jerry were roomies.

'I think she's unhappy,' Jerry said, keeping his voice low.

It was dark, but we each knew the other was still awake.

'You're right about that,' I said.

'But why?' he asked, 'I mean . . . she's freakin' Ava Gardner. Everybody loves her.'

'Not everybody, Jerry,' I said. 'And she doesn't love herself. She keeps talkin' about how she looks.'

'She looks amazin',' Jerry said.

'To you and me,' I said, 'and maybe to most men, but to

herself she doesn't look the way she did at twenty-five, or even thirty-five.'

'Oooh,' Jerry said, getting it, 'she's afraid of gettin' old.' He lowered his voice even more when he said it.

'Like most movie stars, I guess.'

'But . . . she can't even be forty yet. She's got *lots* of time.'

'There maybe more to it than that, Jerry,' I said. 'There's the break up with Frank, the drinkin', she mentioned somethin' about Papa dyin'.'

'Her dad?'

'No, I think she meant Ernest Hemingway,' I said. I folded my arms, stared up at the ceiling. 'They've been friends since she made *The Killers*. She must've taken it hard when he killed himself.'

'So she's got a lot goin' on,' he said.

'Yup.'

'And now a black out.'

We remained silent for a while, and then he said. 'Mr G., you ever black out? I mean, lose some time like that?'

'No,' I said, 'never.'

'Me neither. Must be pretty scary.'

'Yeah,' I said, 'must be.'

Ava was experiencing a lot of fear; fear of getting old, maybe fear of being alone, and now fear of what she might have done during those forty hours.

'We have to find out for her, Jerry,' I said. 'We have to fix it so she at least doesn't have to be afraid of that. She's got enough to deal with.'

'OK, Mr G.,' he said. 'I'm with ya.'

FIFTY-FIVE

It bothered me that the two gunmen Jerry had killed had come from Chicago. The next morning in the kitchen, before Ava awoke and while Jerry was making some eggs, I mentioned this to the big guy.

'Yeah, I know, Mr G. It bugs me, too.'

'Think you can make some calls? Maybe find out somethin'?' I asked him.

'I can sure try,' he said.

'Good. Now all we have to do is find someplace for you to do it from.'

'Why not the Sands?'

I had thought about putting Ava in the hotel, but there were too many ways that could go wrong.

'No, we need someplace else and I can only ask somebody I trust implicitly.'

'The Shamus?'

'Danny's about the only person I trust, without question. Other than you.'

'Not Mr Entratter?'

'Jack would do whatever he had to do for the Sands, Jerry,' I said. 'If that meant givin' up you or me, he'd do it. His loyalties are very clear.'

'Well, we can't call Mr S. What about Mr Martin?'

'I don't want to put Dean into any more uncomfortable situations,' I said. 'If Frank doesn't know where Ava is, Dino wouldn't want to know, either.'

We batted it around over coffee until Ava appeared, wearing my terry cloth robe, which was a shortie. It had been a gift.

'You must have a lady friend who likes your legs, Eddie,' she said. 'I can't see you buyin' this for yourself.'

Both Jerry and I had to tear our eyes away from Ava's thighs. It became easier when she sat down and the table hid her bottom half.

'You got that right, Ava,' I said. 'Of course, it looks a lot better on you than it ever looked on me . . . not that I wear it that much.'

'Really? You'll have to show me some time so I can decide.'

Jerry gave her a cup of coffee and then dished out scrambled eggs.

'What's the subject of conversation this morning?' she asked. 'I mean, besides me.'

'We're tryin' to figure out where to put you and Jerry.'

'Well, like I told you before, I could call Howard.'

Jerry frowned at me.

'Hughes,' I said. He raised his eyebrows. 'I still don't think that's a good idea, Ava.'

'It's up to you,' she said. 'You're the boss.'

She finished her eggs then excused herself to shower and get dressed.

'And pack,' I said. 'Wherever we go, we'll be leavin' here.'

'I'll need to either do some laundry or some shopping,' she said. 'I think you know which one I'd prefer.'

'OK,' I said. 'We'll see.'

Jerry did the dishes while I had another cup of coffee at the table and continued to think about where to put Ava that would be safe.

Tahoe and one of the cabins there would have been good, but we couldn't do that without Frank. And Jerry could probably keep her safe at the Sands, but then I remembered that on two separate occasions I'd had to face a gun at the Sands, being bailed out by Jerry and Dino.

I had plenty of friends in town, but none that I wanted to trust Ava Gardner's safety to.

'Gonna make a call,' I told Jerry, and he nodded.

I had a phone in the living room and made the call from there so I wouldn't disturb Ava.

I dialed Danny's office, wondering if he'd even be there – or even in town.

'Bardini Investigations,' Penny said, professionally.

'I'll bet the boss is away,' I said. 'Does the muse wanna come out and play?'

'If you only meant it, but you're a big tease, as always, Eddie G. How're you doin'?'

'I'm OK, what about you?'

'A little bored. As far as I know Danny's got one case, which he's working for you, but he won't tell me what it's about. I can only assume it involves one of your high-profile clients.'

'Well, if the boss can't tell you it's not my place to. Is he there?'

'Nope,' she said, 'outta town. Can I help?'

'No, just thought I might catch him before he left and ask a question.'

'Well, if you really decide you wanna play while he's away, I'm here,' she said. 'Just come and get me.'

'Don't tempt me.'

'If I only could,' she said, and hung up.

Penny was about as cute as a young gal could be, but there was something going on between her and her boss that even they didn't know about, and I wasn't about to get in the middle of that.

'Anythin'?' Jerry asked. He was standing in the kitchen doorway, drying his hands on a towel.

'No,' I said.

Jerry turned and tossed the towel toward the sink, then folded his arms and leaned against the door jamb.

'So whatta we do? Leave town?'

Earlier that year, when we had needed to put Marilyn Monroe somewhere safe, we'd taken her to Frank's home in Palm Springs. That was out of the question with Ava.

'To tell you the truth, Jerry, I'm not sure what our next move should be,' I said. 'Danny's out there doin' the grunt work, the detective work. We only need to keep Ava safe until he finds out what happened during those hours she lost. I thought that would be easy here, but now we've got two stiffs to worry about.'

'We don't got 'em to worry about no more,' Jerry reminded me.

'But where'd they come from? When will they be found? And will someone be sent in their place?'

'I listened to the radio this mornin',' Jerry said. 'There ain't nothin' there. Should I go out and steal a paper from one of your neighbors?'

'Naw,' I said. 'We'll buy one when we go out.'

'I guess I better pack my stuff, then,' he said.

'I have to pack a bag, too,' I said. 'Then we'll load the car.'

FIFTY-SIX

We got the car packed. I was impressed by the fact that Ava only had two bags, but she said they were both almost filled with dirty clothes, so she was reduced to wearing a t-shirt that fit tight across her full breasts, and a pair of tight fitting jeans. She laid off the high heels and wore flats again. Ava Gardner in high heels was an eye catching sight from any distance, and we didn't want to attract attention. The t-shirt was bad enough. As for her beautiful face she tried to cover that with her big oversized sunglasses.

Jerry wore a sports jacket to cover his .45, and I wore jeans and a windbreaker so I could keep Ava's little gun in a jacket pocket.

We went out to the car and Ava surprised me by shouting, 'Shotgun!'

I looked at her and she stuck her tongue out at me.

'Wherever we're going,' she said, 'I want to have a good seat.'

I was happy to sit in the back, my arms crossed over my chest, deep in thought. In the front seat Jerry and Ava were chattering about nothing. I think she was nervous and he was just going along with her, trying to keep her occupied.

I had a phone number in my pocket that I had only used once before. It kept me out of jail, but was this situation important enough to use it again?

OK, maybe I was making this harder than it should have been. I needed a place to put Ava; one which nobody could trace to her and nobody could trace to me. Putting it in Jerry's name wouldn't have helped that much either because he could be connected back to me.

We could have gone to a no-name hotel off the strip and registered under an assumed name, but the three of us would attract attention together, or Jerry would attract attention, or Ava would. I was the only one who wouldn't be noticed checking into a hotel alone, but I was pretty well known in town. There was a chance somebody would see me and recognize me.

There had to be a way around all of this that didn't involve leaving town, which was the only other thing I could think of.

That is, until something occurred to me.

'Jerry,' I said, 'pull over by a phone.'

'Anywhere special?' he asked.

'Just a pay phone,' I said, 'I've got an idea.'

Nobody who was looking for Eddie Gianelli was going to look through Tony LaBella. That was the logic I was operating on.

Frank Sinatra, yeah.

Dean Martin, definitely.

Jack Entratter, logically.

But not Tony.

In the back seat of my Caddy I remembered Tony talking about his cabin on Lake Mead.

'It's usually empty when I'm doing shows,' I remembered him telling me.

Well, Tony was booked into the Sands lounge for the week. That meant his cabin was empty.

When I called Tony and asked him about using his place he immediately said, 'Anything for you, Eddie.'

'You talked to Frank?' I asked, judging from his tone.

'Yep, he gave me the go ahead. I owe it to you. I might never have asked him.'

'I'm glad it worked out.'

He had a key on him and told me to come and get it; he'd be rehearsing in the lounge.

I instructed Jerry to drive to the Sands and park behind the building, in the lot.

'Stay here,' I told both of them. 'I'll be right back.'

I went in through a back door, made my way to the casino floor, and then along to the lounge. Tony was up at the piano with his arranger, going over a song. If I just walked up to him and got the key the whole room would see.

A little redheaded waitress came within arm's length, so I reached.

'Sweetie, excuse me.'

She turned, saw me and smiled instantly. What a sweet looking kid, I thought.

'Hello, Mr G.,' she said.

'Oh, you know me?'

'Well, of course,' she said. 'I'm new, but the other girls have pointed you out.'

'What's your name?'

'Didi.'

'Well, Didi, can you do me a favor?'

She took a deep breath which caused her cleavage to swell and said, 'Sure.'

'Would you go up to Mr LaBella, up there on stage, and tell him I sent you for his key?'

'His key?'

'That's right,' I said. 'I'll give you ten bucks—'

'Oh, that's OK, Mr Gianelli,' she said. 'You don't have to tip me. The girls have all told me what a right guy you are.'

'Is that so?'

'Oh, yes,' she said. 'You're very popular with the girls.'

'That's good to know,' I said. 'Thanks.'

'Oh, sure, don't mention it.'

She stood there staring at me with wide, green eyes and a big smile.

'Honey? Could you go and do it? Like now?'

'Huh? Oh, sure. Sorry.'

She turned and walked right up to the stage. I saw Tony turn as she called his name, then listen, then look around the room. When he spotted me I just nodded, hoping he wouldn't wave. He nodded back, and handed the girl his key. She said something else to him, then turned and came back to me.

'Geez, that's the first time I ever talked to Mr LaBella. He's sweet.'

'Yeah, he's great.'

'And so famous!'

'Didi?'

'Huh?'

'The key?'

'Oh.' She smiled, reached between her breasts and came out with the key. 'For safe keepin'.'

She dropped it into my palm with a saucy wink. I closed my hand. The metal hadn't had time to get warm.

'Thanks a lot, Didi.'

'Any time, Mr Gianelli.'

'Just call me Eddie.'

'OK,' she said, 'and you can just call me . . . any time.'

I left the lounge and started back through the casino when I saw somebody I didn't want to see. Detective Hargrove, who disliked me even more than Jack Entratter's girl did. Every chance he got he tried to throw me in jail – and Jerry, too, if he happened to be around.

There was no way anybody could connect me and Jerry to the shooting of the two Chicago button men, and yet, there was Hargrove. And what other reason could he have to be there?

I had to get out of the building without running into him.

FIFTY-SEVEN

I couldn't go through the casino. Hargrove and his partner of the moment were busily looking for me. I guess there could have been a chance they weren't, but come on, who else would they be looking for? There was access to other doors, but I'd still have to cross the casino floor. I had to move fast, but I didn't want to run. My only way out was back through the lounge, but I didn't want to raise a ruckus.

I backed into the lounge, then turned and moved briskly

along the wall. There was a door behind the bar, so that's where I headed. By the time I got to the end of the bar, though, Didi was there picking up some drinks.

'Oh!' she squeaked when she saw me. 'You forget somethin', Eddie?'

'Didi, I need to use the back entrance here to get out,' I said. 'There's somebody in the casino I don't want to see.'

'Oh, well, I guess that's OK,' she said. 'Not that you need my permission.'

'No, I don't need permission, Didi, but I may need your help.'

'My help? Sure.'

'There may be a man in here lookin' for me,' I said. 'And he may be a policeman.'

'Police?'

'And I need you tell him you haven't seen me for a few days.'

'You want me to lie to a policeman?' she asked.

'Yeah,' I said, 'Is that a problem?'

She stared at me for a minute, then her face lit up in a smile and she said, 'Hell, no, Eddie. Me and my girlfriends used to lie to the sheriff all the time back home.'

'Back home? Where was that?'

'Hannibal, Missouri.'

'Well,' I said, 'the police are a little different here than in Hannibal, but the principle is the same.'

'Don't worry, Eddie,' she said. 'I can handle it.'

'Can you get Lew the bartender to go along with you?' I asked.

'Eddie,' she said, with a wink, 'I can get Lew to agree to do anything.'

'I'll bet you can,' I said. 'Thanks, doll.'

I used the door behind the bar to get out of there.

'Any trouble?' Jerry asked as I got into the back seat of the car.

'Maybe.'

'What's wrong?' Ava asked. They both turned to look at me.

'Did you get the key?' Jerry asked.

'I got it, but I saw an old friend of ours in the casino.'

'An old friend of ours?' Jerry asked.

I nodded.

'Hargrove.'

'What's that sonofabitch want?'

'Who's Hargrove?' Ava asked.

'Detective Hargrove,' I said, 'Las Vegas Police.'

'The police? Looking for you?'

'That's the only reason I can think of for him to be in the casino,' I said.

'We gotta find out for sure if he's lookin' for you, Mr G.,' Jerry said. 'And if he knows I'm in Vegas.'

'Let's get where we're goin', Jerry,' I said, 'and then I'll call Jack Entratter and find out what's what.'

'OK, Mr G.,' Jerry said, turning around and starting the Caddy's. 'Gimme some directions.'

FIFTY-EIGHT

Tony LaBella had given me directions and advice on the phone. I read them to Jerry, and when we got within a mile of the cabin I took Tony's advice. We stopped at a small convenience store and stocked up on some groceries.

When we reached the cabin I realized that it was nearly perfect. It stood alone on the Lake, the nearest neighbor at least half a mile away. It was rustic, built on stilts, with a deck running completely around it. Jerry and I grabbed the groceries and followed Ava up the steps to the front door. She took a bag from me while I unlocked the door, and we entered.

We found ourselves in the living room; Ava pulled the drapes so we'd have some light to look the place over. We left her to it while we went out and got the bags.

'Two bedrooms, and a nice couch,' she said. 'All three

of us can stay here comfortably. And it doesn't smell musty.'

'No, Tony was here recently, before his Sands engagement,' I said. 'But we can open some windows and air it out, anyway.'

'I'm going to put the groceries away,' Ava said. 'Jerry, put my suitcases in the big bedroom, will you?'

'Yes, ma'am.'

Jerry did that, came out and made sure Ava wasn't in the room before saying to me, 'This place has a lot of windows, Mr G.'

'I noticed,' I said.

'Later I'll scout around, see where somebody might set up,' he said. 'That way I can keep Ava from certain windows. Or off the deck.'

'Nobody should be able to find us here,' I said. 'She should be able to sit on the deck. But go ahead and take a look.'

'That's a big, solid sofa,' Jerry said. He was right, it looked as if it had been hand crafted by somebody who knew what they were doing. 'You take the second bedroom, I'll take the sofa.'

'OK,' I said. 'I'm gonna call Entratter now and see if he's talked with Hargrove.'

'I'll put your suitcase in the bedroom, and then make some coffee.'

'Sounds good.'

The phone was next to the sofa. I sat down, realized Jerry was going to be very comfortable. I dialed the Sands, got Entratter's girl.

'Is he in?'

'Yes.' So much disapproval in one word. Maybe I should have told her how the waitresses felt about me. Entratter came on the line.

'Eddie?'

'Yeah, Jack.'

'Where are you? Wait, don't tell me. I don't wanna know. Is Ava with you?'

'Yeah, Ava and Jerry. Jack, I saw Hargrove in the casino. Did he come to see you?'

'Yeah, he was lookin' for you.'

'For what? I didn't do anythin' to attract his attention.'

'Since when do you have to do somethin' to get on his wrong side?' Entratter asked.

'He didn't say why he was lookin' for me?' I asked.

'No, just that he was. He warned me to tell you to call him.'

'Yeah, right away,' I said. 'Jack, did he mention Jerry?'

'No,' Entratter said. 'No mention.'

'That's good, anyway.'

'What did you do, Eddie?'

'I'm just tryin' to keep Ava safe, Jack,' I said. 'And find out what's goin' on. Like Frank wanted.' I knew all I had to do was mention Frank and Entratter would back off.

'Yeah, OK,' he said, 'OK. Look, here's his number.' He read it off to me. 'Just keep in touch. And stay safe. All of you.'

'Sure, Jack,' I said. 'Thanks.'

I hung up, sniffed the air, smelled the coffee. Ava came into the room, also sniffing the air.

'This must seem small to you,' I said.

'It's nice.'

'You've probably got a big villa in Spain.'

'Big enough.' She sat down beside me on the sofa, put her hand on my thigh. It was a sexual gesture that was decidedly non-sexual at the moment. 'Are you all right?'

'Yeah,' I said. 'Just got off the phone with Jack Entratter at the Sands. The cops are lookin' for me, but not Jerry.'

'That sounds good and bad,' she said.

'Good for Jerry,' I said. 'Definitely.'

'What about you?'

'I'm gonna have to talk to Hargrove sooner or later and see what he's got,' I said. 'I can't run from him. He's not the kind to give up.'

'So what are you going to do?'

'I'll have to drive back to Vegas, leave you guys stranded here.'

Suddenly, her hand tightened on my thigh and the situation became very sexual. She also leaned over so that her shoulder was against mine, she lowered her voice.

'I'm getting pretty horny, Eddie,' she said. 'If we don't do something about that soon your friend Jerry might be in jeopardy.'

I turned my head and looked into her eyes. I almost said that I'd bet she could *not* get Jerry into bed, but I didn't want to challenge her. But I was pretty sure Jerry's loyalty to Frank would keep that from ever happening – unless, of course, Ava pulled out the big guns.

So I just gave her a stern look and said, 'Behave,' and slapped her hand away.

'Fine,' she said.

FIFTY-NINE

I had something to eat with Jerry and Ava, then Jerry took a walk before it got dark, while Ava and I sat on the deck with glasses of wine.

'Franks and beans,' Ava said. 'I can't remember the last time I had that.'

'Me, neither.'

'It was good.'

'Surprisingly good,' I agreed.

'But because I'm eating, and trying to keep up with you and Jerry, I'm getting fat.'

'You're not fat, Ava,' I said.

'What am I?' she asked, sipping her wine. She batted her eyes at me over the rim.

'Oh no,' I said, 'you're horny enough without me making it worse by telling you how beautiful and sexy you are.'

A self-satisfied smile spread over her face.

'Thank you, Eddie, for not telling me.'

We clinked glasses.

'What's he doing out there?' she asked

'Making sure there's nobody in the bushes with a gun,' I said.

'Really?'

'Kinda,' I said.

'Are you staying here tonight?' she asked.

'I don't know,' I said. 'I was planning to, but now that the cops are lookin' for me I should call the detective and see what he wants.'

'And?'

'He might want me to come back to town.'

'Tonight?'

'Maybe. If he does, it's not that late, and only thirty miles.'

'Why can't it wait until morning?' she asked.

'Maybe it can,' I said. 'That's what I'm going to find out. I've had trouble with him before,' I said. 'Me and Jerry both. He's got it in for me.'

'Fuck him, then,' she said. 'Don't call him.'

'Well, if it was just me I might do that, but there's you and Jerry to consider.'

She tapped the nail of her forefinger against her glass.

'Well then, why don't you go and call him now and get it over with?' she suggested.

'You know what?' I said. 'That's what I'm gonna do.'

'Do you have his number?'

'Yeah, Entratter gave it to me.' I stood up, left my glass on the deck rail. 'I'll be right back.'

As I headed for the door Jerry came up the steps.

'What'd you find?' I asked.

'Nothin'. Looks good so far.'

'I'm gonna make a call,' I said. 'Go ahead and sit with Ava.'

'OK, Mr G.'

I went inside. I'd left the number on a piece of paper next to the phone, so I sat and dialed.

'Detective Hargrove,' he said, after four rings.

'If you're lookin' for somebody, Detective, maybe you should answer your phone on the first or second ring.'

There were a few moments of silence and then he said, 'Fuck you, Gianelli. Where the hell are you?'

'I'm around,' I said. 'Not far. What's goin' on? I heard you were lookin' for me.'

'I'm lookin' to throw your good for nothin' ass in jail, that's what I'm lookin' for,' Hargrove said with not a hint of humor.

'What for?' I asked. 'What did I do now? Or what didn't I do that you want to pin on me?'

'Never mind,' he said, 'just get your ass in here so we can talk.'

'OK, I'll be there first thing in the mornin',' I said.

'No, not mornin',' he said. 'Now, so I can call off my men and not waste their time lookin' for you.'

'What, you got an APB out on me? Am I gonna be charged with somethin'?'

'I told you, I just wanna talk.'

'No, you said you wanted to throw my ass in jail, but I thought you were just talkin' like you always do, in general. You got somethin' specific you wanna toss me in a cell for?'

'Eddie,' he said, 'if you run I'll find you.'

'What the hell, Hargrove,' I said, 'what reason do I have to run? Look, I'll be there in an hour.'

'I thought you said you were nearby?'

'I'm an hour away,' I said. 'I'm on my way. Call off your dogs so they don't shoot me on the way.'

'Don't worry about that,' he said. 'If you need to be shot I'll do that myself.'

SIXTY

Jerry wanted to go with me.

'If this is about poppin' those two Chicago goons I should tell 'em I did it,' he said. 'I can't let them pin that rap on you.'

'They're not gonna pin anythin' on me, Jerry, because I didn't do it. And I'm not about to give you up.'

'I never thought you would, Mr G.,' he said.

'OK,' I said, 'so I'm gonna drive back now, and I'll return tomorrow.'

'If you're not in jail,' Ava said.

'I won't be in jail.'

'If you are,' she said, 'it'll be my fault.'

We were sitting on the deck, staring out at the darkening sky.

'I leave now I can make most of the drive before it gets dark,' I said. I handed my wine glass to Jerry.

Ava stood up abruptly, set her glass down, and put her arms around me. Once again, what could have been a sexual situation was really just a warm one.

'Be careful.'

'I will.' I hugged her back. 'Look after the big guy.'

'I will.' She let me go and stepped back. 'Call if you're not in jail.'

I smiled.

'See ya, big guy.'

'Mr G?'

'Yeah?'

'You got Miss Ava's gun on ya?'

'I do.'

'Don't take it into the police station with you.'

'Thanks for reminding me,' I said. It was so light in my pocket that I might have done just that.

I drove to the police station on West Russell, just off Las Vegas Boulevard. Inside I asked for Detective Hargrove. When the desk Sergeant asked me my name I gave it to him, half expecting to be handcuffed moments later and dragged to the floor. Instead he said, 'Wait here.'

Moments later Hargrove's partner of the month came out. I recognized him from the casino. He was young, white and polite.

'This way, Mr Gianelli,' he said. 'My name is Detective Holman.'

'Really?' I asked.

'I'm afraid so,' he said.

I followed him to an interview room where, I knew from experience, Hargrove would let me cool my heels for up to an hour.

'Detective Hargrove will be with you in a minute.'

'Yeah, sure,' I said. 'Tell him to bring coffee, black, no sugar.'

Holman nodded and backed out.

Fifty minutes later Hargrove came walking in. To my surprise he had two cups of coffee with him. To my further surprise, he pushed one across the table to me.

'Black, no sugar.'

'Thanks.'

He sat down across from me.

'What's this about, Hargrove?' I asked. 'It's been awhile since you came lookin' for me.'

'I know,' he said. 'You been keepin' your nose clean, huh?'

I shrugged.

'I've pretty much been bein' myself.'

'Which, to me, is enough reason to throw you in jail,' Hargrove said.

'Luckily, you need more than that,' I said. 'You need evidence that I did something illegal.'

'You're right, I do.'

'Do you have it?'

'I have some questions.'

'About what?'

He sat back in his chair. I sipped the coffee. It was hot, and toxic. I put it down on the table. Maybe he was trying poison so he wouldn't have to figure out how to jail me.

'I've got two dead wise guys from Chicago on my hands,' he said. 'What do you know about them?'

'Dead? How?'

'Shot,' he said. 'In the front seat of their car, with a .45'

'How do you know who they were?'

'We found the hotel they were stayin' in,' Hargrove said. 'Their registration card said Chicago. We found their guns on the roof of their car, more in their room, and their names. Checked them out with Chicago P.D. Wise guys.'

'Workin' for who?' I asked.

'Whoever has the money to hire them, apparently.'

'Did you ask Jack Entratter about them?'

'No,' Hargrove said, 'I wanted to talk to you first.'

I'd been trying for a couple of years to convince Hargrove that I was no wise guy just because I worked for the Sands casino.

'Why me?'

'Because of where we found them.'

'Where?'

'The same place you and your big friend found a body in a dumpster a couple of years ago, when your buddies were here makin' *Ocean's Eleven.*'

'And you think that's enough of a reason to try to connect me to this? That's not evidence, Detective.'

Now he leaned forward.

'You're at the top of my list, Eddie, for whenever somethin' happens in this town that concerns the mob, the boys, whatever you want to call them. This was enough for me to want to ask you some questions.'

'And that's it? That's all you've got to?'

'No, I've got one more thing,' he said.

'What's that?'

'I checked on your buddy, Jerry Epstein, in Brooklyn. He's not there. You got any idea where he is?'

'No,' I said, without hesitation, 'I have no idea, at all.'

Hargrove sat back again.

'And why don't I believe you?'

SIXTY-ONE

'Look, Hargrove,' I said, 'I know you think I'm up to my ears in the Mafia, but I'm just a pit boss at the Sands who does favors for some famous clients.'

'Yeah,' he said, 'and I'm Sherlock Holmes.'

'I don't know anything about two button men from Chicago gettin' wasted in Vegas,' I said. 'That stuff's not part of my life.'

'Yeah,' he said, 'you and dead bodies, you just happen

to fall over each other. I'm trackin' your buddy through the airlines. When I find out that he's here, I'll be lookin' for you again – and him. So don't make me look too hard.'

'Am I done here?' I asked, standing up.

'Yeah, you're done. Stay in town. Stay available.'

'Look,' I said, 'I can just about guarantee that you're not gonna find that Jerry Epstein flew here from New York.'

'Why?' Hargrove asked. 'Did he drive?'

That was too close to the truth and I'd already told enough lies.

'Next time you want to talk to me, you better do it through Jack Entratter's lawyer.'

'Yeah, hide behind your hood boss and tell me you're not mobbed up, Eddie.'

'Fuck you, Hargrove,' I said, and got out of there before he could decide to toss me in a cell just to be a dick.

I didn't want to go to my house just in case somebody was watchin' it – cop or otherwise. I drove to the Sands and went up to Entratter's office. It was after hours and his girl was gone, so I sat at her desk and used the phone to call Jerry. I told him about my conversation with Hargrove.

'He's tryin' to track you through the airline, Jerry,' I said. 'Eventually he'll find out you flew to L.A. And from there it's no big leap for him to figure you drove here, even for a lunkhead like him.'

'It don't matter, Mr G.,' Jerry said. 'He can't prove it, and he don't know that you was in L.A.'

'You're right,' I said – I hoped. 'How's Ava?'

'Beatin' me at gin again – and one of her movies is on TV later, so we're gonna watch it.'

'Which one?'

'*The Killers.*'

That was the one based on a Hemingway short story, with Burt Lancaster. Her hair was long and luxurious in that film and she looked amazing. That was also when she became friends with the writer.

'Wait – what?' he said to Ava. 'Oh, she wants ta know if you're comin' back tonight.'

'I don't think so,' I said. 'Jerry, did you make some calls to Chicago?'

'Yeah, Mr G., but I got no answers yet. I should be gettin' some answers tomorrow.'

I didn't think there was any danger in his making those calls from Tony's cabin, so I didn't protest.

'Since those two guys were from Chicago, somebody should know somethin', right?'

'Don't worry, Mr G.,' he said.

'OK. I'm gonna stick around the Sands tonight, but I'll be out there tomorrow.'

'See ya then. And watch your back.'

'I think I'm starting to get pretty good at that, Jerry.'

I called Jack Entratter's suite next.

'Where the hell are you now?' he asked.

'In your office,' I said. 'I just got back from talkin' to Hargrove.'

'What the hell does he want?'

'He didn't tell you?'

'No, all he said was that he wanted to talk to you.'

'Well, he'll probably talk to you next.'

'About what?'

I told him how two guys from Chicago had been killed in their car, and why Hargrove was trying to connect me to the killings.

'That sounds like a half-ass reason to suspect you of murder,' he said. 'And he doesn't even know that Jerry's in Vegas?'

'No. He's gonna track him to L.A., but the trail will stop there.'

'Eddie,' Entratter said, 'you and Jerry didn't have anythin' to do – no, wait, don't tell me. If you don't tell me then I won't be lyin' to Hargrove when I tell him I don't know nothin'.'

I didn't comment. I didn't really want to lie to Jack, either.

'You got Ava stashed someplace safe, right?' he asked.

'Yeah, with Jerry. And I'll be there tomorrow.'

'You want me to make some calls to Chicago?'

'Jerry's makin' calls, but it wouldn't hurt if you did too.'

'My calls will be a little further up the food chain,' Entratter said. 'Where can I get in touch with you?'

'I'll call you tomorrow,' I said. 'How about one?'

'I'll be at my desk,' he said. 'Watch your ass, Eddie. Hargrove's had a hard-on for you for a couple of years now.'

'Don't I know it.'

I hung up, remained seated at the desk. With Jerry and Entratter both calling Chicago we should have word soon on who sent the two goons to Vegas. Once we knew that, we should also know who was after Ava. What we still had to find out was why.

I started to get up, then slapped my forehead. I hadn't checked with Penny to find out if she'd heard from Danny. But at this time of night? And if he had tried to get me during the day, I had no idea who to check with about a message. Just on the off chance, though, I called the front desk of the hotel and asked if there were any messages for me. The clerk on duty said he didn't see anything.

I left the office and went up to the room I used when I slept at the Sands. As soon as I walked in I stepped on something and looked down. It was a pink message slip. I closed the door and picked it up. It was from the front desk, which explained why the clerk hadn't known about it. It had already been delivered.

I sat down on the bed and unfolded it, figuring it was from Danny. It wasn't. It read: 'You ain't out of the woods yet, Eddie.'

It wasn't signed.

SIXTY-TWO

I slept fitfully. I didn't like the idea that someone knew which door to slide a message underneath – a threatening one at that. I probably should have changed rooms, but I was tired – so tired.

*   *   *

I got up early the next morning, had breakfast in the coffee shop, then went to the front desk.

Sean was working and I asked him about the message.

'I swear, Eddie, it wasn't me. I didn't take a message, or slide one under your door.'

'OK, then somebody grabbed a sheet of your paper,' I said. 'Who? Did you see anyone hangin' around the desk yesterday?'

He thought a moment, said, 'No, not really.'

'OK, what do you mean "not really"?'

'Well, there was somebody hangin' around the desk, but he wasn't suspicious.'

'Why not?'

'Because he was flirting with Rose.'

We both looked over at Rose, a stunning blonde who worked behind the desk and had a jealous husband. Who wouldn't flirt with her? And what better ruse to not seem suspicious, waiting for your chance to grab a slip?

'You can ask her about him, but I know for a fact that she never remembers guys who flirt with her. She puts them out of her mind.'

'I'll ask her anyway,' I said. 'Maybe there was something memorable about this one.'

'There *was* something memorable about him,' Rose said, moments later.

'What was it?'

'He was a creep,' she said. 'He wasn't charming at all. He was smarmy and made me feel dirty.'

'Why didn't you have him tossed out?'

She lowered her eyes.

'I can't have every man who flirts with me thrown out, Eddie,' she said.

'No,' I said, 'we wouldn't have any men in the place. Can you tell me what he looked like?'

'I guess some women would think he was good-looking. He had strong features, an almost hawk-like nose, slicked back black hair – oh, and he had a pinky ring on, with a big diamond. I think I was supposed to be impressed.'

'OK, Rose. Thanks.'

'Have I gotten myself in trouble, Eddie?'

'No,' I said. 'You didn't do anythin' wrong. Don't worry about it.'

She'd just described every would-be wise guy who ever came out of Chicago and New York.

Damn it, what had Ava gotten herself into?

I was wishing Danny would call with some information or, at least, Jerry, when Sean called my name.

'I got a call for you.'

'Who is it?' I asked, hoping it was Danny.

'I don't know,' he said, 'but he says it's important. About somebody named Danny Bardini?'

With a cold feeling in the pt of my stomach I grabbed the phone and put it to my ear.

'Hello?'

'Eddie?'

'That's right.'

''ey, how you doin'?' the voice asked. A familiar voice, too, one I wasn't expecting to hear. 'You know who this is?'

'Yeah, I know, Mo—'

'No names!' Sam 'Momo' Giancana growled.

SIXTY-THREE

Giancana told me to get to a phone I felt secure with and call him back. To me that meant nothing in Jack's office, and nothing in the Sands. In fact, nothing in any casino. I told him I'd get to a pay phone, hung up and left the casino. I walked a couple of blocks to a phone booth outside a gift shop. But before I called Momo back, I called Jerry.

'No, Mr G., I didn't call Mr Giancana. But I called some guys who work for him. They said the two dead guys wasn't with any crew. They freelanced, but they wasn't really good enough to be with a real crew.'

'Well, somehow Momo heard about it,' I said. 'And he wants to talk to me about Danny.'

'Did Danny go to Chicago?'

'I don't know, probably.'

'Maybe he got himself in trouble again,' he said, referring to Danny's problems earlier in the year.

'Well,' I said, 'I guess there's only one way to find out.'

'Let me know what happens, Mr G.,' he said. It sounded like Momo Giancana even made Big Jerry nervous.

I hung up and dialed Giancana, who I assumed was waiting by a secure line.

He picked up on the second ring.

'What took ya so long?' he asked. It wasn't a demand, just curiosity.

'I had to find a phone booth,' I said. 'What can I do for you, Mr Giancana?'

'It has come to my attention that you've had some trouble with a couple of boys from Chicago.'

'Um, well, that's not really somethin' I'd want to confirm, right now.'

'Hey, Eddie,' he said, 'you're talkin' ta me, not the cops, *Capice*?'

'Yeah, I understand, but—'

'Lemme tell you what I know,' he said, cutting me off. 'You're tryin' ta help out Ava Gardner, who's had some problems of her own, but now your problems and hers are the same. Hey, ya know what?'

'What?'

'We can't be doin' this over the phone. You come here to Chicago, we'll go have some dinner, hit the Ambassador, and see if we can't solve everybody's problems. Maybe catch Sammy at the Chez Paree.'

'You want me to come to see you?'

'Sure. Is that a problem? Jack Entratter gives ya time off, don't he?'

'Well, sure—'

'I mean, like when ya gotta help Frank and Dino?'

'Yes.'

'So ya fly out here and I'll see ya tomorrow. Somebody'll pick you up at O'Hare.'

'Uh, Mr Giancana—'

'Hey, just call me Momo, hah?'

'OK, Momo, did you say something to the desk clerk about Danny Bardini?'

'Oh, your buddy the P.I.? Yeah, he's my guest. He was askin' some questions and it got back ta me. Also, I heard Jerry Epstein was makin' some calls and me, I talked to Jack Entratter. Ay, I'm gettin' it from all sides. But you, you're the horses mout', so I figured I'd get the story straight from you.'

'I see.'

'So I'll see ya tomorrow, Eddie G.,' Momo said. 'First flight inna mornin', hah?'

'If I can get on it I'll—'

'You try,' he said, before hanging up, 'real hard.'

I thought it over for a while before I finally called Frank in Tahoe. I didn't know if he was still there, didn't know if he was in his cabin, but I was leaving it up to fate. If he answered, I'd ask him what I was thinking of asking him.

He answered.

'Hey, Frank, it's Eddie.'

'What's up? Ava OK?'

'So far,' I said, 'but I just got off the phone with Momo. He wants me to come to Chicago.'

'Why?'

'Because I've been askin' questions about some Chicago button men,' I said.

'There are some assholes from Chicago after Ava?' Frank asked. 'Is that what you're tryin' to tell me?'

'I'm still lookin' into it, Frank, but I've got a question for you.'

'What's that?'

'Momo,' I said. 'He seems to have Danny. Do I have any reason not to go and see him?'

Frank hesitated before answering.

'If he wanted Danny dead, he's dead already, Eddie,' he

said. 'If he wanted you dead, you'd be dead, too. I don't think he'd invite you – he did invite you, didn't he?'

'Sort of.'

'Yeah, well, I don't think he'd invite you to Chicago to bump you off. Is that what you're worried about?'

'That's it.'

'I'd say go,' Frank said, 'but I've got some help for you, if you want it.'

'I want it.'

'OK,' he said. 'I'll make a call . . .'

SIXTY-FOUR

After hanging up on Frank I went back to the Sands. I had a few things to do before flying to Chicago. Jack Entratter agreed to get me on a flight, and cover for me if Hargrove came sniffing around while I was away.

I called Jerry and told him and Ava that I wouldn't be driving out the next morning because I was going to Chicago.

'I should go with ya, Mr G.,' Eddie said, sounding worried.

'That's OK, Jerry. Those guys weren't sent by Momo, right?'

'That's the word I got,' Jerry said. 'But I still don't know who did send 'em.'

'Well,' I said, 'maybe Momo can tell me.'

'Wait, Miss Ava wants to talk to ya.'

When Ava came on I could hear the anger in her tone.

'Eddie, except for those lousy hours I have a perfect memory. And I have never had anything to do with Sam Giancana. I hate that animal.'

'But he and Frank are friends.'

'That was something Frank and I always argued about,' she said. 'I didn't like his mob friends. You be careful. That man is vicious.'

'I'll be OK, Ava,' I said. 'I had a sit down with Momo once before, and I walked away from that alive.'

'That's only because he let you,' she said. 'Don't get over-confident.'

'Believe me, Ava,' I said, 'when dealin' with these people I am anything but over-confident.'

She put Jerry back on the line.

'Gimme a call from Chicago, Mr G. . . . if you can.'

'I like your optimism, Jerry. Keep your eyes open.'

'Gotcha, Mr G.'

When I got off the plane at O'Hare the crush of humanity reminded me of New York airports. A nervous feeling erupted in the pit of my stomach which had more to do with me never wanting to go back to Brooklyn to see my family. I had to do it earlier in the year when my mother died, but that convinced me never again. If anybody else in my family died they could send me a postcard and tell me about it.

I went to the baggage claim to grab my suitcase and headed for the exit. I hadn't reached it when I saw a man standing with a piece of cardboard with 'EDDIE G.' written on it. He had wide-shoulders stuffed into a cheap suit, stood about five-five. He looked like an ice box in pinstripes.

'I'm Eddie G.,' I said, standing in front of him.

He lowered the cardboard, looked me up and down.

'You want I.D.?' I asked.

'Mr Giancana says I should bring ya.'

'Bring me where? Do I get to register at a hotel?'

'Mr Giancana says to bring ya right away,' the goon said. 'He says maybe ya won't need a hotel room.'

He said that with no trace of humor in his eyes. There could only be two reasons I wouldn't need a hotel: if I was going home right away, or . . . I didn't like the second one.

'Well, OK,' I said, looking around. 'You better bring me then.'

He nodded. I waited for him to take my suitcase, but he just turned and walked away. I was staring at his broad back when I heard my name.

'Hey! Eddie G.. How you doin', babe?'

I turned and saw Sammy Davis Jr. walking toward me in that cool, bouncy way he had. Apparently, Frank had made that call he was talking about.

The ice box turned around and frowned.

'Sammy Davis,' I said to him. 'An old friend of mine.'

Sammy reached me and we shook hands. He was as dapper as ever in a suit and tie.

'What's shakin', baby?' he asked. 'Whataya doin' in the Windy City?'

'I'm on my way to see Sam Giancana,' I said. 'He invited me.'

'Uncle Sam? I ain't seen him in a while. Mind if I tag along? I was supposed to meet somebody here, but they stood me up.'

I went along with the scam.

'It's OK with me, Sam,' I said.

The ice box walked back to us.

'Mr Giancana didn't say nothin' about him,' he said.

'Hey, baby,' Sammy said to him. 'Me and Uncle Sam go way back. Sam and Sam, ya know? Maybe you wanna call him and tell him you left me behind? Or how about we call my other good friend, Frank Sinatra? And we let him call Uncle Sam?'

Ice box stared at Sammy, then at me.

'Come on, man,' Sammy said to him. 'Just drive.'

The wide man started to turn to walk away.

'Hey!' Sammy shouted. 'My friend's bag!'

Ice Box turned, stared at Sammy, then picked up my bag. Carrying it, he headed for the exit.

'Nice job,' I said to Sammy.

'The Leader said not to take no for an answer,' Sammy said. 'Besides it has been a while since I've seen Momo.'

'I appreciate this, Sam,' I said, as we slowly followed our driver.

'Hey,' Sammy said, 'the worst that can happen is that Frank's wrong and Momo kills both of us.'

'You got a gun?' I asked.

'Not this time, Eddie,' he said. 'Not to see Momo. That would not be a good idea.'

We followed the Ice Box out the door and to the parking lot. He opened the trunk of a black Chevy and put the suitcase inside, then got behind the wheel. I got in the back, and then so did Sammy.

Giancana's headquarters was in the Armory Lounge in a suburb of Forest Park. We pulled in front and got out. When I stopped at the trunk to get my suitcase the goon said, 'Uh-uh. You ain't gonna need it inside.'

We followed him into the building. Just inside the door we encountered two more men. Their suits cost a little more, fit a little better, but underneath they were cut from the same cloth.

'What's the nigger doin' here?' one of them asked.

'Hey, baby,' Sammy said, good-naturedly, 'now that ain't kosher, ya know?'

'He's friends with Mr Giancana,' our goon said.

'Hands up,' one of the others said.

I raised my hands and he patted me down, checked the pockets of my sports jacket. I could smell something in the air, something cooking. It smelled really good.

'What is that?' I asked, sniffing the air.

'Mr Giancana's sauce,' one of them said. 'He makes a batch in the kitchen every day.'

'OK,' the other one said, 'Hands down. He's clean.'

They did the same search on Sammy with the same results. The one who met me at the airport said, 'OK, come on.'

We followed him towards the back of a large room with lots of folding chairs in it, to a kitchen. Inside I saw Momo standing at a stove with an apron on over his suit. He was still wearing his Fedora, and dark glasses.

'He's here, Mr Giancana,' the man said. 'And he's clean.'

'Of course he's clean,' Momo said. 'Eddie's my guest. You frisked him?'

'The boys thought—'

'*Stupido!* Get out.'

'Yessir.'

As the hood hurried out of the kitchen Momo looked at me, saw Sammy and smiled.

'Hey, Sam,' he said.

'Momo.'

'You the bodyguard?' Momo looked at me. 'Did you think I was gonna snuff ya?'

I shrugged, not sure what I could say that wouldn't offend him.

'I'm sorry about the boys, Eddie,' he said. 'They're idiots, but they keep me safe.'

'I understand.'

He put a wooden spoon into the pot on the stove, took it out and extended it to me, keeping his other hand beneath it.

'Taste.'

'That's OK—'

'Come on, one taste. You don't want to insult me.'

'No,' I said, 'no, I wouldn't wanna do that.'

I let him put the tip of the spoon into my mouth. It was the best sauce I ever tasted. I wondered if he was going to ask Sammy to taste, but he didn't.

'You got anything like that in Vegas?'

'Nope.'

'Taste that garlic?' he asked. 'All my ingredients are natural.'

'It's great.'

That made Momo happy.

'I'll give ya a couple of jars to take back home with ya.'

'Jars?'

'Yeah, I give it to family and friends. It's too good to keep it all for myself. Whataya like? Meat sauce? Marinara?'

'Uh, marinara's fine.'

'OK,' Momo said, 'you got it.'

He went back to the stove and put the wooden spoon down, then picked up another one and stirred another pot.

'The pasta's ready. Now we eat.'

Because of the time difference it was afternoon. A little early for pasta, but not unheard of.

He got some plates down, filled them all with spaghetti, then covered it with the sauce. He stuck a spoon, fork and cloth napkin in his jacket pocket.

'Take one each,' he said.

We picked up a plate, while he carried two.

'Come on.'

'Um Momo, where's Danny Bardini?'

'Don't worry about your buddy,' he said, over his shoulder. 'Like I said, he's my guest.'

We followed him down a hallway into a back room where some tables were set up. At one of the tables sat Danny, with a fork and spoon. There were two more settings on the table. Momo set his plate down, then the fourth setting. He set one plate in front of Danny, who smiled up at me.

'Best food I ever ate,' Danny said, with a smile. He picked up a fork and dug in with gusto.

'Have a seat, Eddie, Sammy,' Momo said. '*Manga!*'

SIXTY-FIVE

'A h, *stupido!*' Momo said, suddenly. 'I forgot the *vino*. I'll be right back.'

He jumped up and hurried back to the kitchen, leaving me and Danny alone.

'Nice to see you, Mr Davis,' Danny said.

'It's Sammy,' Sam said. 'Damn, but this is good. Ya gotta give it to Momo, he can cook.'

'What the hell is goin' on?' I asked.

'I'm not sure,' he said. 'I came to town, found the hotel Ava said she woke up in, started askin' some questions. When I came outside three of Giancana's men were waiting for me and brought me here. Momo wanted to know what was goin' on and I didn't see any reason not to tell him the truth.'

'Good.'

'They put me in a hotel. Momo says I'm his "guest".'

'Could you get up and walk out of here if you wanted to?' I asked. 'For that matter, could we?'

'To tell you the truth, Eddie, I don't know if I'd wanna try. But the food is great!'

I put some spaghetti in my mouth and I had to agree with him.

'I don't know what's goin' on,' Sammy said. 'Frank only asked me to meet you at the airport, told me what to say. Do I want to know more?'

'I'll tell you later,' I promised.

Momo reappeared, carrying one of those bottles of Chianti with wicker on the bottom, and four glasses.

'Here we go,' he said, pouring the glasses full with a flourish. 'Now, enjoy, and we'll talk.'

He sat down and took a huge forkful of pasta in his mouth. I decided to let him chew and swallow and start the conversation himself.

'So, I hear Frank's wife, Ava, has been havin' some problems,' he said.

'Um, ex-wife,' I said.

'*Basta*!' Momo said. 'When you marry, you marry for life. Frank and Ava, they are – how do you say it? – *caldo*. Hot? They are hot.'

'Yes, hot,' I said. 'Hot for each other.'

'*Esattamente!* Like you say. Anyway, your detective friend, Danny, tells me she has lost forty hours.'

'That's right.'

'And woke up in a hotel here in Chicago with blood on her?'

'Yes.'

'*Terribile*,' he said, shaking his head. 'And I got a call from Jack Entratter about two Chicago guys who came after you and Jerry in Vegas.'

'Yes,' I said. 'They ended up dead which, I hope, is not a problem for you.'

He shook his head with his mouth full, chewed, washed it down with some wine, and then said, 'No problem for me, Eddie. A problem for whoever sent those *stronzo* after you.'

'And do we know who that was?' I asked.

'Not yet,' Momo said, 'but we will, and soon. I will find out. Meanwhile, you finish eating. Later, we go to the Chez Paree and listen to Sammy sing, eh?'

'Suits me,' Sam said. 'I'll get you the best table in the place.'

'Then I put you in the same hotel with Danny and in the morning you go home. Leave this to me. Frank should've called me right away.'

'I don't think he wanted to bother you with this, Momo,' I said.

'*E una sciocchezza!*' he said. 'Nonsense. It was not him, it was her. That one never liked me.'

I knew that was a fact, but I didn't say anything.

'*Mangiare!*' he said. 'Eat up! Then I will have Vicenzo take you to the hotel to change. Tonight we go out, tomorrow you go home.'

I liked the sound of that because it meant if we were going home, we'd be alive.

Unless, of course, we left in a box.

SIXTY-SIX

S ammy had left us when Momo's man drove us to the hotel. We saw him later at the Chez Paree. He was in rare form, singing, dancing, playing the drums, doing impressions. He took me away from everything for over two hours. Afterwards, Momo took us back stage, where we congratulated Sam. But there were a lot of other people there, and I had no time to fill Sammy in.

'That's OK,' he said. 'I'll call Frank – that is, if I want to know more.'

'Thanks a lot, Sammy,' I said. 'You took a chance.'

'Momo wouldn't hurt me. He knows Frank wouldn't like it.'

'I thought you were friends—'

'Friends?' he said, laughing. 'You notice he didn't ask me to taste any sauce off the wooden spoon?'

'Sam—'

'Ah, it doesn't matter. I'm glad you enjoyed tonight,

Eddie. Go back home tomorrow and finish what you have to finish.'

We shook hands.

On the plane the next day Danny and I had seats together so he could tell me what he'd been doing.

'I spent a day in Madrid just to see where the trail started,' Danny said. 'Ava had really been burnin' the candle at both ends over there. Lots of men: bull fighters, actors, race car drivers. I found out what flight she took to the US, and I took the same one.'

'To Chicago?'

He shook his head.

'New York first,' he said. 'Same thing. Hittin' the clubs, lots of men . . . I talked with the hotel staff at the Waldorf. They were happy to have her, but she appeared to be drunk most of the time, people on her floor complained about the noise . . . and then she flew to Chicago.'

'Anybody go with her?' I asked. 'From Spain to New York, or New York to Chicago?'

'No,' he said, 'she flew alone, but that doesn't mean somebody didn't follow her.'

'Any fights, anything that made the police necessary . . .' I said.

'No,' he said, then, 'not yet.'

'But . . .?'

'Apparently, things got messy in Chicago.'

'How so?'

'Somebody got killed.'

'Who?'

'A man named Vito Napolitano.'

'Great,' I said. 'A made guy?'

'Actually, the son of a made guy,' he said. 'Tony Napolitano.'

'How was he killed?'

'Shot with a small caliber gun.'

'Where did it happen?'

'That's the part you're not gonna like.'

'The Drake Hotel?'

'Yes,' Danny said. 'The body wasn't discovered in his room until after Ava got on a plane to Vegas.'

'Are the police lookin' for her?'

'No, but Napolitano's father is.'

'Did you see Napolitano?'

'I was on my way when Momo made me his guest.'

'So Momo knows Napolitano?'

'Apparently.'

'Fellow businessmen?'

Danny shrugged.

'I didn't have time to get the goods,' he said. 'You should ask Entratter.'

'Yes,' I agreed, 'I should.'

At the airport we took separate cabs.

'Want me to keep lookin'?' he asked. 'I could get the next flight back to Chicago. I didn't get to have one of those famous Chicago hot dogs while I was there.'

'They don't compare to a Nathan's hot dog' I said.

'I was sort of hopin' to make the comparison myself,' Danny said.

'No,' I said. 'You go back and Momo's liable to make you his guest again. A more permanent one. If Napolitano is made, then he's off limits to anybody but another made guy.'

'That's their code, not ours.'

'Well, they kill to uphold their code, we don't,' I reminded him. 'Go home, see Penny, work some normal cases.'

'If you need me for anythin',' he said, slapping me on the back, 'don't hesitate.'

'When have I ever?'

He got in the first cab in line, I walked to the second.

I had left the Caddy at the Sands, stranding Jerry and Ava until I came back. I was going to drive out there, but I stopped at Jack's office first.

'Napolitano,' he said, shaking his head. 'I heard the kid got hit.'

'Well, apparently his father thinks Ava did it.'

'If that's the case,' Entratter said, 'he won't stop comin'.'

'Napolitano's a boss?'

'Let's say he aspires,' Entratter said. 'He's got a crew made up of misfits. He's tryin' to establish his own "family".'

The Five Families were based in New York, and were ruled over by the Commission. While the Chicago Outfit was separate from the Five Families, it was still ruled by the Commission. Giancana was 'the man' there, but he was in a constant struggle to keep his territory. Entratter said that Napolitano was one of those who were trying to muscle in.

'You can forget all about this now, Eddie,' he said. 'Momo will take care of Napolitano. He won't let him kill Frank's Ava.'

'I hope not,' I said. 'And I hope his protection will also extend to Ava's friends.'

I picked up my suitcase, hefted it, then put it down and opened it. I took out one of Momo's jars.

'Here,' I said, putting it on Jack's desk. 'A gift.'

I left Entratter's office to make the drive to Tony LaBella's cabin on Lake Mead. He was examining the jar as I walked out.

SIXTY-SEVEN

When I walked up on to the deck I noticed the broken window in front, now covered by some cardboard. Then I saw the bullet holes in the side of the building, some chunks taken from the wooden railing.

'Jerry?' I shouted. 'Ava?'

I rushed into the house, found Jerry and Ava sitting in the living room. They both looked unharmed.

'Hey, Mr G.'

'What the hell happened?' I asked. 'Are you two all right? Ava?'

'I'm fine,' she said, 'thanks to Jerry. Where've you been?'

'Danny and I were guests of Momo Gianacana's.'

'Guests?' Jerry asked.

'That's what he called it,' I said. 'We never tried to walk off on our own, so I don't know what would have happened if we had. But what happened here? And when?'

'Last night,' Jerry said. 'After dinner. I made a nice roast—'

'I'll get something for us to drink,' Ava said, standing up from the sofa, 'while Jerry fills you in.'

She went into the kitchen.

'She's a real trooper, Mr G.,' he said. 'Didn't go into shock like the other day.'

'What happened, Jerry?' I said.

'Come outside,' he said, 'and I'll tell ya . . .'

The previous night, Ava and Jerry had just finished their dinner, the pot roast Jerry had prepared with potatoes and carrots.

'I'll make the coffee,' Ava told Jerry. 'It's the least I can do.'

'OK, Miss Ava,' Jerry said. 'I'm just gonna go out on the front deck and get some air. I'll wash all the dishes after we finish.'

'I'll bring it out there,' she promised.

'Sounds good.'

Jerry went and stood on the deck, looking out at the dying light and breathing in the fresh air. This was a lot different from trying to breathe in Brooklyn – but Brooklyn had a lot of other things to recommend it. He wasn't about to trade in Brooklyn for Vegas or Lake Mead. Not permanently, anyway.

He was still standing at the rail, leaning on it, when Ava came out of the house with two mugs of coffee.

'Here you go, Jerry—'

Before she could get another word out there was a shot, and the front window shattered just behind Ava.

'Wha—' she said, dropping the mugs.

'Get down!' Jerry shouted. He grabbed Ava and dragged her to the ground with his left hand, while pulling his .45 from his belt with his right.

'What was that?' she asked.

'That was a shot, Miss Ava,' Jerry said.

'B-but I didn't hear a shot, only the glass breaking.'

'Trust me, it was a shot. You better get back inside.'

'Where inside?'

'Away from any windows,' Jerry said. 'In fact, get in that closet outside the bathroom and stay there until I come for you.'

'But Jerry, you can't – I can get my gun—'

'No,' Jerry said. 'Get in the closet. Now!'

'All right.'

'And keep low.'

Ava crab-walked back inside while Jerry went to the rail, keeping low and looking out for the shooter. What he saw was two men coming toward the house, guns in their hands. One of them had obviously gotten anxious and fired too soon.

Jerry decided staying out in the open was a bad idea so he went back into the house, figuring he'd have an advantage because they would have to come in after him.

He closed the front door, locked it, and then peered through the shattered window.

The two shooters thought better of coming up the front steps. Jerry was just able to see them as they split up, each going around the other side of the house.

There was a back door in the kitchen. The deck wrapped around, but the only other access was in the back. They'd have to climb up on to it from the side, which wouldn't be easy with guns in their hands.

Jerry left the front of the house and went into the kitchen. It would have been helpful to use Ava as a look-out, but he decided to leave her in the closet, where she'd be safe from flying lead.

He peered out the back window, saw one man appear at the base of the steps. He stopped there. That meant the other man was probably climbing up on to the deck.

This man had come from Jerry's left, so he assumed the other man was climbing up on the right. He hurried to that window, saw the man sweep one leg over the rail, then the other. Then he drew his gun from his belt. Jerry did not break out the window pane the way they did in movie westerns. Rather than warn the man with breaking glass he simply fired through it. Oddly, the hole appeared in the window, but the pane didn't shatter. The bullet struck the man in the chest. His eyes went wide, his mouth opened, and then he toppled backward over the rail. Jerry heard the body hit the ground, but didn't waste any time in running back to the kitchen. As he reached the doorway the back door slammed open from a kick, and the second gunman rushed in with his gun out. They saw each other and fired at the same time . . .

From inside the closet Ava sat with her little gun in her hand. She'd made a point of grabbing it before she obeyed Jerry and hid in the closet. She held it in both hands, flinching when she heard the first shot, then again when she heard two shots fired almost at the same time.

Then it was silent, and that was even scarier.

She held the gun tightly, waiting. She heard footsteps approaching the closet, and then the door swung open. She pointed the gun . . .

. . . Jerry saw Ava pointing the gun at him with both hands and said, 'It's OK, Miss Ava.' He was shocked when she fired, her eyes wide with fright. He waited for the impact of the bullet, but none came, despite the fact that she pulled the trigger again and again.

The he turned, saw the man behind him and fired once. The man staggered back, the gun dangling from his hand. Finally, he dropped his gun to the floor, and then fell over on to it. Jerry went to the body and turned it over.

'Did I . . .' Ava asked.

Jerry told her the truth.

'You missed every shot,' he said. 'But you gave me time to put one hole in him, and that was enough. Thanks, Miss Ava.'

*   *   *

'The bullets are small and didn't do much damage to the walls.'

'I saved your butt and you're talking about the walls?' Ava asked, coming back in with the coffee.

'You did save my ass, Miss Ava,' he said. 'I don't know how that guy got behind me.'

I knew, but I didn't say it out loud. Jerry was so concerned about Ava that he'd made a mistake, and it had almost cost him.

I looked at Ava. Actually killing a man did not seem to have affected her as much as seeing Jerry kill the two in the parking lot. Maybe she was becoming hardened to this kind of life.

'OK, hold on,' I said. 'What happened to the bodies?'

'Oh,' Jerry said, 'they're out back. I covered 'em up with some branches to keep animals away, but they're gonna start to stink soon.'

'When did all this happen?'

'Yesterday evenin',' Jerry said. 'I woulda taken Miss Ava away from here, but we didn't have no car and it's too far to walk.'

'We can talk about that later,' I said. 'We've got to get Tony's house fixed up, and those bodies taken care of. We can't have him come back here and find a stack of dead, decaying Chicago hoods – they are from Chicago, aren't they?'

'Oh yeah,' Jerry said. 'Here.' He walked to a small writing desk that Tony had against the wall and opened a drawer. He came back and handed me two wallets.

'Daniel Pierce and Gino Capetti,' I read off, 'Chicago driver's licenses. Even Chicago union cards. But Pierce isn't Italian.'

'Don't matter,' Jerry said. 'I ain't Italian and I work for the families.'

'You're right.'

'So what do we do?' Ava asked.

'We can stay here another day or two. They won't be lookin' for these guys until then. Meanwhile, Jerry and I have to cart them off someplace and bury 'em.'

'That's gruesome work,' she said.

'Yes, it is. After that we'll have to fix that window. I don't know what we can do about the bullet holes in the outside wall.'

'Maybe Mr LaBella will think they lend the place some character,' she offered.

'You know?' I said. 'He just might, at that.'

'I can heat the leftover roast up and make sandwiches for lunch,' she said. 'I mean, if you can be hungry after burying three men.'

'I can,' Jerry said.

'Yeah,' I agreed, 'I'm afraid to say I'll probably be hungry too.'

SIXTY-EIGHT

There was no other way to do it. Jerry carried two of the bodies – one over his shoulder and one under his arm – and I carried the other, smallest one. We walked as far as we could into the forest and then dug one big hole to bury them in. Tony had a couple of shovels in a shed behind the house, so we used them to go down at least three feet

But before I shoved my guy into the mass grave I noticed something.

'Jerry, this guy's got the same ring.'

'With the snake?'

I nodded, leaned over and took it off him.

'This must be somethin' Napolitano's guys get from him,' I said. It was the only explanation I could think of. 'They don't all have it,' Jerry said, 'but maybe you gotta make your bones first.' He shook his head. 'Tacky.'

I rolled my guy into the grave.

We covered them up.

We couldn't call the police, even though Jerry had killed them in self defense, Hargrove would have used the incident to try to put him away – and probably me, too. There was no way we'd get an even break from the cops. Not when almost everybody involved was a wise guy.

When we got back we were, indeed, hungry. We washed up and sat and had a kind of grim lunch with Ava, who surprised herself by having an appetite as well.

'Man, this roast was great, Jerry,' I said. 'I'm sorry I missed the whole meal last night.'

'Maybe you shouldn't be,' Ava said. 'If you were here you might've got shot.'

'Yeah, well . . .'

'You gotta tell us how Chicago went, Mr G.,' Jerry said. So I did . . .

'Napolitano,' Jerry said. 'That's the name I got.'

'When?'

'Yesterday,' the big guy said. 'I didn't have a chance to tell you.'

'What did you hear?'

'Just that the two guys I wasted worked for Napolitano.'

'And what do you know about Mr Napolitano?'

'That he ain't as big as he thinks he is, and won't ever be,' Jerry said. 'Eventually, Mr Giancana's gonna have him taken care of.'

'Well,' I said, 'now may be the time.' I looked at Ava. 'What do you know about Vito Napolitano?'

'I've been trying to remember ever since you said the name,' she said. 'I remember a handsome young man – but I remember a lot of handsome young men. Oh, I can't believe this!' She held her head in her hands.

'Take it easy, Ava,' I said. 'I don't think you killed him.'

'That's not what I mean,' she said. 'I spent so much of the time I was married to Frank trying to get him away from those men. I can't believe that I did something to get myself involved with them.'

'Don't be hard on yourself,' I said. 'If you were so drunk you lost forty hours, you can't be held responsible—'

'Oh, but I do hold myself responsible,' she said. 'After

all, I'm the one who apparently went on a goddamned bender. Sex, booze and, who knows, maybe drugs, and I get involved in the murder of some would-be Mafioso's son? What the fuck is wrong with me?'

I looked at Jerry, who seemed about to speak, and shook my head. Then I jerked my head to indicate I wanted him to walk outside with me.

'Jerry and I are just gonna have a look outside, Ava,' I said.

'I'll do these dishes,' she said. 'Might as well make myself useful.'

Jerry and I went out on to the deck.

'What are we gonna do?' he asked.

'We can spend the night here,' I said. 'If Napolitano doesn't hear from his men by tomorrow night he might send more. We should be safe tonight.'

'What about the window?'

'I'll have Jack Entratter send someone out here to replace it. Maybe even dig out these bullets and fill the holes. But I'll tell Tony what happened, anyway. He has a right to know.'

'About the bodies we buried?'

'No,' I said, 'I don't want anybody to know about that. That's between you and me.'

'I agree.'

We were both raking the landscape with our eyes while we were out there.

'Just to be sure,' I said, 'maybe one of us should stay awake tonight. We can go four hours on, four off.'

'Suits me, but where are we gonna take Miss Ava tomorrow?' he asked.

'I hate to do it,' I said, 'but maybe the Sands will be the safest place. According to Jack Entratter, we just have to wait for Momo to take care of things for us.'

'What's that mean?' Ava asked. We hadn't seen her come to the door.

I looked at her. 'Apparently, Giancana is gonna take care of Napolitano.'

She came out on to the deck.

'But that wouldn't help me,' she said. 'I want to know if I killed that man.'

'Ava—' I said.

'I know you don't think I did, Eddie,' she said, 'but that doesn't mean I didn't.' She put her hands on my chest. 'I still need to know what happened!'

I put my hands on her upper arms and rubbed them.

'OK, Ava,' I said. 'We'll find out for you.'

SIXTY-NINE

I took the first watch, sitting on the sofa with Jerry's .45 either in my lap, or on the cushion next to me.

It seemed to me I hadn't done all that much for Ava, except run her around L.A. and Las Vegas. If wise guys from Chicago stopped coming after her it would be because Sam Giancana put an end to Tony Napolitano. But if I could find out for her who actually killed Vito Napolitano, and prove to her that she didn't do it, then I would have done something real for her.

Of course, if Giancana killed Vito to get at Tony, and then later killed Tony, he wasn't about to admit any of that to me. But then I didn't really have to prove who *did* kill Vito. I just had to convince Ava that, during a drunken black out, she hadn't.

I picked up Jerry's .45 and walked to the front window – the one without Jerry's cardboard patch. I didn't think the two goons Jerry had killed had help out there, but if they did we had to be aware and ready. There was plenty of moonlight and I could see the front of the house clearly. Then I walked to the kitchen door and looked out. The lock had been shattered by a kick. Jerry had found some tools the same place we found the shovels, and nailed it shut.

Satisfied, I got some water from the tap, carried the glass back to the living room with me and sat down on the sofa with the gun on the cushion next to me. We were taking a chance that I was right, that the two dead men were working alone, and that no one would come looking for them for at least a day. I was ready, though, in case someone kicked in the front door.

My four hours were about up and I was in mid yawn when Jerry came walking in, looking refreshed. I knew from past experience that he could operate on remarkably little sleep.

'Hey, Mr G,' he said. 'Why don't you turn in?'

'Jerry, there's a chance Hargrove will be waitin' to catch me at the Sands,' I said.

'So if he catches you, he catches me, is that what you're gettin' at?' he asked.

'Pretty much.'

'I'm sure you can get us into the Sands without goin' through the front, Mr G.,' he said. 'I got lots of faith in you.'

I stood up, and his .45 changed hands, as did Ava's little gun. We decided not to let Ava hang on to it herself. Less chance she might shoot one of us.

'I hope I can earn your faith, Jerry,' I said.

He grinned and said, 'Hey, Mr G., no worries. You already have.'

SEVENTY

We packed up the next day, locked down Tony's house. I took his key with me so I could give it to Jack Entratter. I wanted Tony's house back to normal before I returned the key to him.

As Jerry drove us back to Las Vegas with Ava once again riding shotgun, I told them I had come up with a better idea.

'Better than the Sands?' Jerry asked.

'Hargrove may have the Sands bein' watched front and back,' I said.

'Looking for you?' Ava asked.

'He knows how to find me,' I said. 'If he tracked Jerry from L.A. to here, he could be lookin' for him there.'

Jerry looked at me in the rear view mirror.

'How's he gonna do that?' he asked. 'Track me, I mean?'

'I don't know,' I said, 'but just to be on the safe side I'm gonna call Danny when we get near town.'

'The handsome private eye?' Ava asked. 'I'm going to stay with him?'

'Not exactly,' I said.

On the outskirts of town I had Jerry pull over at a pay phone. If this was going to keep up I was going to have to get a phone put into the Caddy. On Jack Entratter's dime, of course.

I called Danny's office and Penny put me through along with a little flirting.

'I need a favor,' I said.

'Name it.'

'I put Ava at a house in Lake Mead owned by Tony LaBella,' I explained. 'She was there with Jerry while I was in Chicago with you. Last night, they found them.' I hadn't even mentioned to Danny, when we were flying back from Chicago, where I had stashed her.

'Uh-oh,' he said, 'does that mean what I think it means?'

'Yes,' I said, 'it was a mess and now we're on the road.'

'Where are you going?' he asked.

'That's the favor,' I said. 'I need someplace safe to stash Ava.'

'Mine?' he asked.

'No, we're too connected.'

'You want me to find a place?'

'I was thinking of Penny's place,' I said. 'Do you think she'd mind rooming with Ava for a few days?'

'I think she'd love it,' he said. 'But what about Jerry?'

'I might need Jerry,' I said, 'so I'd be taking him with me.'

'Well,' he said, 'Penny's got a gun permit and knows how to use one, and she's always buggin' me to let her work on a case.'

'Would you ask her for me?'

'Hold on.'

While he spoke with Penny I thought about it. Using Danny was chancy, because we were so connected, but using Penny might give me a few days. And the fact that she could use a gun freed Jerry up for – what? I wasn't sure. Maybe just to watch my back.

'Eddie? No problem. Penny's thrilled to meet Ava.'

'OK,' I said. 'I don't think we should come to your office.'

'No, take Ava right to Penny's. We'll meet you there.' He gave me the address. 'Warn Ava that it's a small place.'

'At this point if there's no shooting I don't think Ava will mind the size.'

'OK, then. See you there. Half an hour?'

'Twenty minutes,' I said.

'Done.'

I called Entratter quickly and told him I'd be there in an hour.

'Any sign of Hargrove?' I asked.

'He was here earlier, but only to talk to me,' Entratter said.

'Did he ask about me?'

'You were one subject we discussed,' he said. 'I'll talk to you when you get here. This has gotten way out of hand. I'm thinkin' about just dumpin' it on Frank.'

I knew that wasn't what he was thinking, at all, but I said, 'Don't do anything until we talk.'

'I'll see you later.'

I hung up, went back to the car and gave Jerry directions to Penny's place.

Penny lived in a neighborhood that was on an upswing. It was only a few blocks from Freemont Street, which meant she could walk to work each morning. It was a fourplex on a residential block where one end was burnt out and the other end was being renovated. She was right in the middle.

We pulled up in front and Jerry got out first, followed by me, and then we opened the door for Ava and stood on either side of her. She was wearing a plaid shirt that was too big for her, jeans and her dark glasses.

'I feel like the goddamned president,' she said.

'He ain't bein' guarded as well as you are, Miss Ava,' Jerry said.

'Yeah,' she said, 'but his bodyguards would take a bullet for him.'

I swore Jerry looked as if she'd smacked him. I knew Jerry would take a bullet for me, or for Ava.

I give Ava credit, she also saw the look on his face.

'I'm so sorry, sweetie,' she said, giving him an impulsive hug. 'I know you'd take a bullet for me.'

'Of course I would, Miss Ava.'

'Don't pay any attention to me, Jerry,' she said. 'I have a big mouth.'

'Can we take this love fest inside?' I asked. 'It's way too wide open out here.'

Jerry and I walked Ava to the door and inside. Luckily, neither of us had to take a bullet for her.

SEVENTY-ONE

Danny and Penny were waiting for us, so when we rang her bell – second floor, back – Danny opened the door immediately.

Penny tried not to gush, tried her best to be professional, and she almost made it.

When she went to her kitchen to get coffee Ava said to all of us, 'She's sweet, is she really the one who's going to be responsible for my safety for the next few days?'

'No,' Danny said before I could respond, 'she's not. I'll be staying here, too.'

'And what will the sleeping arrangements be?' Ava asked with a grin. 'You and Penny in her bed and me on the sofa?'

'No,' Danny said, 'you could share the bed with Penny,

or you could have the bed, Penny will take the sofa and I'll take the floor.'

'Or—' Ava started, but I cut her off.

'You three can work that out,' I said, 'and I'm hoping it won't be more than one night. If Momo is true to his word, that is.'

'I'll go help Penny and get acquainted, then,' Ava said. 'I'll see you boys later.'

'That was good thinkin', Danny,' I said.

'You had a good idea, Eddie, bringin' her here, but you didn't think it through, and neither did I, until now.'

'You're right,' I said. 'I don't know what I was thinkin'.'

'Well, we've got it straight now,' he said. 'You and Jerry go and do what you gotta do. We'll just wait here for the good word.'

'OK,' I said.

'Remember,' Jerry said to Danny, 'she's a lady.'

'You mean a threesome is out of the question?'

Actually, knowing Ava, I didn't think it was, but I dragged Jerry out of there before he could belt Danny.

When we got to the front stoop Jerry stopped and looked around.

'Were we followed?' I asked.

'No,' he said. 'I'm sure we weren't. I'm just bein' careful.'

'And to that end,' I said, 'we should find a place to drop you off while I go back to the Sands.'

He grinned.

'I know just the spot.'

I dropped Jerry at Benny Binion's so he could eat at their coffee shop, then drove to the Sands. A couple of stacks of pancakes would keep him busy.

Jack was waiting for me in his office. His girl didn't bother looking up at me.

I walked to his desk and dropped the rings on it, next to a jar of Momo's sauce, which was still there.

'You know what these are?' I asked.

'Rings?' He picked one up, looked at it, and set it down.

'One of the two guys who beat up the cabbie in L.A.

wore one. And two other Chicago goons who came after me wore them.'

'Two others? There were four altogether?'

I held out my hand, fingers and thumb extended.

'Five?'

'But only three wore these rings.'

'Wait a minute,' he said. 'What happened to the five men?'

'They're dead.'

'You?'

'Jerry,' I said. 'And Ava.'

'Ava?' He dry washed his face with his big hands several times. 'This is gettin' way out of hand.'

'Getting?' I asked. 'It's got. But Momo's gonna take care of it, right?'

He looked uncomfortable.

'Isn't he?'

'He wants to,' Jack said, 'but I got a call this morning.'

'What about? Is Momo—'

'No, not that,' he said. 'Napolitano, he's gone.'

'Whataya mean, gone?'

'Disappeared,' Jack said. 'Left Chicago.'

'To come here?'

Jack shrugged.

'Momo thought I should warn you. He said he was sending some guys.'

I sat down heavily.

'Yeah? When will they get here?'

'Any time now.'

'Any time could be too late.'

'Is Ava safe?'

'Yes, but any time I say that, something happens.'

'Meaning?'

'Meaning somehow they always find us,' I said. 'How does that happen?'

'I don't know. Momo is probably bugged.'

'Momo didn't know where we were.'

'Then who did?'

'Nobody,' I said. 'Nobody but me, Jerry and Ava.'

'And Tony.'

'Tony only knew I asked for the key,' I said. 'He probably thought I was taking a girl there.'

'So? He could've told somebody.'

'I don't think—'

'Ask 'im' Jack said. 'See what he tells you. Sometimes the simplest answer is the best, Eddie.'

'But not always . . .' another voice said.

Jack abruptly looked past me. I turned in my seat, saw a man in his fifties standing in the doorway, wearing a very expensive black suit.

'Napolitano,' Jack said.

'Tony Napolitano?' I asked.

'Antonio,' the man said. '*Don* Antonio Napolitano, at your service.'

He stepped into the room, hands in his trouser pockets. Behind him two men came in, with Jack's girl between them, looking very frightened. Both men had guns. One of them was wearing a silver snake ring.

Great, I thought, just fuckin' great.

SEVENTY-TWO

'I'm surprised it was so easy for us to walk in here,' Napolitano said.

'This is a casino,' Jack Entratter said, 'not some Mafia enclave that needs to be guarded.' I had heard Jack wax eloquent before, so it didn't surprise me.

I also knew Jack had a gun in his top drawer. And I had Ava's in my pocket. Was I waiting for him to make a move, or was he waiting for me? Make a move? Why did I sound like a bad movie in my head? My hands began to sweat, and I could feel the perspiration at the small of my back.

'What do you want, Napolitano?' Entratter asked.

'What do I want?' Napolitano asked. He was walking around Jack's office, looking at things. His hands still in

his pockets. 'I want the bitch who killed my son. I want
the whore who has caused the death of five of my men. I
want Ava Gardner.'

'I don't know where she is,' Entratter said.

'You're probably telling the truth,' Napolitano said. He
took his hands out of his pockets and pointed at me. 'But
he does.'

On the third finger of his right hand was a gold snake ring.

Up close I could see he was closer to sixty than fifty.
His hair looked as black as shoe polish.

'Where is she?' he said, looking directly at me for the
first time.

'Let this girl go,' I said. 'And Jack.'

'And then you'll tell me? Is that your bargain?'

'No,' I said. 'This is my bargain. Let them go and I'll
see if I can stop Sam Giancana from killin' you.'

'Sam can do what he wants to me,' Napolitano said, 'after
I've avenged my son's death.'

'What makes you so sure she killed him?' I asked.

'She came to Chicago and beguiled him,' he said. 'Plied
him with sex and drink and then killed him. The only reason
she is still alive is because of you. And yet,' he added, with
a shrug, 'if you give her to me, I will let you live.'

The only thing I could think to do was keep talking.

'You've managed to find us every time,' I said. 'How did
you do that?'

Napolitano smiled.

'It was not hard to find her in L.A.,' he said. 'What other
hotel would a woman like her stay in? But after we heard
that you were coming to help her, we knew we had to do
something.'

'So you sent two men to the Beverly Hills Hotel to put
me in the hospital, only they got the wrong guy.'

'That was unfortunate,' he said, 'but after that we assumed
you would come to Las Vegas.' I wondered who the 'we'
was he kept referring to, or if he really used the royal 'we'
when referring to himself?

'You managed to kill two of my men and disappear again.'

'But you found us again.'

'And, since I have not heard from those three men, I assume they are dead, as well. You and the woman have cost me a lot.'

'I think you got it wrong, Napolitano,' I said. 'Ava didn't kill him, and you've wasted your time and your men tryin' to kill her.' Whether she did or not, this man needed to be convinced she didn't. He could reach out for her even from behind bars,

'No,' Napolitano said, 'you can't deter me with lies.'

Entratter slammed his hand down on his desk top, getting everyone's attention.

'You have somebody in my hotel and casino, don't you?' he demanded.

Napolitano smiled at Jack.

'That's right,' I said, 'the man who slid the message under my door. Did he find out from Tony LaBella that I'd gotten his cabin key?' I stood up. 'Did you do anything to Tony?'

'Sit down, Mr Gianelli!' Napolitano roared. He startled not only Jack's girl, but his own two men. However, I was too mad to be startled. If they had hurt Tony LaBella it was my fault.

I turned my head, spotted the two rings I'd left on Jack's desk.

'What's with the tacky silver rings, Napolitano?' I asked. I walked to Jack's desk, picked one up. 'I notice you wear a gold one. What is it supposed to be, some kind of badge of honor?'

'I give them to men who have been loyal to me,' he said.

'Yeah, well, they can't be very good men, can they? I mean, I'm just a casino pit boss, yet I have three of their rings right here.' I picked up the others, held them all in my palm and rattled them at him. I noticed there was a line of Momo's sauce down the side of the jar that had made a small pool on the desk.

'Give them to me!' Napolitano said, his eyes flashing.

'Yeah, sure, here ya go,' I said, tossing them to him.

He put his hands out to catch them. As he did I grabbed the jar of sauce, flipped the lid off and tossed the contents into Napolitano's face.

His two men were stunned by the move, didn't know where to look or what to do. They did release the girl's arms and she slid to the floor, unable to stand.

Jack had opened his top drawer when I moved and grabbed his gun. At the same time I pulled Ava's little gun out of my pocket.

Jack stood up, extended his gun and fired twice at Napolitano's men. The sound was deafening within the confines of the office.

I moved in on Napolitano, who was still wiping sauce from his eyes. I jammed the barrel of Ava's gun right under his chin.

'Eddie! Don't!' Jack shouted. He obviously thought I was going to pull the trigger.

Napolitano dropped his hands and looked at me from behind a marinara mask.

'Go ahead, pull the trigger. I am done, anyway. If you don't kill me I'll keep going after the woman, and you.'

'I don't think so, Napolitano,' Jack said. 'For one thing I don't think you've got many more men.'

'For another, I'm still gonna prove that Ava Gardner didn't kill your son,' I said.

'Then who did?'

'That's what I'm gonna find out.'

'As well as who the traitor in my house is,' Entratter said.

'That I will not tell you,' Napolitano said. He licked some sauce from his chin. 'What is this?' he demanded.

'Sam Giancana's marinara sauce,' I said. 'You owe me a new jar.'

SEVENTY-THREE

Jack had to call the cops.

I had no choice but to stay and wait for them. Napolitano was sure to tell Hargrove I was there, and then he'd be looking for me – again.

Jack took his girl out to her desk, made her sit down and gave her a small brandy. She insisted she was fine and he told her she was a trooper.

I kept Napolitano company until Hargrove arrived with three uniforms and they took him into custody.

'What is all this?' Hargrove asked, looking at the orange stains on Napolitano and the floor. 'It doesn't look like blood.'

'Marinara,' I said.

'How the hell—'

'We'll tell you the whole story,' Entratter said, coming back into the room.

'You two?' Hargrove asked, folding his arms. 'That will be a switch.'

'Where's Ava Gardner?' Hargrove asked.

'She's someplace safe.'

'With your buddy Jerry?'

'No, with my buddy Danny.'

'Hmph, Bardini.' He was almost less of a fan of Danny's than he was of me. 'Well, I'm going to have to talk to her.'

'Have to, or want to, Detective?' I asked.

'I ain't a starry eyed movie fan, Eddie,' he said. 'I'm just tryin' to do my job.'

'OK, but I can't tell you where she is. I'll bring her to your office.'

He was about to object, but I'm sure what went through his mind at that moment was having Ava Gardner show up at the police station, asking for him.

'OK,' he said. 'Today.'

'Sure.'

'I got a statement from your secretary, Mr Entratter,' Hargrove said. 'She's pretty shook up. You might want to send her home.'

'Yeah, I'll do that,' Jack said.

'And I'll need you to come to headquarters with me,' he said. 'As long as you're stickin' to the story that you pulled the trigger.'

'I did pull the trigger,' Jack said.

Hargrove looked at me.

'I threw the sauce,' I told him.

When I picked Jerry up he said, 'You got sauce on your sleeve.'

Leave it to him to immediately recognize the red stuff for what it was.

'Come on, I'll tell you about it in the car.'

By the time we arrived at Penny's I had filled him in. Now I was going to have to repeat it for Danny, Ava and Penny.

'That was pretty smart,' Jerry said, as we got out. 'And lucky.'

'I know,' I said. 'About the lucky part, I mean.'

We went up to Penny's place and she opened the door.

'Thank God,' she said. 'We're losing all our money in gin.'

'I shoulda warned ya not to play with her,' Jerry said.

'Hey, look who's back!' Danny said, from the kitchen table.

'How did everything go?' Ava asked.

'Actually, it went pretty good,' I said. 'We got Napolitano.'

'How'd you manage that?' Danny asked.

I told them the story. Ava actually laughed when I got to the part about throwing the jar of sauce.

'So that's what's on your sleeve,' Danny said.

'I spotted it right away,' Jerry said, proudly.

'You would,' Danny said.

'So it's over?' Ava asked. 'Napolitano is the one who's been trying to have me killed?'

'He's the one,' I said, 'but we still don't know who killed his son.'

'How about Giancana?' Danny asked.

I frowned.

'That would mean he was willing to let Ava take the blame,' I said. 'Since Frank's his friend, would he do that?'

'That animal always hated me,' she said. 'Probably because I hated him. I can believe he'd let me take the rap.'

'I guess that makes sense,' I said.

'Can't prove it, though,' Danny said. 'Maybe you can get Giancana to admit it to you, but you still wouldn't be able to prove it.'

'You could tell Mr S.,' Jerry said.

They all looked at him.

'I mean, then he'd have to explain himself to Mr S.,' the big guy said.

We all thought that over for a few moments, and then Ava broke the silence.

'As much as I used to try to get Frank to dump Momo,' she said, 'I don't like that idea.'

'Why not?' I asked.

'It would hurt Frank to know what Momo did,' she said. 'And like Danny says, we don't have proof.'

'OK' I said, 'nobody says anything to Frank.'

'So what do we do now?' Penny asked.

'The cops want to talk to you, Ava,' I said. 'They want me to bring you to headquarters.'

'What should I tell them?'

'Almost the truth,' I said.

'How much is almost?' she asked.

'I'll coach you on the way.'

SEVENTY-FOUR

Hargrove was a damned liar.

When Ava Gardner walked in he jumped to his feet and gushed.

'We can use my Lieutenant's office,' he told us. 'Can I get you something? Coffee? Tea?'

'No,' she said. 'I'm fine.'

'I'll have some coffee,' I said.

'Forget it!' Hargrove said. 'And you stay out here while Miss Gardner and I have a talk.'

She looked at me and said, 'I'll be all right.'

There was no reason why she shouldn't be all right. We

had all coached her on the way. I had left Danny and Jerry off at a bar down the block. I didn't remember if the two of them had ever spent anytime together, alone. I hoped they would get along.

Hargrove closed the door of his Lieutenant's office, leaving him and Ava alone. Entratter was nowhere to be seen, so I assumed he had made his statement and gone home. Of course, he could have been in a cell. I had no idea if the gun he'd used in his office was registered or not. Meanwhile, Danny was going back to his office after dropping Jerry off at the Sands.

I sat in the chair next to Hargrove's desk. On the desk I saw a plastic evidence bag with the two silver snake rings, and the gold one.

If Entratter was back at the Sands he was probably already looking for the man Napolitano had somehow inserted in to his Sands staff. It was because of that man I still wouldn't be able to take Ava back to the Sands when Hargrove was done with her.

I spotted a coffee pot across the room, so I got up and poured myself a cup. Nobody tried to stop me. I went back to Hargrove's desk and sat down. His partner came over and sat at the desk closest to me.

'So, what happened to Hargrove's other partner?'

'The negro?' he asked. 'He's moved on to other employment.'

I guess if I cared I would have asked what that meant.

'You're supposed to be a pretty big shot in this town,' he said.

'I'm just a casino pit boss.'

'That's not what Hargrove says.'

'Hargrove isn't the detective he thinks he is.'

'I'll tell him you said so,' he said, with a grin.

'Please do.'

He applied himself to some paperwork on his desk and I drank my coffee, staring at his right hand.

After about half an hour the office door opened and Hargrove came out with Ava.

'Thank you for your statement, Miss Gardner.'

She smiled at him and said, 'Always my pleasure time with a handsome man.'

I could see by the look on Hargrove's face that he been totally charmed.

He walked over to me and said, 'Your turn.'

I saw Holman getting Ava a cup of coffee as Hargrove closed the office door.

'How's your new partner workin' out?' I asked Hargrove.

'What's that got to do with anything?' he asked.

'I noticed his right hand,' I said.

'What about his right hand.'

'Used to have a ring on it,' I said.

'Let's just get on with the statement.'

'Sure,' I said. 'Anything you say.'

It took me twenty minutes, probably because Hargrove wasn't flirting with me the whole time.

'Don't leave town,' Hargrove said. 'Any of you. Remind Entratter of that.'

'Jack never leaves town,' I said.

'Fine. See that you and Miss Gardner don't. Not until I tell you.'

I looked around.

'Where is she?'

He did the same.

'I don't know.'

I looked at Holman's desk. He was gone too.

'Where's your partner?' I demanded.

'Beats me,' Hargrove said, with a shrug. 'He's supposed to be here.'

'Ask somebody,' I said.

'What?'

'Find out where they went!'

'Who do you think—'

'Unless you want to be held responsible for the death of Ava Gardner,' I said, 'ask!'

SEVENTY-FIVE

Hargrove came back into the squad room.
'An officer saw Holman leaving with Miss Gardner.'
'Does he know where they went?'
'No.'
'Damn it!'
'What's this about, Eddie?' he demanded.
'Come on,' I said, 'I'll explain on the way.' I headed for the door.
'On the way where?' he asked, trailing after me.
'I don't know!'

We were in Hargrove's car, driving around aimlessly, trying to see if Holman had stopped somewhere close by with Ava.
'You think Holman works for Napolitano?' he asked. 'That's crazy.'
'You have never seen the ring he wore on his right hand?'
'Well, sure . . .'
'What does it look like?'
Hargrove thought.
'Damn it, I can't remember!' he said, finally.
'Come on, Hargrove,' I said, 'a trained observer like you? You can't tell me you can't—'
'It was silver!' he said, suddenly.
'Ah,' I said, 'silver like the ones on your desk in the evidence bag? Like Napolitano's gold one?'
'But Napolitano's in jail,' Hargrove said. 'Why still go after Ava?'
'Because,' I said, 'with Napolitano's lawyers he'll probably be out by morning.'
'So even if we manage to save her he'll be after her again.'

'I don't think so,' I said, thinking of Giancana.

'Why not?'

'Wait,' I said, suddenly struck by a thought. 'Head for the Sands.'

'Why?'

'Is Holman a killer?'

'Yesterday I would've said no. But that ring . . .'

'Maybe it doesn't mean what we think it means,' I said. 'Maybe it's not made guys that wear it, just . . . guys who have worked for Napolitano for a certain amount of time.'

'What's your point?'

'If he's not gonna kill her himself, he's got to take her to someone who will.'

'And where do we find that guy?'

'At that Sands.'

SEVENTY-SIX

We pulled up in front of the Sands. There was some commotion, people complaining, valets running around. I spotted Kenny, and Hargrove spotted the car.

'That's Holman's,' he said.

'Kenny! What's happening?' I asked.

'Some guy drove up and ran inside with Ava Gardner,' the valet said. 'Just left his car here with no key in it. Now we're blocked.'

'I'll take care of it,' I said.

Hargrove and I ran toward the front door while Kenny called out, 'You can't leave yours here, either.'

Hargrove turned and tossed Kenny the keys.

We ran into the hotel lobby with Hargrove harping in my ear.

'I don't know why I'm goin' along with this, Gianelli,' he said. 'My own partner—'

'You saw the ring, Hargrove.'

'Yeah, but why would he wear the ring on the job?'

'How about arrogance?' I asked. 'You've run into that on the job, haven't you?'

He ignored my theory.

'Where do we look?' he asked.

'All over,' I said. 'You go into the casino, I'll check the hotel. Napolitano put a man in here to spy on us. It's my bet he's still here.'

'I hate to have to gamble on you . . .' Hargrove said, but he didn't go on. We split up.

I turned and looked toward the front desk. I couldn't very well go floor by floor, checking rooms. I noticed Rose was on duty, and something occurred to me.

I walked to the desk, caught her attention and waved her over.

'Yes, Eddie?'

'The man we talked about the other day,' I said. 'The one flirting with you?'

'Yes?'

'He works here, doesn't he?'

'Well, yes.'

'Why didn't you tell me that before?'

'Y-you didn't ask me.'

She was right, I hadn't asked.

'Do you know what his job is?' I asked.

'I—I think he works in the office.'

'What office?'

To the front desk staff of a hotel everything else was 'the office.'

'I'm not sure. Employment?'

A job that gave him access to employees' records would be very helpful to a spy. For instance, he'd know what room I was staying in so that he could slide a threatening message beneath my door.

'OK, Rose. Thanks.'

She started to return to her position when I called, 'Rose?'

'Yes?'

'You said you noticed his pinky ring,' I said. 'Does he wear any other jewelry?'

'Oh, yes,' she said, 'he has a silver ring on his right hand. I didn't get a close look, though.'

'That's OK,' I said. 'Thanks.'

I left her and took the elevator to Entratter's floor. I needed something from him.

Jack's girl's desk was empty. She was probably still at home recovering. I barged into Jack's office, saying, 'Jack, I need your gun—' I stopped short when I saw Frank sitting at the desk, Jack standing nearby.

'Hey, Frank.'

'I just came in to see what was going on with Ava,' he said. 'I didn't hear from you after Chicago. Whataya need a gun for?'

'Ava's in the building,' I said, quickly, 'and she's in trouble. She was snatched from the police station.'

'By who?' Frank demanded, jumping to his feet.

'A cop,' I said, 'but I think he brought her here so one of Napolitano's men can kill her.'

'The damn spy of his?' Entratter said.

'Yeah,' I said, 'but they're gonna be armed, and I'm not.'

'Well, I'm not,' Entratter said. 'The cops still have my gun.'

'Well, I am,' Frank said, and took a .38 out of his pocket. I wasn't surprised to see he had a gun. He'd once showed it to me in the steam room. 'Let's go!'

'Frank, you can't—' Entratter started, but Frank ignored him. If he weighed a hundred and fifty pounds every bit of it was vibrating.

'Forget it, Jack,' I said, firmly. 'This is Ava we're talking about.'

We took the elevator to the second floor, where the business offices were. Marcia Clarkson pretty much ran the offices there, and was a good friend of mine. When I entered her office she looked up from behind her wire-framed glasses and smiled. Under normal circumstances I would have told her how pretty she was, but I had no time

'Marcy, I'm looking for a man who works here. Dark-hair, hawk nose, pinky ring.'

She recognized the urgency in my manner, but she also recognized Frank and it threw her.

'Mr Sinatra?' she said, catching her breath.

'Hiya, doll,' he said. 'Answer Eddie's question, OK?'

'Oh, uh, his name's Jeff Smith,' she said.

'How long has he worked here?'

'A few weeks.'

'Where does he work, Marcy?'

'Across the hall.'

'Is he there now?'

'He was a few minutes ago.'

We rushed out of her office into the one across the way. It was empty. Marcy came in behind us.

'What's going on, Eddie?'

'We've got to find him, Marcy,' I said. 'Where would he be if he's not here?'

She hesitated.

'Come on, Marcy!'

'I don't want to get him in trouble,' she said. Jesus, she had a thing for the guy?

'He's already in trouble, Marcy,' I said. 'He doesn't belong here. He was sent to spy on Entratter. There's a good chance he's about to kill Ava Gardner. If you know something, tell me.'

She stared at me as if I'd gone crazy, but said, 'Well, I know he likes to go to the roof when he has a break—'

'The roof!' Frank said, and he took off.

'Call down to the casino,' I told Marcy, 'find Detective Hargrove and get him up here. And tell Entratter where we went.'

'But, Eddie, what—'

'Do it now!' I said.

I started after Frank.

SEVENTY-SEVEN

I caught up to Frank, who sheepishly admitted he didn't know how to get to the roof.

'Come on,' I said.

We took the elevator again, this time all the way to the top. Then we ran down the hall with me in the lead until we reached the doorway to the roof.

I put my hand on Frank's chest. I could feel him vibrating.

'Frank, we have to be careful,' I said. 'There's two of 'em, and they're both gonna have guns.'

'While we're talkin' here, Ava could be in more danger,' he said.

'OK, we're goin',' I said, 'just . . . watch out.'

I knew we couldn't wait for Hargrove to catch up, but all I needed was for this to end with Ava and Frank dead.

I opened the door and we went up the stairs to the roof door. Frank's tension was contagious, but I kept him from barging right through the door. I put my ear to the door, thought I heard voices but it could have been my imagination.

'We've got to go easy—' I started, but Frank had had enough.

'Bullshit!' he said, and slammed the door open. He went through with his gun held out in front of him.

'Damn!' I swore, and followed.

No one. The voices *had* been my imagination, but then we both heard them. We moved away from the door and saw them over toward the edge, near the front of the building.

Holman was standing behind Ava, holding her by the shoulders. The other man – Smith or whatever – was standing in front of them, holding a gun.

'Shoot her!' Holman shouted.

'Toss her off the roof!' Smith shouted back.

Each man seemed reluctant to kill her themselves, which

may just have saved Ava, which might have been the only reason we'd be able to get there in time.

'Hold it!' Frank shouted.

All three turned and looked at us.

'Frank!' Ava shouted.

'Frank Sinatra?' Smith said, staring.

'Let her go!' I yelled at Holman. 'Your partner's on the way, Holman. The jig is up.'

'Damn it!' Holman swore at the other man. 'You see what happened because you couldn't do your damned job, Nico?'

'It can still get done,' Nico said.

Holman let Ava go and she slid down to her knees. She didn't seem to have the strength to run.

'It's OK, baby,' Frank said.

'Holman—' I said.

'Stay back!' the detective shouted. He moved his hand towards his holster.

'Don't!' Frank said. 'I know how to use this. You, put your gun down!'

Nico looked at him and said, 'You're a goddamned singer.'

'Try me,' Frank said.

'He can't get both of us,' Holman said. 'We take care of them, and then the woman.'

'You touch your gun and I'll kill you first!' Frank said.

I felt helpless. The whole situation was in Frank's hands. I knew he carried a gun, but I didn't know if he'd ever used it before. I didn't have a lot of confidence.

Nico was still facing Holman and Ava with his gun.

'Put yours down,' he said to Frank, 'or I'll kill the woman.'

'That's not a woman, you idiot,' I said, 'that's Ava Gardner. You kill her you'll never walk away from this.'

I was trying to make him think twice. I was willing Frank to go ahead and pull the trigger, but that was easy for somebody like Jerry. It wouldn't be so easy for Frank. I knew because I'd been in that position.

'Kill her!' Holman said. 'Do it.'

'You haven't killed anybody yet, Nico,' I said. 'Not that I know of. Maybe you *can* walk away from this.'

'Don't listen to him,' Holman said. 'You brought her up here against her will. That's kidnapping. That's a federal offense. Neither of us is walkin' unless we kill them all.'

'It'll be a blood bath,' I said. 'Maybe none of us will survive it.' I knew I wouldn't. I was the only man without a gun.

I could see the sweat running down Frank's face. I knew the palms of his hands must be wet, too. Mine were.

'Frank . . .'

Holman reached for his gun.

'Frank!' I shouted.

'Holman, don't!' someone shouted from behind us.

Hargrove had made it to the roof. Holman pulled his gun from his holster and I heard a shot from behind me. There was a burst of red on Holman's chest. Some of it showered down on to Ava.

Nico started to turn and Frank pulled the trigger. I don't know where he was aiming, but he hit Nico in the hip. The force of the bullet spun him around, and his gun flew out of his hand.

Hargrove raced past me and pinned Nico to the ground so he could cuff him.

Frank ran to Ava and took her in his arms, speaking to her softly.

I hadn't had to move.

SEVENTY-EIGHT

Las Vegas, 2003

After the movies I had the limo take us to Caesar's Palace. With all the old places gone they had the best coffee shop on the strip.

Jennifer was talking about how much she loved *Mogambo*.

I nodded, but I stared out the widow at the passing marquees: Tom Jones, Danny Gans, Wayne Newton, Rita Rudner, Howie Mandell. Jones and Newton were power houses, but it just wasn't the same strip. It couldn't be, not without the guys.

I was wondering if I should tell her the whole story over a snack. Or which parts to leave out? Like sleeping with Ava. I'd never told anyone about that, all these years. How many men would have done that, slept with a Goddess and not told anybody?

I decided to wait and see if she asked. Then I'd make the decision.

We entered Caesar's with her arm linked in mine. A couple of valets, a doorman, some dealers and pit bosses greeted me by name as we went by.

'My God, Eddie, this town never forgets, does it?' she asked. 'You're a legend.'

'You live long enough somebody's bound to hang that word on ya,' I said. 'But the real legends are long gone . . . long, long gone.'

'You miss them, don't you?' she asked.

I nodded.

'I miss them, and I miss my Vegas. I still love this town, but I hate the bells and whistles. Look at this. There are lights everywhere. All the slots light up, the table games have neon signs above them, and then when somebody hits they start to blink. It's blinding sometimes.'

We got seated in the coffee shop by a young waitress who didn't know who I was. She treated us like a couple of old codgers who were in a big casino for the first time.

'Have you ever been here before?' she asked.

'Yes,' I said, 'many times.'

'Do you need help ordering?'

'No,' I said, 'I've been ordering for myself since before you were born.'

'Eddie,' Jennifer said, 'she was just trying to be helpful. You didn't have to snap at her.'

'Believe me,' I said. 'She didn't even notice.'

'Well,' she said, 'let's get some coffee and pie, and then you were going to tell me about you and Ava Gardner.'

'There's not much to tell,' I said.

'I'll be the judge of that.'

While she looked over the menu I thought back to the last time I saw Ava . . .

Sept. 1962

Ava went off with Frank after the events on the roof and I didn't see her.

The Vegas cops got together with the Chicago cops and discovered that Napolitano's kid had been hit. They still didn't know if it had been Giancana's men, or somebody else, but what we did know was, it hadn't been Ava – even though she had been there.

They found a witness – a bell boy – who put Ava with the Napolitano kid in that hotel room. Danny had determined that by that time she'd been wandering around for most of the lost hours in an alcohol induced stupor. Spain to New York to Chicago . . .

The kid had apparently been killed in the room, and Ava left to take the rap. With his blood on her, the cops figured she'd been set up. But she had come to, panicked and ran. If she'd stayed she might have been cleared. Turns out the detective in Chicago didn't buy the kid's death as anything but a hit. They were looking for a woman who'd been seen with him, but Ava had done a good job of keeping her face hidden. Or the bell boy had just been too young to know who she was. And whoever the killers were, they probably hadn't recognized her, either, because at the end of a forty-hour bender she wouldn't have looked like Ava Gardner. Somehow, Napolitano knew about her, though, and blamed her for the death of his son. So he kept sending his men after her, until he actually came himself.

But in the end both the law and Napolitano were convinced of Ava's innocence. The Chicago cops had even accepted a statement taken from Ava by the Las Vegas police.

There wasn't much, because she still had holes in her memory. They might come back some day, but she probably hoped not.

I still didn't know why the manager of the Beverly Hills Hotel had been killed. Obviously, he'd called somebody about Ava being there. The beating Larry the cab driver had taken had been meant to scare me off. Why kill the manager, but leave me alive? Not all the questions ever get answered.

I was in my pit two days later when I saw Ava walking across the floor towards me. I went to greet her.

'Eddie,' she said. She embraced me warmly, then kissed me on the mouth. My lips and toes tingled. Dealers and gamblers were staring. Let 'em.

'I'm leaving and wanted to say goodbye. And thank you. The police said by keeping me ahead of Napolitano's men you managed to keep me alive.'

'Me and Jerry.'

'Where *is* Jerry?' she asked.

'Took a plane back home yesterday,' I said. 'Had to get back to his life.'

'Life as a leg breaker?'

'That's what he's good at.'

'I know better,' she said. 'So do you.'

'You may be right. I thought you and Frank—'

'Two days, Eddie,' she said. 'We've been together for two days. That's usually more than enough for us. We had a huge fight this morning, and now I'm off.'

'To where?'

'Back to Spain.'

'To make more movies?'

'I don't know,' she said. 'Right now that doesn't seem so important'

'What does?'

'Finding the fountain of youth, I guess.'

'Ava—'

'Don't say it.' She covered my mouth with her hand. 'I'm forty, Eddie, and it's only going to get worse. I'll have to find a way to live with that.'

'How are your memories?'

'I think some of it's coming back,' she said. 'In fact, I'm afraid it is. I see a face, in bed with me . . . and blood . . .' She shook her head, as if to dispel the memories.

She gave me a powerful hug.

'You come and see me in Spain,' she said. 'We'd have a helluva time together.'

'For how long?'

'Who knows?' she asked. 'Maybe two days?'